Beverly Bonnefinche Is Dead

Kristen Seeley

RISING ACTION

Cover Illustration © **Ashley Santoro**

Distributed by **Blackstone Publishing**

ISBN: 978-1-990253-50-8
Ebook: 978-1-990253-63-8

FIC044000 FICTION / Women
FIC045000 FICTION / Family Life / General
FIC071000 FICTION / Friendship

#BeverlyBonnefincheisDead
Follow Rising Action on our socials!
Twitter: @RAPubCollective
Instagram: @risingactionpublishingco
Tiktok: @risingactionpublishingco

For Lyric.
Your beautiful, complex mind is one of my favorite parts
about you (and there are a lot of parts that are my favorite).
I am me because of you.

A Note From The Author

Thank you for reading Beverly's story. Books should always bring pleasure, and never cause harm, for this reason if you have any content that may be harmful to your mental wellbeing, I encourage you to visit **https:// mariestill.com/contentwarnings** to ensure Beverly's story is one you wish to read.

Please know that you are never alone.

For my US readers, if you are in crisis or in need of someone to speak with, I encourage you to dial 988. UK readers, text 85258. Canada readers, call 1-833-456-4566.

Beverly's story, more than any of my other stories, is a personal one. As a society we get physicals annually, we talk openly about physical diseases, and support those battling them. Mental health isn't treated with the same care and openness. While we have taken great strides, there is still more work to do. Preventative mental health is a lifesaver. You deserve to be happy just like you deserve to be healthy.

Each person's journey with a mental health crisis or disorder is different. This story, while completely fictional, has been my way of processing one of the hardest battles I've had to fight. Please show empathy for each other, you never know what demons someone is fighting internally, or if they are fighting a battle for someone they love very much.

Take care of yourself and those around you. No matter how different and unique your mind is, you, like Beverly, are perfect the way you are.

XOXO,
Marie

Beverly Bonnefinche is Dead

Now

On an ordinary October morning, *death's spindly hands tickled my throat. Outside, the leaves stole the show with their blood reds and burnt oranges. A chill gripped the New England air, while winter's frigid blanket patiently waited in the background, ready to suffocate autumn. The neighborhood children's high-pitched squeals occasionally disrupted the quiet hanging over the cul-de-sac. The distant rise and fall of their voices reached me from my position, sprawled on my back on the living room floor.*

My listless gaze wandered the room. Familiar furnishings came in and out of focus. Dust spun lazily in the spotlight provided by the low morning sun.

My view sharpened, bringing the cavernous area under the loveseat into clarity, along with the film of dirt making its home in that usually inconspicuous space. And I thought, as the darkness which crept into my vision threatened to take over, oh dear, I should have vacuumed under there.

This wasn't my first time standing on the edge of life's cliff while the wind howled: jump, jump, jump. *My mind, long broken before that fateful October morning, not quite ready to take the leap. Death didn't frighten me, but I wasn't ready to go, not then, despite all I'd done to those I'd loved. I had also imagined my last thoughts to be cleverer or even more appalling than lamentations about a messy floor.*

One

Now

"WELL BEVERLY, that's certainly a dramatic beginning."

"Is it? I'm usually not one to have a flair for the dramatic. I suppose things change as we grow, get older, experience life."

"It sounds like you're writing a book rather than sitting here, talking to me."

I snort. "I don't write books, I read them."

"That you do. I don't think I have the patience." His head shakes and the chair creaks as the rocking chair glides easily on the front porch's wooden planks.

Better than any song, the rustling of animals and insects in the forest surrounding us, the chair creaking, and a quiet mind.

"My story is... well, it's not like other stories I don't suppose. Though I'm not like other women, never have

3

been. Perhaps that's part of the problem. No, that's actually where most of my problems began. Being different."

"I like your differentness. Too much of the same out there if you ask me."

"Kind and appreciated. We've known each other, what, two years now?"

"Sounds about right." He stops rocking as if he knows how hard this is for me, but how could he? I've never divulged the full truth to him, or to anyone who didn't already know. However, those people couldn't be helped. Partly from embarrassment, mostly out of fear of being left truly alone—again.

"I suppose now as good as a time as ever."

He remains quiet. He's always been an excellent listener.

The memories come flooding back. They tend to do that. Laughing on a bench. Gossiping over steaming mugs of coffee. A shared hidden giggle behind the back of a certain someone placing a drink on a coaster.

"What are you grinning about over there?"

More memories. A horrified look. The light catching the metallic badge on a uniform. A round belly. Blood. Mistakes.

I sigh and wave away the question as if it floats in the air between us. "Oh, nothing. Just silly moments that popped into my head."

We take a moment to look in front of us, a view that still has a way of stealing my breath and words. One that makes you feel small and large all at the same time. I force my eyes from it and turn my head to him. "That's not the beginning, though. You know this already, though, don't you?"

He nods, his silence an invitation to further explain.

"It was one beginning. But not *the* beginning."

"Why don't you start from the beginning, then? Tell me your story, Beverly."

"It's not a very interesting one,"

"I think I'd disagree." His knowing smile and warm eyes, eyes that have always reminded me of—I resist the urge to swat at the air again, that smile may twist into confusion. Pity, confusion, horror, all looks I'm more familiar with than I'd prefer. Pity being the one I despise the most. I want to keep his face soft, his lips smiling, and his eyes twinkling for as long as I can. So the beginning is where I begin.

Part One

Two

Before

AFTER PARKING MY CAR, I strolled down the street, ready to start another day. My dependable and well-loved loafers clicked and clacked on the brick-lined sidewalk. Summer's oppressive heat hadn't yet taken over the day, and I let a smile tug up my lips while I admired my beloved Newport, Rhode Island.

Breathing in the salt air and enjoying the omnipresent crash of the sea, I made my way under the colorful awnings shading the street. Many towns were too carefully planned, or their historic buildings too crumbly. Not Newport. Newport had character with its beautiful architecture well-kept despite age. The rows of restaurants and shops stood connected in their own unique converted townhomes.

"Bev! Good morning. You, my love, are looking absolutely amazing, as always," a gravelly voice called.

I didn't look amazing, and far from absolutely. But Bill —my one and only friend—was always too inebriated to notice. Even at eight on a Monday morning.

"And you look drunk." I handed him a thermos filled with coffee.

"That's because I am," he replied, a slight slur melting his words.

He winked, taking the thermos. My hands swept behind my gray pleated, ankle-length skirt, then smoothed the front of it as I took my seat next to him on our white wooden bench. Located a few streets down from the bookshop—aptly named Bookshop—which employed me, our bench sat against the back of a stone building in one of the squares that broke up Newport's blocks.

Bill and I had a connection most wouldn't understand. We were both outcasts. Both misunderstood. We had our differences, though. The most obvious being Bill's lack of housing. And there was the matter of Bill's alcoholism. Everyone has means to numb their pain and quell their anxiety; Bill used vodka—or whatever alcohol he could get his hands on—and me, well, I had my own vices, so who was I to judge?

I retrieved a brown paper bag from my purse and handed Bill what would probably be his only non-liquid meal of the day. My mother prepared these meals for him on days I was scheduled to work.

Yes, I still lived at home, which I'm aware is quite unusual for a twenty-five-year-old. An old soul, my mother calls me. Would an old soul still be living at home with her parents well into her twenties? Not someone who particularly cared for change, I didn't let the answer to that question trouble me.

These morning meetups became our ritual. I provided Bill with sustenance, and he provided me with friendship. Perhaps I provided him the same, but I never considered myself capable of bestowing companionship. At least not in a meaningful or fulfilling capacity.

"Think they realize how captive they are by the expectations of society?" Bill asked as he jutted his chin toward the thin crowd of people moving through the square in front of us.

"I'm sure they're just glad to have a job and to not be drunk this early in the morning," I said, nudging him with my shoulder and chuckling.

"Always so judgmental, Beverly." His laugh turned into a fit of coughs. With a shaky hand, he reached into his pocket and retrieved a rusted flask, which he used to spike the coffee with its clear contents. I turned my face away and chewed my inner cheek.

He continued, "What they don't know is this. The feeling of freedom you and I enjoy. *We're* the lucky ones, Bev, because we don't give a hoot what other people think. And that makes you and me the *real* feelers of freedom."

"Are we, though?" I asked. My vision unfocused, and the colors from the foot traffic and buildings blurred into a meaningless swirl. "Perhaps we're missing out? Maybe they know something we don't."

Bill gasped rather theatrically. "Do I not fulfill you? Have my conversations and friendship become boring?" He smacked his hand to his chest and feigned offense.

I rolled my eyes. "No, no. I'm being silly." I leaned my

head on his shoulder. The rough fabric of his dirt-encrusted jacket that it was entirely too hot to be wearing, scraped against my cheek. The sharp scents of Bill filled my chest with comfort. Even the most casual conversation devoured my energy, leaving me bled out and bruised, except those with Bill. With Bill, I could be myself. Maybe it was the haze of vodka filming his eyes that kept my insecurities at bay. In reality, even slowed by the fog of drunkenness, Bill's mind was sharper than most. He had so much potential, but I accepted the things I wanted for him —stability, soberness, a home—weren't the things he wanted for himself. And he also accepted me. Coarse edges, social ineptness, and all.

"There really is no use, is there? Trying to fit in, to be one of them, I mean," I said.

"Heartache and hurt, Bev, heartache and hurt." Bill leaned his head against mine.

Two middle-aged women, a blonde and a brunette, walked by whispering and stealing glances at us as if they smelled a dead body. Their matching chin length bobs tipped toward each other. Not a strand out of place, their hair framing their faces reflecting the light, shining in ways hair shouldn't be capable of. My hand subconsciously reached up to my own flat hair.

"Dare you to bark at them." Bill wagged his eyebrows, encouraging me with his bad influence.

My lips pursed. "You behave. They aren't worth it." I shook my head.

A squirrel skittered across the now empty square. The squirrel seemed much less judgmental; Bill and I preferred his company to the women's.

We sat, sipping our coffees and enjoying the warm morning breeze. After some time, I stood and threw my purse strap over my shoulder.

"Well, regardless of what we think or say, I'm not completely free from those shackles of society. I, like them, have a job. And I'm going to be late for that job if I sit here any longer staring at nothing and debating philosophy with you."

"I bid you farewell." He held up the thermos in mock cheers.

"I'll see you tomorrow morning, Bill."

With that, I left Bill to do whatever it was he did with his days and joined the society-shackled crowd to walk to work.

I turned the key and unlocked the bookshop's door. On my second step in, I tripped over a large stack of brown shipping boxes. A groan escaped my mouth at the manual labor the boxes signified, something I despised more than small talk with customers. Careful to avoid another incident, I stepped around the packages to discard my belongings at the front counter. Once there, I rifled through the drawer filled with various bits and bobs, muttering annoyances to myself until I found what I was in search of. Box cutter in hand, I approached the inconveniently placed boxes.

Slicing open the first one revealed a stack of hardcovers, a debut expected to be the breakout of the year. Comparisons to Stephen King fueled the excitement of its release.

I picked one up to read the inside flap and inspect the cover. A stark black knife with remnants of blood drying on the tip was debossed on the glossy red cover. Murder, mystery, secrets—a plot dark and twisted enough to pique my curiosity.

I set the novel down and stood facing the boxes with my hands on my hips. My meticulous attention to detail and propensity for order were two areas of my life in which I took great pride, but the books were heavy, and I had more pressing matters to attend to, like *Carrie*—a novel written by the bona fide King—waiting for me. I rushed through the task, stacking the novels haphazardly on the table next to that month's other major release, a romance book by a much-too-hyped, in my humble opinion, author. I can read almost every genre but romance. Perhaps it's jealousy. All those happily ever afters.

As a reward for my hard work, I brought one of the new novels with me to the counter and slid it into my purse. An act which could be considered stealing, but John—the bookshop's aging owner—never explicitly stated free books wasn't a work perk. A gray area I had no qualms about exploiting.

Regardless of occasional manual labor, I loved my job and the bookshop. Not being the most scholarly of students, coupled with my lack of social connections, left my prospects after high school graduation limited. Armed with the knowledge that I had to do something with my life, and with no hopes of higher education or of marriage, my love of books drew me to the bookshop. John happily obliged my inquiry of employment. It wasn't the most bustling establishment, making it the perfect complement to my thorny disposition.

That occupational choice also came with some additional advantages: a paycheck and no colleagues. This left no need to compete or fret over promotions and awards, no drama to be entangled in, and no watercooler rumors to hope didn't involve me.

Back on my stool, behind the scuffed wooden counter and vintage cash register, I rubbed my lower back and cursed the novel's page length contributing to its girth. I picked up my well-worn copy of *Carrie* to spend my day how I spent most days: reading and hoping no customers would disturb me. While I didn't particularly care for the customers or working, I found the clacking of the aged cash register's large buttons satisfying. The exchanging of germ-infested money, not so much.

During the hazy time between morning and afternoon, the bell above the door jingled. I had just reached a critical point in the story where Carrie stood horrified in front of her classmates, the thrill of winning prom queen drowned by the pig's blood dripping down her face in thick scarlet streaks. My nails dug into the book's cover, annoyed by the interruption.

I placed *Carrie* on the counter and gave this new arrival a proper once over. *Sci-fi or war-themed, but most likely sci-fi.* I liked to play this game—guessing which books or genre a customer preferred. After seven years, I prided myself on my accuracy.

A man stood backlit in the doorway. I guessed him to be about my age, but his typical-looking face matched most mid-twenties men I knew, not that I knew very many. However, I wasn't as adept at guessing ages as book preferences. He oozed *not too*: not too short and not too tall, not too fat, but also not too skinny, not too handsome, yet not too homely. His hairline, unfortunately for him, foreshadowed baldness. He wore jeans, a plain white T-shirt, and nondescript sneakers. Not the most noteworthy first impression.

My passing judgment made my thoughts wander. What stories did people craft in their minds about me? Did they see me and think I'm 'not too' as well? Or did they think the opposite and believe me to be much too?

Much too plain.

Much too ugly.

Much too boring.

Or was I so insignificant I left no imprint? Was I so inconsequential that when eyes slid over me, my body was water, too slippery to stick in the depths of their consciousness? I'm not sure what's worse, being stuck in the movie of another's mind, having no control over what the actress portraying you is saying or doing, or leaving no impression at all.

I imagine an apt impression of me would be Plain Jane. My thin hair, a mousey brown, hung limply below my shoulders, usually curtaining my face and widely spaced eyes, eyes on a face usually buried in a book. Those brown eyes as beautiful as a muddy river—or a pile of cow dung. And the final forgettable feature of my forgettable face was my thin lips which unconsciously pressed between my teeth and disappeared even further in most social situations.

My nose being my only redeeming feature. It was a lovely nose, a button nose one might say, but a good nose doesn't serve much of a purpose when surrounded by such an uninspired face.

"Help you?" I asked, making no move to get up.

As with most days, I spoke my lines like a good little shopgirl. I may not have been the best bookseller, but I hadn't burned the place down yet, so I had that going for me.

"Morning!" he hollered in reply.

I attempted to hide my wince. His booming greeting, too loud and too cheery, took up too much of the room. My initial impressions proved themselves to be inaccurate. He did, in fact, have some 'much too' characteristics after all.

He marched toward the counter and continued unfazed, asking where he might find that new romance release.

At that, I gave him my full attention, opening my eyes wide and looking him up and down, meeting his broad, friendly smile with my own surprised expression.

"It's for my mom." He chuckled. "I'm more of a horror fan myself." He tipped his head toward my abandoned copy of *Carrie*.

"Are you now?" My eyes narrowed and my chin tilted down.

"Yes indeed. I've read just about every one of his. Have you read *The Stand*? It's one of my favorites. Man, that ending, what Stu says, really makes ya think. And when he—"

"I have not," I cut him off. I, in fact, had read *The Stand*. But had no desire to extend the impromptu book club meeting, especially with someone rude enough to spoil a book before confirming whether I had read it.

"You'll find it over that way," I said, pointing him in the right direction.

He walked right by the table on his way in. A table impossible to miss.

"Not much of a talker, are you?" he asked. His light-hearted delivery proved he wasn't trying to be vicious, only attempting to break the ice with friendly banter. Still, passing remarks, even in jest, always slice a bit deeper when they cut with the truth.

He cleared his throat and continued when I assume he realized I would not be participating in the exchange. "Thank you kindly."

After taking two confident steps in the correct direction, he swiveled his head, looking everywhere except the location of the book he had come in for, which sat directly in front of him. If he had stopped flinging his head around like an owl, he would see it.

I wanted to scream, *It's right in front of you, knucklehead!* But I held my tongue.

Once realizing his mistake, he laughed and bent to grab a book with fumbling fingers. While doing so, he knocked over the surrounding stack of hardcovers. They thudded to the floor around his feet, sending my shoulders shooting to my ears.

His head whipped back around, and his eyebrows jumped toward the ceiling. No red hue of shame colored his face—he looked more surprised than embarrassed—leading me to conclude he had no problem making an ass of himself in public. My head cocked curiously to the side, and I couldn't help but stifle a giggle behind my hand.

Committing each detail to memory, I couldn't wait to share this story with Bill. I could already picture him doubled over with laughter. I didn't mean to be impolite or curt with people. And I was fully aware that making fun of this man behind his back was mean. I couldn't help myself, though. Social interactions might not be easy, but pretending I didn't care, and making someone else the butt of jokes, now that wasn't as hard.

The surprises from this much too and not too man continued, as he filled the room again with a laugh straight from his belly. I found myself a bit fond of him—only a bit though.

After sloppily returning the fallen books to their table, he walked back to the counter with a copy of the brightly covered book in hand. That goofy smile still taking up half his face. How unfortunate for him to walk around with his mouth stuck like that. Faces use smiles to show happiness, but smiling like that *all* the time doesn't make you look happy; more unhinged, on the verge of something evil. I certainly couldn't imagine anyone that truly delighted with life all the time.

I assumed this man didn't have a friend like Bill, one honest enough to tell him he looked like a serial killer. And not the charming, blend-right-into-society ones. The ones who are more easily caught. I considered telling him as much, but instead chose to return his smile with a less serial killer one.

Ready to complete his purchase and be rid of him, I rang up the book on the old register. The tap, tap, tapping of the keys soothed my frayed nerves, releasing the strange knot in my stomach. I pushed the credit card machine forward and my pinched smile fell when he held out a fist clutching cash. I resisted the urge to jerk my own hand away when our skin brushed upon completing the exchange.

It wasn't his touch specifically I didn't like. It was any touch, really. Another aspect of human interaction that nettled me.

Gripping his change, I turned my knuckles toward the counter so I could drop the coins into his outstretched hand and avoid any further skin-to-skin contact. I reached across the counter to place the bag with the book in his hand. That is the point when most customers would take the bag and finalize their transaction. Sensing he hadn't taken complete possession of it, and not wanting it to plummet to the floor like the stack of books he'd knocked over, we stood there frozen and staring at each other uncomfortably. Me fully gripping the bag, him partially.

The simple gesture dragged on while the second hand of the hanging wall clock rhythmically ticked off the passing time. His eyes refused to leave mine. The relentless smile remained frozen on his face.

Finally freeing me from the absurdity of the drawn-out exchange, he removed the bag from my grip and cleared his throat.

He pointed at his chest with that clumsy thumb of his and said, "Henry."

A name gave me an identifier to provide the police with if he were to attack, possibly with a knife hidden in his jeans. Or perhaps his hands were his weapons of choice, and a beating would need reporting. Of course, I would need to survive the attack first. I scanned the back of the counter for a blunt object of protection.

Unable to find a weapon, I sighed and remembered

my social graces. If he wasn't a serial killer and simply an average friendly guy, it would be strange of me to treat him more unkindly than I already had. I often lacked the knack for distinguishing simple gestures of kindness from more nefarious ones. Besides, if he had in fact held murderous intentions, a bit of kindness could be the life-saving substitute for the blunt object I was unable to locate.

"Beverly," I replied.

"Well, Beverly, it was a pleasure to meet you," he said before leaving.

The door closed behind his back, and my mind wandered off to that dark place it liked to go when left to its own devices.

I'm in a dirty alley with a single streetlight illuminating overflowing trash cans. My back against the crumbling brick, my body pinned by Henry's menacing form. His forearm crushes my chest, holding me in place, and he grips a knife at my throat. I crane my face to the side, pressing my cheek against the rough surface to avoid his twisted features. His fiery breath tickles my neck. With a fluid swipe of his knife, he opens my throat, spraying my blood across his smiling face. The remaining reserves pour down my chest in a river of red, pooling at my feet. My life leaks out with it.

I sharpened my vision and brought the bookshop back into focus. A hundred versions of the knife from my imagination peered innocently from across the room on their hardcover homes. My shoulders shrugged, and I dove back into King's story, my fingers tingling with the anticipation of Carrie's great revenge.

Lost in the novel, I almost missed the chiming of the

bells above the door announcing another customer's arrival. I looked up from my book and froze.

The blonde and brunette women from earlier that morning sauntered through the store engaged in conversation, too wrapped up in chitchat to notice me staring at them. The blonde slapped her friend's arm with the back of her hand. Their conversation halted. The brunette and I made eye contact. She whispered something to the other that I couldn't make out, and they both tried to hide their snickering behind cupped hands at their mouths, a perfect impersonation of ridiculous teenagers. Still, a flush of embarrassment set my cheeks on fire, and I hated myself for allowing them to burrow under my skin, *again*. They continued through the store. I placed my book on the counter and followed them with my gaze.

Their heads bounced up and down the aisles over the squat, cramped shelves, before the blonde approached the counter. My eyes flitted around for something to occupy my hands, something safe. I liked my job and didn't want to do anything rash like throw a stapler at her head and get myself fired.

"Hello, dear," the blonde said, spoken like a woman used to getting everything she wanted in life. My fists clenched. I knew their type. Simply finding and buying a book was a concept as foreign to them as divorce. Instead, their requests extended into monologues detailing which girlfriend—or group of girlfriends—loved the book, couldn't put it down, and why they *had* to see what all the fuss was about.

I never could figure out why they assumed I cared about the opinions of women whose vanilla tastes in books matched their dull lives. If I had to guess, their desperation for someone to listen to them caused the needless flow of words to spill from their mouths. I played a part, someone who made them feel acknowledged and real before returning to their empty homes, kids too busy with their own lives and husbands too busy screwing their secretaries to listen.

I shook the bitter thoughts from my head. I'm sure many of them had lovely lives, and lovely husbands, and lovely children.

"How can I help you?" I asked, attempting to emulate Bill and stuff my awkwardness deep down into the depths of my interior.

Her brunette friend joined her and answered, "Have any suggestions for some light beach reads? We're heading to the Cape this weekend for a girls' trip and want to stock up." Her bright white smile didn't reach her eyes, not as Henry's had. I reassessed my thoughts about him and wished he'd return.

There was a time when I aspired to be like these two women, or at least their younger versions. When I tried, it felt like having your shoes on the wrong feet. I gave up on those notions many years ago.

I offered the pair a few suggestions of books I had never bothered reading that most women of their sort seemed to be buying those days. They stood in the aisle browsing a few selections. The blonde one tugged on her friend's arm and suggested they go to Barnes & Noble instead. John the owner may disagree. I, on the other hand, was fine with that.

The blonde leaned her head toward the brunette's and

whispered something to her as they walked out. They both peered over their shoulders at me. The front door shut, cutting off their high-pitched cackles.

My toes curled in my loafers. I hung a sign on the front door letting potential customers know we'd be *Closed for 15 Minutes—Back in a Jiffy* and went to the bathroom to compose myself with my secret coping mechanism. One, if discovered, would surely give those women something to discuss on their upcoming girls' trip.

Three

TUESDAY MORNING. The smell of fresh coffee tugged me from sleep. The rich scent rolled up the dark staircase, whose third step groaned with annoyance whenever stepped on. It swirled down the muted hallway, whose walls overflowed with photos of me at various awkward stages of adolescence. The fragrance greeted me in my narrow twin bed, completing my transfer from the murky world of dreams into the harsh reality of my bedroom. The same bedroom I'd slept in my entire life.

Begrudgingly, I rolled out of bed. I'd never been a morning person. Then again, I'd never been an afternoon or evening person either.

I shuffled down the hallway past those embarrassing reminders of every regrettable haircut, and into the small bathroom where I rubbed the sleep from my eyes and began my simple, yet effective, morning routine. Shower—water lukewarm—teeth brushed, a good wash of the face to help jolt me to life, and a bit of moisturizer, because I saw a television commercial claiming users of the brand would retain their youth. I may not have had the face, hair, or clothing other women did, but that didn't mean I couldn't have the same smooth skin.

Downstairs, I slid into my seat at the round table in the center of the kitchen. Some may consider the room dated and cramped, but I considered it cozy and comfortable. Much like my life, that kitchen was frozen in time. Artifacts from the past displayed like a museum. This might be the reason I had no desire to leave the kitchen, my parents, the house. It fit perfectly, and I wasn't one for change.

As usual, my father attended to his own morning ritual, hidden behind his newspaper, with a barely touched breakfast and half-drunk coffee in front of him. My mother fluttered around the kitchen, unfazed by dad's grunts in reply to her attempts at conversation.

I took after my dad in most respects. We were both perfectly fine going through life speaking as few words as possible. I'm not sure if he possessed all my same quirks, though. If his mind—unprompted—would transform everyday situations into gruesome and disturbing scenarios. I'm also not sure if he consumed toilet paper to calm his anxiety. Because I did.

I don't claim to have a firm grasp of the human psyche, but I wouldn't doubt everyone walking this earth has their own flavor of strangeness. I also wouldn't doubt the secrets everyone carries—and the things people do when alone with their thoughts—are every bit as peculiar and shameful as eating toilet paper.

"Morning, Bev," my mother chirped while she placed

my fresh cup of coffee and a plate with buttered toast on the table.

Mom was one of those annoying people who woke up peppy. But she provided me with much-needed nourishment and caffeine, so I pushed away my irritation and took a deep breath through my nose, enjoying the coffee's scent that had tugged me from bed. I took a long swig and ignored the trail the bitter liquid burned from my tongue down to my stomach.

"Thanks," I muttered, picking at a small tear in the plastic floral tablecloth, trying to match my mother's cheeriness, yet failing miserably.

Seemingly unbothered, she continued with her routine, clearly taking no offense to my usual morning grumpiness.

My family had never been what one would consider verbose in their interactions. The din of family chatter never filled the rooms I grew up in. That perpetual quietness was where I developed my comfort in being alone, lost in my thoughts, and my discomfort in small talk.

We also weren't a family who felt big. While my mom always opened up more, my dad and I preferred to keep our emotions tucked away. Life stayed tidier that way. I have never understood people's incessant need to fill every space with babble and fuss. Or to display every thought, feeling, and emotion through their body language and facial expressions. It's so unnecessary and disorderly. I certainly felt feelings. I wasn't comatose, but I preferred my feelings to remain tucked away from the prying of others.

I gulped down two cups of coffee in amiable silence,

only the background music of dishes interrupting the quiet. As plates clattered in the sink, I gathered my keys, Bill's fresh thermos and his lunch, and headed out the door with a quick wave to my parents.

A gesture most likely unnoticed.

I ARRIVED at our bench to a sprawled, snoring Bill.

"You stink," I said, pushing him over to make room for myself.

"Bev, delightful as usual," he slurred, rolling himself into a sitting position. Gravity wasn't helping, as he promptly slumped forward.

"You obviously need this. Perhaps try it with no additions this morning." I handed him the thermos. His haggard face and eyes, mapped by bright red lines, shot a pang of worry into my belly. I expected a drunk Bill, but the Bill of that morning looked a half-step away from death.

I frowned, remembering how Bill came into my life. To graduate high school, all students had to perform mandatory volunteer hours. That's how Bill and I met, at a soup kitchen where I completed my hours. I'd half-heartedly scooped sad lumps of unidentifiable food into bowls held out by people who wanted to be there even less than I did. I wasn't there to make friends or even to do something good for the world. A signature on the form proving I did my time was my only goal. But Bill, not satisfied with a scoop of food, insisted on holding up the line, forcing me into a conversation.

Against my better judgment, I fell victim to his charms.

He quickly became my favorite person. I learned his history, which he delivered with such gumption you would think he lived a life filled with adventure and not heartbreak.

Somewhere in the world, Bill had two children around my age and an ex-wife who threw him out after he lost yet another job due to his excessive drinking. Ten years had passed since he'd seen them. I often found myself wondering if they missed him or even thought of him. It was evident in the way his eyes watered when he spoke of them, he longed for the life he'd drank away—the closest he ever came to admitting regret.

His former self would sometimes shine through, past the disheveled clothes, toothless grin, and foul stench, though I couldn't deny it was clear why his wife threw him out on the streets. Regardless of his flaws, he needed a friend. And so did I.

I never considered myself lonely. Yes, I spent most of my time alone, but alone to me never equated to lonely. I'd tried to make friends growing up. Those friendships never lasted long. They'd push me away, call me clingy, annoying, or weird. Sometimes, I wondered if I was born broken. A girl too different and too odd for this world or for friendship. After years of rejection, I had all but given up on the notion. Books would be my friends. But humans aren't built for a life of solitude. Everyone needs companionship of some sort. And Bill gave me that. Eventually, our friendship moved from the soup kitchen to our white bench where we met most mornings.

"I must tell you about the strangest encounter I had yesterday," I said.

"You had me at strange," he replied, perking up a bit.

"This man called Henry came into the shop. He was an odd one. This big smile just stuck on his face. The whole time he talked, just smiling away. And then he knocked over an entire stack of books. He didn't even have the good sense to be embarrassed about it." I imitated Henry's bumbling, leaving Bill doubled over in laughter, which quickly turned into a fit of coughs.

I continued when he'd recovered himself. "Wait, it gets stranger. I go to hand him his bag with the book he purchased, and he just stands there staring at me like this." I held out my hand, imitating Henry's maniacal smile to demonstrate.

"Do I really have to explain this to you? My beautiful, brilliant friend. Think, love, think." He poked the side of his head with a dirty finger.

"About what? How a potential serial killer may be lurking in the shadows, waiting to capture me and turn my bones into wind chimes?" I clucked my tongue and watched the people crossing the square in front of us, wondering which ones had dark secrets. Desires they had either acted on or were alarmingly close to.

Bill barked a loud laugh, attracting the attention of a few of those potential murderers. "I think he was flirting with you, love." He wiggled his eyebrows.

I choked on my coffee. "Utterly ridiculous assumption. I won't hear another word of the sort."

I jumped to my feet, *hmphed*, turned on my heels, and walked to the bookshop. Shaking my head.

A few more steps and I found myself smiling, then quickly pushed those preposterous thoughts from my head.

Flirting. Impossible.

LATER THAT AFTERNOON, Henry came bounding back into my store and into my life. Bill's outrageous suggestions re-played in my mind while I tried to hide the flush on my cheeks.

Oh my, do I have a stalker? That would be something new. The idea both thrilled and terrified me. Bill would love this twist.

Henry barreled through the store and met me at my usual spot tucked behind the counter. "I have a present for you."

He dropped a heavy book I hadn't noticed him holding onto the wooden counter. The thud made me start. A stranger bringing me a present made no sense. Also, why a book? He knew where I worked. He must be too dense to realize a perk of my employment was unlimited access to the very thing he was gifting me. Even if that unlimited access was possibly a very minor version of theft, potentially.

He pointed to the book, like a child displaying an art project only a mother could conjure up a compliment for.

"You said you hadn't read it. I needed to remedy that."

My lie stared back at me from the counter as Stephen King's book *The Stand.*

I had several decisions to make.

First, do I accept the book?

Second, do I admit I had lied? Tell him I already owned and had read *The Stand*—three times to be exact.

"Uh." A lame response was all I could muster. Perhaps I *was* unfit for life in a world where conversations were the kings and queens reigning over their chaotic kingdom. Such a simple situation, and I was in a tailspin. Almost two-hundred-thousand words comprise the English language and there I stood, only able to produce an unintelligent noise.

However, Henry didn't let the minor inconvenience of conversing with a lobotomy patient stop him. "Read it, and it will give us something to talk about when I take you out for dinner." He waited patiently—his grin more sheepish and less homicidal—anticipating my reply.

I narrowed my eyes, utterly perplexed by his persistence. I had never been on or even been asked on a date.

Was this some sort of practical joke? I wasn't ready to rule out my serial killer theory yet, either. Perhaps he was the one with plans for my bones and homemade wind chimes. Pretty ones, that hopefully made beautiful sounds when the breeze brushed through them. And grating screams when the wind blew with an angry force.

"No thank you." My words were the hammer that pounded in my stance with each syllable. "Can I help you find something else? Another romance, perhaps?" I smirked.

Henry's smile faltered, but he remained undeterred. "Oh, come on, it will be fun. Just one date."

"I don't date," I replied flatly.

A flicker of pity crossed his face which erased any feelings of affection that had begun to plant their seeds within me.

Visions of elementary school rushed in, and the sour belly that always accompanied those memories. A smaller, but no less awkward version of myself, weighed down by a backpack as large as a Sherpa's, always hiding in the back of the classroom, head bent into a novel.

One day in particular I had a similar unexpected invitation from perfect Claire Taylor. Her smile exposed her perfect teeth, complemented by her perfect blue eyes, and paired perfectly with her shiny blonde hair.

My interactions with Claire—and her loyal posse of Claire wannabes—alternated between being ignored and being picked on. While I preferred the ignoring, Claire and her cohorts preferred bullying. But on that day, she had something new in mind, and sidled up to my desk with a hint of mischief twinkling in her eyes. While twirling a shiny lock of hair around her slender finger, she drawled out my name with a sugary sweetness.

"You have no one to eat lunch with. And that is so sad to us." Pausing, she replaced her megawatt smile with an over-exaggerated frown. Her lapdogs nodded in agreement, and she continued, "We've decided that just won't do. We can't have our Beverly eating alone every day. It's not right!"

I was sure there was a catch. But it's so easy to believe pretty people, isn't it? As if there is some unwritten law stating a pretty face is incapable of delivering a lie.

I hadn't entirely constructed the wall keeping other humans out at that young age. I naively agreed and am ashamed to admit I did so with little pushback or consideration of my hasty acceptance's adverse consequences.

At lunchtime, I stood nervously gripping my tray in the center of the busy cafeteria. My eyes landed on a table of unbothered faces surrounding an animated Claire waving me over from across the room.

Gathering my courage, I walked over and carefully placed my tray on the table, taking a seat in the center across from Claire and between two girls whose names I can't be bothered to remember. A twisted smirk replaced the welcoming expression Claire used to call me over enthusiastically.

"What do you think you're doing, Beastly Beverly?" Claire asked. I froze with my peanut butter and jelly sandwich paused halfway to my mouth.

"This table is reserved for *normal* people. And only for our *friends*." She sneered.

Out of the corner of my eye, I caught a hand gripping a carton of milk and watched it twist. My ruined lunch swam in a white bath. I gathered my backpack and ran red-faced to the exit. The shrill of laughter punched me in the back with each step.

From that day forward I became Beastly Beverly. Beast when they were particularly lazy. Brick by brick, I completed the wall's construction, built to keep people out and my feelings in.

With a head shake, I brought myself back to the present and pushed thoughts of Claire and her stupid mini-Claires back into the recess of my mind.

The girl scarred by Claire screamed at me to run from

Henry and his proposed date. But the other, much quieter version, piqued with curiosity.

Henry's face became pages of a book, I easily read each emotion like the words on a page. "Oh, I'm sorry. I— are you in a relationship?" The last page landed on embarrassment.

"What?" My head jerked back. "No. Of course not."

His back straightened. "Oh phew, then what do you say?"

There were many things I wanted to say. No for starters. Perhaps I should have. Every second of every day we are faced with decisions that continually alter the course of our lives. I stood on the bank of an imaginary lake rolling a smooth rock in my hand. Would I throw it in and watch the ripples form on the water, or would I drop it and walk away?

I let the two competing opinions battle it out a bit longer. If he didn't fill the pregnant pause with unnecessary words, I would go against my better judgment and say yes. What the hell, I couldn't remember the last time I'd been out to eat. How much damage could come from one meal?

He, much to my chagrin—or was it delight?—patiently waited. The world felt off-kilter. Like I had followed the white rabbit down the hole, and everything had flipped upside down and turned inside out. The extra exertion of complicated human interaction left me exhausted.

"I suppose a meal with you wouldn't be the worst thing I could do with my weekend. And I happen to be free this Saturday evening."

"Great!" He slammed a blank sheet of paper on the counter. I jerked in my seat and almost reconsidered.

As if sensing my retreat, he quickly continued, "Just go ahead and add your address and phone number here, I'll pick you up at six-thirty on Saturday—evening, of course."

He watched intently. Despite my inner voice screaming at me not to, I—carefully, and in neat, practiced penmanship—wrote my information down. When the last *t* was crossed and *i* dotted, Henry snatched the paper and sped-walked for the exit. *Making your escape before I change my mind, I see.*

He called his goodbyes over his shoulder, lifting his hand in a quick wave. The shop door closed behind him, leaving me alone and unsure how to feel or what to do with my hands. I faltered between regret and panic. *What have I gotten myself into?*

By the time the clock signaled closing time, I assured myself he'd cancel; worrying myself over it was unnecessary.

Yet, later that evening, while lying in bed—hanging on the rim of wakefulness and sleep—a face floated behind my eyes. A face consumed by a broad smile that stretched all the way to its eyes. A smile that didn't hide murderous intentions after all. And a face whose eyes crinkled ever so slightly at the edges in the most pleasing way.

That all occurred on a Tuesday. Which gave me exactly two days to remain confident Henry would call to cancel and two days to fret he would not.

Four

Now

"Now WAIT A MINUTE," he says. I'm so caught up in my story I forget I have an audience for a second.

I lift my eyes to his. "Go on."

"No offense—" he starts.

"Usually when people start a sentence with that, what follows is offensive." I grin to let him know I'm teasing.

"True. Let me go ahead and offend you then. You were terrible to Henry, why in the world would anyone torture themselves? He sounds like a nice guy, that Henry."

I close my eyes and picture Henry's face. "He was. Henry and I both made mistakes. We could sit here and argue about whose were worse. I understand your point, though. As you can see, I wasn't always the endearing woman you see today." I wink. "That's exactly why I was so weary. Why me? No one ever picked me or wanted me.

At that point in my life, I'd accepted my fate. I didn't want more."

"Want comes with disappointment."

"Precisely. Did I treat Henry poorly? Of course. I treated everyone poorly, including myself."

"You're not answering the question."

My chair creaks as I rock. My head turns forward and I gaze out at the sea of green. Bloated clouds tumble over themselves above the trees. "Looks like rain."

He nods. "News said a storm's coming tonight."

"I love the rain."

"Did your parents know?"

"About Henry?"

His chin tilts and his bushy eyebrows speckled with gray rise.

"Oh, you mean my little habit? The toilet paper." I shake my head. "No. I never told them. Mostly from embarrassment, partly because I didn't want them fretting over me."

"I get that."

A breeze picks up lifting my hair and tickling my neck. "Why don't we go inside? I have chili in the slow cooker. We can eat and I can tell you more. I think things will become clearer."

He pushes himself from the rocking chair and pats his belly. "I'm starved, chili sounds great."

"It's my mom's recipe. She's always been the best cook." I stand and grab our empty mugs.

"I know where you get your skills from then."

I smile. My mother and I are so very different, it warms me to think there are ways I'm like her after all.

Five

Before

BILL TEASED me relentlessly about the upcoming date. After realizing he had taken it too far, he switched to encouragement. Bill's flavor of encouragement, of course. He told me if Henry didn't like me, well, that was his problem, not mine. A big fan of free meals, especially good ones, he said if I needed any further justification for going, a free meal should be enough. All reasonable and excellent points.

By Saturday morning, though, I transformed into a bundle of nerves. As I lay in bed, I pondered my situation, the realization sinking in, this date was probably going to occur. I argued with myself internally, if only I could summon some of Bill's confidence, or at least, his unwavering faith in me.

To help, I focused on the critical items still entirely within my control. I rolled out of bed, hands on hips, and stood frowning at my closet, contemplating what women wore on first dates. Nothing hanging in there, for certain.

My unmade bed called to me with its comfort. To avoid the temptation of crawling back in and avoid the situation entirely, I walked back and pulled the covers up. An uncharacteristically sloppy bed making job. I had to be quick so as not to give myself the chance to change my mind.

I needed help from a more experienced woman. After racking my brain for where I could find one of those, I came up with the clothing boutique near the bookshop. I had never ventured inside, but the women I'd seen going in and out the front door seemed like women who dated and married.

I dressed quickly and ran downstairs. My parents' curious stares followed me out the door.

RATHER THAN GOING STRAIGHT to the boutique after parking my car, I chose to visit our white wooden bench, hoping a conversation with Bill would ease my nerves. An empty bench greeted me. It was Saturday, and we typically only met Monday through Friday, so the empty bench wasn't a surprise. I wandered down a few blocks, peeking in alleyways in search of him, before determining my efforts were in vain. I was on my own.

Chin lifted, shoulders rolled back, I faked confidence as I walked to *My Lady Boutique*, trying my hardest to project the poise of a woman who knew what she was doing. Once there, I swung open the door and stepped through the entryway, only to stop short. The thick scent of lavender and rose petals smacked me in the face, the saccharine smell an affront to my olfactory system—immediately nauseated, my mouth filled with warm saliva. I brought a fist up to my nose and took deep breaths, begging myself not to puke.

Once certain I had swallowed my bile into submission, my other senses ignited. The blindingly bright lights and music screaming through the overhead speakers made it hard to think. Realization hit me; I had made a mistake. I turned to leave when a girl whose looks perfectly complemented her surroundings assaulted me.

"How can I help you, darling?" Her thick New England accent made the r non-existent.

Auburn hair stretched down her back in waves. Beach waves I think they would be called. Her ripped jeans hung baggy on her thin frame, and her arms were so full of bracelets, she sounded like a hurricane blowing through wind chimes. This reminded me of Henry, and bones, and other horribly scary things like first dates, or overly friendly shopgirls.

My eyes flitted in their sockets, desperately searching for an alternative employee to assist me. No such luck. Dejected, my only hope was she would be more successful in dressing me than she had been herself.

"I have a date tonight," I explained, trying to hide how foreign the statement felt on my tongue, "and as it so happens my wardrobe does not contain the appropriate trappings for this type of social engagement."

She laughed. Not getting the joke I didn't join in. She swallowed back her giggles and her face fell serious. "Ok."

She recovered quickly and her cheeriness returned. "I can help with that for sure. We have all sorts of options. I'm Quinn by the way."

She reached out her hand, indicating she wanted me to grab hold of it.

I clasped my hands with interlaced fingers across my belly button. Just because she'd provided me with her name didn't mean this was an invitation for contact.

"Beverly," I said. "Nice to meet you."

Without a beat, and clearly taking no offense, she turned and retreated deeper into the store. I let her get two steps ahead so she wouldn't make the mistake of trying to touch me again.

She called over her shoulder, "Do you have any idea what type of outfit you're looking for? Dress, skirt? Something more casual?"

The options were overwhelming. Bill wouldn't be welcome in such an establishment; still I longed for his presence. We could have at least giggled behind her back at the absurdity of it all.

"I suppose something conservative will do. A dress, perhaps."

Quinn nodded while moving amongst racks of clothing. I moved with her as if a rope tethered us together. She pulled articles of clothing off the racks, *mmhmming* as she went. As the pile draped over her arm grew, she disappeared behind it.

"Alright, let's get you set up in a fitting room and find your date dress!"

I shuffled to the back of the store following her bouncing stride. She hung her selection on a hook inside the bright changing room. One glance at my reflection in the back wall mirror had any bit of courage I had left leaking out through my toes. A pale and petrified face stared back at me. The glaring lights accentuated my every flaw.

With the door shut, I undressed and quickly pulled a dress over my head to avoid any prolonged visuals of my half-naked body reflected in the unflattering mirror. *Not terrible.* I twisted at the hips so I could observe myself from multiple angles. Quinn babbled from outside the door, but I only half-listened and didn't bother to reply.

By the time I tried on the third option, I started to enjoy myself—despite my best efforts to hate the process. The dresses Quinn picked weren't too garish, and they all fit nicely. Even more surprisingly, they flattered my body. She turned out to be good at her job. I was pleased with myself for making the right choice in coming here.

I found my winner in the fifth selection. A navy-blue sleeveless dress, with a red belt. The skirt flared slightly right above my knees. I stepped from the dressing room to model for Quinn, suddenly realizing how important her approval was.

"You look beautiful," she proclaimed. "So sophisticated, and look at the curves that cinched waist gives you; the perfect hourglass figure!"

Hourglass, ha! Nevertheless, I was satisfied with my selection and appreciative of Quinn's help.

I glanced at the larger mirror hanging at the end of the dressing room hall and smiled at myself. I wished again for Bill's presence. I would have twirled for him, showing him a different side of me. He would have laughed and told me to put my regular clothes back on. He, like me, didn't slide readily into change.

I stepped back into the dressing room. Getting into the dress had been no problem. Removing myself from it, however, proved to be a challenge. With one arm bent above my head and the other arm reaching from below, I desperately grasped at the zipper like a floundering contortionist. After spinning in circles, my efforts in vain, I dropped my arms to my sides and stared at my sweaty reflection. I considered asking Quinn for assistance, but no, I couldn't bear the thought of her undressing me.

With no other option, I stuffed my clothes into my purse and stepped out, declaring I loved the dress so much I would wear it home.

Quinn tilted her head and shrugged. "Works for me."

At the counter, I gripped the tag from the armpit of the dress and leaned closer so Quinn could scan it. She obliged, not looking too pleased with the idea.

Quinn smacked her gum in the most annoying way, then stopped and stared at my face as if she was trying to read my thoughts. My gaze dropped to my feet, and I wished she'd hand me my card so I could leave.

"Any plans for hair and makeup?"

My brow furrowed. "I'm not sure what you mean. My face and hair will look like they always do, as they do now."

She appeared to grow a few inches and reached for her phone. I opened my mouth to let her know I was ready to leave when she held up a finger. "My girlfriend is *the best* hairdresser in Newport, let me see—Cora, hi! It's Quinn, can Rowan squeeze in a girlfriend of mine? Special date night." She winked at me, and I stared at her with a dropped jaw, stunned speechless. Quinn continued to "mmhmm" and nod enthusiastically, then ended the call.

Before I fully processed what was happening, or had a chance to decline, she gave me directions to Rowan's shop three doors down, hoping I didn't mind—telling me I wouldn't regret it.

"She will take the very best care of you, I promise," Quinn said. "You'll feel so pampered and pretty and have the best night ever."

I stood on the sidewalk in front of the boutique, my legs twitching with the urge to skip the appointment and walk straight to my car. The courtesy of cancellation wasn't my responsibility, as I didn't make the appointment. But the newness of it all intrigued me.

I found myself two doors down in Rowan's swiveling salon chair, draped in a black plastic cape, the sulfuric smell of rotten eggs from what was hopefully more invasive hair treatments than I'd be receiving permeated my nostrils. Rowan slowly pushed the chair around in a circle, inspecting my hair and face like a scientist analyzing her new specimen. She tsked and tutted, and hummed and hawed, then finally—a plan likely in mind—began gathering an array of devices that appeared to have no other use than torture.

She went to work with my back facing the mirror, so I couldn't monitor the ongoing situation. The anticipation buzzing through my limbs made it hard to sit still and not fuss. I sat on my hands under the cape to keep them from reaching up and getting in her way.

"Who's the lucky guy?" she asked.

An unplanned appointment meant I was ill-prepared with no book to use to avoid idle chitchat. It was a day to break free from my comfortable refuge. I obliged rather than sought out some other way of deflecting.

I told her about Henry, at least what I knew of him, which at that point wasn't very much. My attempts at blasé fell flat. Even the thought of a stranger knowing I was hopeful and excited sent a sliver of fear up my spine, especially when the likelihood of disaster soared so high.

"It sounds like he's quite smitten with you," she said when I finished. Henry's thoughts had never occurred to me before that moment. That was one of my faults. I wasn't selfish, or I tried not to be, but I often found myself so overcome by my own thoughts and fears, I didn't give proper consideration to other's feelings.

"Hmm, I suppose he must be," I replied partially to myself, "otherwise, why would he be so resolute with his request?"

Maybe I *would* have a pleasant time, and the date wouldn't end in hurt and sadness and disappointment? The hope growing inside my chest drudged up unwelcomed loneliness with it, which I didn't care for one bit. Up until that point, I was convinced a life of solitude and sameness was the life I wanted. I didn't need other people, as other people complicated things. I had my job, my books, Bill, and my parents. That was enough. Anything more, and an opportunity opened for someone holding my heart to turn their hands palm down, smash my feelings to the floor, and stomp on them with their enormous feet as they walked away.

Could I be a normal girl? Could someone see past my

weirdness and find something likable? Hard to imagine someone else liking me when I didn't care for myself very much.

What felt like hours had passed, grinding on my patience, when Rowan finally stepped back to admire her work. With a smile, she swiveled my chair to face the mirror.

Startled by the sight, I jerked forward and brought my hand up to a face that no longer looked like mine. I wanted to make sure it was real and still connected to my body. Rowan had teased and curled my normally flat and uninspired hair. It now occupied a significantly larger area of the atmosphere surrounding my head. My eyes, rimmed with black, popped, and the dark shadow smeared across my lids somehow transformed the brown of my irises into the color of chocolate rather than the brackish water they typically resembled. My lips, surely breaking some laws of physics, were plump and glossy, and my cupid's bow plunged in a deep V. Moving my head from side to side, I watched those shiny lips transform into an O.

"I—" I stammered, "I can't believe—that face?" My voice rose at the end of my partially formed sentence, unsure if I had a question or a statement.

The tiny seed of excitement that had planted in my belly earlier began tingling and budding. I gave my face a break and abstained from self-deprecations. I let myself admire the reflection in the mirror for once in my life. If I could like it, maybe someone else could, too.

"I love it!" I proclaimed, after drinking it all in; an uncharacteristic glee accentuated my words. It was best that Bill wasn't there after all. He wouldn't like that unfamiliar face occupying my head, and I wouldn't like his scrutiny.

Rowan smiled back at me in the mirror and removed the black cape, then handed me a tube of lipstick she explained was for touch ups. After I paid, she lavished me with more compliments; I had never been complimented so much in a day.

I could understand why people liked them so much.

I walked quickly to my car, no longer looking for Bill, afraid of what he might say if he saw the new—potentially improved—Beverly.

My sweaty palms gripped the steering wheel while I drove home. Unable to focus on the road, my eyes kept drifting to the rearview mirror, examining the stranger reflected in it. Twice, I dangerously drifted into the lane next to me, eliciting a chorus of angry beeping and furious glares.

Visions of a fiery crash flashed through my mind. My body flying through the windshield, skin shredded by the glass. Body smashed on the pavement; contorted appendages twisted in the wrong directions—not so pretty anymore.

A very cautious driver, I chuckled and returned my attention back on the road. It would be my luck to get asked on a date, finally be excited by such an endeavor, only to die in a crash from my own negligence before having the chance to enjoy it.

Once in my driveway, I shifted into park and turned the car off. Without the engine's sound, my heartbeat pounded loudly in my ears. Its tempo sped up to match my breathing. The familiar pricks crept under my skin as anxiety replaced the giddiness I'd been floating on. Thoughts of my parents' reaction made it hard to swallow. I sat in the driver's seat, hands gripping the wheel, gulping deep mouthfuls of hot summer air.

Finally, I walked up the driveway and braced for their reaction.

The familiar scent of my mom's perfume and a meat and potatoes dinner greeted me when I stepped through the front door. My parents were in their usual Saturday evening spots. My dad in his brown leather recliner, with a Coors Light sweating on the small end-table next to him, and my mother on the floral print couch, both engrossed in the local news.

My mother looked up and her eyes widened briefly. She forced the edges of her lips into an unnatural smile. Her face resembled Bozo the Clown rather than a welcoming mother. I mumbled my hellos and walked past them with my chin tucked to my chest. My dad grumbled something that sounded like *huh*, and my mom chirped an overly cheery—even for her—hello.

"Dinner will be ready in a bit," my mom said.

"I'm not eating here tonight," I called, while scurrying up the stairs to my bedroom in my new dress, with my new face, and my insecurities. It wasn't my mom who looked like an overdone clown—it was me.

In the safety of my bedroom, I stood before my mirror and rubbed the fabric of the dress between my finger and thumb. It truly was a beautiful dress, but was it a dress meant for a beautiful girl? A girl who wasn't me.

I walked across my room and lowered myself to my bed. My reflection caught my eye and my cheeks burned with shame. I saw myself through my parents' eyes. Ridiculous. A strange girl playing dress-up to fit in a world she didn't belong.

I pounded the sides of my head with my fists to dislodge the negative thoughts from my brain. The self-doubt wormed its way in.

You aren't like other girls, it hissed in my ear. *This isn't you. You don't want these things. Dating and love are for other girls, they aren't for you.*

Cheeks puffed, I slowly released the air and tried to calm my shaking hands by sitting on them. Emotions clashed within my head. I felt claustrophobic in my own skin. *Hush you, leave me alone.*

Henry became the target of my frustration. Why did he have to walk into my bookshop and disrupt my life? I was perfectly fine. Now, look at me. A wreck. The waves of anxiety continued to roll over me.

Elbows on my knees, I went to put my face in my hands but stopped short, not wanting to ruin my makeup. I moaned in exasperation. Henry was to arrive in fifteen minutes.

I got moving.

I lifted my arm and removed the dress's sales tags then leaned toward the mirror over my dresser. My lipstick needed a touch up. Thank heavens Rowan thought of this detail. I ran the stick she'd given me across my oh'd lips. One final check in the mirror and a fluff of my hair, and I was ready to go.

At the top of the stairs, I paused and gripped the railing. I had two options—neither of which was less awkward than the other. I could turn back and sit in my room to wait for Henry's arrival. This course of action would give Henry and my parents several unattended minutes together. Or, I could continue downstairs and await his arrival in the living room *with* my parents. This could result in a barrage of questions concerning my looks, plans, and Henry.

I preferred maintaining some semblance of control over the situation, so I walked down the stairs trying to steady my breathing and shaking hands.

The third stair up from the bottom betrayed my entry, groaning under my weight. Both parents occupied the same spots I had left them in. They looked up from the world news at my arrival. Clearly, in better control of her faculties, my mother's smile was much more pleasant. I placed myself on the opposite side of the couch from her.

"Going somewhere, sweetheart?" she asked.

"A very nice man, Henry, asked me to join him for dinner tonight," I responded, keeping my attention on the television.

"Well, isn't that nice," my mom replied.

"Henry, huh?" my dad interjected, apparently that revelation worthy of his attention.

"Yes, Henry," I replied.

My parents turned their attention back to the television screen.

Everyone seemed pleased with the amount of detail they had on the other family members' comings and goings. The old grandfather clock announced the arrival and departure of six-thirty from the formal dining room. A trickle of sweat trailed down my spine. I wrung my hands to occupy them.

A slumped stature makes one look nervous, so I straightened my back, thanking myself for not telling my parents Henry's expected arrival time. The thought of their doubt intermixing with my own was just too much to bear.

If he didn't show up, I'd have to walk right back upstairs. The image of this in my mind made my temperature rise even more. As the minute hand continued to creep past the six, I pressed my hands on my legs to stop them from bouncing. If my parents noticed the turmoil roiling within me, they had the grace not to call attention to it.

Finally, at six-forty—ten minutes late—the ringing of the doorbell announced Henry's arrival. My dad raised a single eyebrow, and my mom's face lit up with a hopeful smile.

I dragged my feet to the front door, ready to calmly, yet pointedly, explain the rudeness of being tardy.

I never got the chance.

Henry's signature smile greeted me when I opened the door. But his smile wavered from genuine to confused. And then he began to laugh. Unable to maintain control of himself, he doubled over with tears in his eyes.

"I'm sorry, Bev," he said after regaining his composure.

He wiped the tears from his eyes. "It's your face! Your hair! It's so different. You took me by surprise."

The heat of humiliation spread like wildfire from my chest up to my hairline. A stone formed in my throat. Tears pricked my eyes, and I slammed the door right in his stupid grinning face before my leaking eyes could betray me.

Mortified, I ran back upstairs to my room, leaving Henry standing on my front porch, gripping three sad carnations. That silly grin still taking up half his face, I'm sure.

Sitting on my bed and staring at my reflection I knew what was coming. The ocean roared in my ears. I clasped my hands together, turning my knuckles white, trying to control what I had no control of. With a resigned sigh, I reached down to my hiding spot under my bed and pulled out the battered shoebox, from which I retrieved a roll of toilet paper. I began eating it, square by square. I ate until I devoured my fear, my sadness, heartbreak, loneliness, anger, and embarrassment.

With each bite the thin paper melted on my tongue. I consumed those emotions, locking them back in their rightful place, hidden deep in the depths of my belly.

Six

I woke up the next morning after the date that wasn't meant to be with a brain still foggy from sleep. For a brief, blissful moment, I forgot the dreadful prior evening. Then, the memories and humiliation slammed into me. I prayed for a catastrophe. The ceiling collapsing perhaps, pinning me to the bed, forcing me back into an endless state of oblivious slumber.

Glaring at the ceiling, I cursed its resilience.

I resigned myself to the fact it was the perfect outcome, the result of a necessary experiment. Last night categorically proved that love is a messy affair, one which I had no room for in my organized, well-controlled life. I decided then and there I would not waste one more minute on Henry or notions of love.

Books and Bill were all I needed.

Sundays were always lazy days in my house. Besides the occasional meetings in the kitchen, we all tended to keep to ourselves. That Sunday was much the same, making it easy to avoid my parents and conversations about Henry, dates, and dinners. Enjoying my meals in the comfort of my bedroom, I spent the day huddled under the covers, below the annoyingly stable ceiling, while disappearing into a book well into the evening.

I didn't yet know that Henry was also hidden away in his own bedroom for most of the day. Nursing his emotional bruises and a terrible hangover. If I had been privy to that information, my mood might have lightened.

Close to dinnertime, the phone rang. Another artifact in our museum of a home. We were probably the last family left who still had a landline. Moments later, my mom called my name from the bottom of the stairs. Confused, I walked downstairs to see what she needed.

"You have a phone call," she said, holding out the cordless phone.

I'm not sure why I was surprised. Henry had already proven himself a nuisance. A persistent mosquito whom I couldn't swat away.

"Beverly? Hello? You there?"

His voice had an edge of desperation to it, causing me to recoil and extend the headset at arm's length. He rambled on, his muffled voice barely discernible, especially over the rush of anger barreling through my ears. I had no clue what he'd been thinking; one would think a door slammed in one's face would be hint enough.

Apparently, he was denser than I realized.

I pushed the button to end the call harder than necessary, cutting him off mid-sentence.

"Wrong number," I mumbled to my mom, handing her the phone and returning to my bedroom.

I sat on my bed and stewed, a boiling pot of bubbling anger threatening to spill over. My breathing shortened into staccato puffs. To hell with Henry for making me hope, only to discard me and my feelings like a used tissue. I grew furious with myself for going against my better judgment and agreeing to go out with him in the first place.

I let him in, albeit a smidge. Still a lot farther than I allowed most people. Everyone else stood on the bank of the moat circling the stone walls safeguarding my heart. If I had let down the drawbridge and welcomed him across, rather than just calling to him from the ramparts, the damage that dimwit could have done!

I allowed myself two squares, nibbling slowly. Their elixir melting in my mouth, I drew out my meal, letting the thin paper perform its magic. The colorful chaos of my thoughts turned to a dull, relaxing gray.

I'd discovered this remedy on a day when my classmates' teasing was more relentless than usual. I'd retreated to my safe place, hidden in the bathroom with my legs pulled up on the toilet seat so no one could see me. The toilet paper roll hung on the side of the stall. After grabbing some to wipe my tears and blow my nose, I paused and chose instead to stuff my mouth with a crumpled ball to stifle the scream I so desperately wanted to release. The paper liquified in my mouth, delivering a consolation I'd never experienced. I stayed in that bathroom, eating through what remained of the roll until the final bell rang releasing us from school. Disgusted with myself but not able to stop, I had discovered my vice. My secret. A secret I would have to hide from the world, even from my parents. But at that moment, in that bathroom, I wasn't sure how I'd lived without it. The more my insecurities grew, the more toilet paper I ate.

A stony expression was now permanently stitched on my face. From that point forward, I was armed with the knowledge that there was always a meal of paper close by whenever things got too hard. I vowed to never let another human steal my power again. And even if I exploded in a shower of bones and blood from the hoard of emotions I packed inside, the Claires or Henrys of the world would *never* earn a single tear from me ever again.

That was why I ate toilet paper; it felt good. If anyone were to discover my carefully concealed quirk, it would repulse them, I'm sure. But I was never one to give credence to the opinions of others, at least most days.

Seven

Monday meant I had to crawl out of my cave and reenter the world. I left for work early, foregoing breakfast at home, and went straight to the bench. In my haste to avoid my parents' sympathetic stares, I had forgotten Bill's coffee and lunch, but I desperately needed to speak with him.

"You look as terrible as I feel." I perked at the sound of his voice and looked up, recoiling at the sight of him.

Despite the early hour, the summer heat was thick and sticky, but something else ailed Bill besides the weather. His cheeks sunk deeper than usual, and his pale skin glistened with sweat. I scolded myself for being too wrapped up in my own problems to remember his food.

"You need to see a doctor. When was the last time you ate? I haven't had breakfast yet. Come with me to the coffee shop so I can buy you breakfast."

"I refuse. That place is for suckers. Trendy, overpriced. Psht. They won't see a dime of my hard-earned money."

Bill didn't have any money, certainly none hard-earned, but I decided against pointing out it wasn't his money we would exchange for the meal. I did, however, agree with him on several of his other points. It *was* trendy and overpriced. Crowded as well, and I hated crowds. But I needed caffeine to survive the day. And he needed food.

"I'm going over there, so if you change your mind, you know where to find me. I'm desperate for caffeine and willing to sacrifice my standards for it."

"What's got you down, love?"

I explained the situation and angrily wiped away the disloyal tears sliding down my cheeks.

"I'm so humiliated. I should have known not to expect a different outcome. Things don't work out for people like you and me."

"Now stop right there. Don't you put yourself in the same category as me. You know as well as I do, there are only three people responsible for my situation—me, myself, and I. You aren't like me, and you aren't like any of these other pigs either." He gestured to the few people within sight. "You *are* better. You are the best."

Bill jumped up, standing on the bench. He cupped his hands to his mouth and called, "My friend Beverly is amazing, and any of you fools would be lucky to date her!"

I pulled on his tattered T-shirt, laughing through my tears. "You're making a spectacle of us. Sit down this instant."

He collapsed back onto the bench in a fit of coughs.

"It's true, though. You don't realize it, but I do. I know the opinions of an old drunk don't matter much in this world. But any man, any person, would be lucky to be acquainted with you. And you deserve a good man in your life, someone who's going to cherish you for the diamond you are."

"Your opinion matters to me, very much so. More than anyone's, really." I grabbed his hand and squeezed.

I wondered what a Bill without alcohol would be like. Perhaps that was another one of life's cruel jokes. To give me the most amazing friend in the world, only to give him a debilitating disease, hindering our friendship beyond morning meetings on a bench.

"You really don't look good. I want you to see a doctor. In fact, I demand it," I said, forcing him to meet my eyes.

"Fine, fine," he replied. I knew he was simply saying it to placate me and wouldn't follow through. That made me want to cry all over again. I had cried more tears in two days than I had in my entire life. I crossed my fingers, praying he would listen this time.

"I'm going to skedaddle, love. You go into that coffee shop and get yourself the most expensive thing on the menu. You deserve it. And don't you let this Henry situation bother you. Don't let that pretty head of yours worry over it."

"He's been trying to call me. I've ignored him. What should I do about that?"

"Well, remember, people make mistakes." With a wink, he rolled himself off the bench, swayed slightly, then hobbled off.

With Bill gone, I pondered his words. Was he alluding

to his own mistakes? His yearning for forgiveness from his long-lost family? I could only imagine what they had endured before making the hard decision to kick him out.

Newport's song of seagulls played distantly. A woman walked by pushing a stroller over the rough brick, the baby asleep inside. I imagined what I would be like as a mother. Then remembered babies cry, a lot, and come with dirty diapers and other bodily fluids that always seem to leak from one end or the other. I scrunched my face right in time for the woman to turn toward me and make eye contact.

Her smile faltered, and she returned my dirty look before quickening her step. Bill's face materialized behind my eyes. His wife must be more compassionate than me. After one mistake, Henry was dead to me. But I had never considered myself tolerant, so I shrugged and rose from my seat.

Coffee was more critical than Henry. However, Bill's health was not, and remained heavy on my mind as I walked to my destination. My stomach rumbled. Unlike Bill, I couldn't function without food. It made me even grumpier than usual.

DESPITE ITS GEOGRAPHIC CONVENIENCE, I'd never visited the coffee shop before. I opened the front door and stepped into the cozy space. Dimly lit and decorated in welcoming hues of browns and tans, the sweet aroma of complicated coffee concoctions filled the air.

An overly perky girl stood behind a curved glass

display case filled with delicious-looking pastries, whip-
ping together fancy-looking drinks with practiced precision. I waited in line with my arms crossed, tapping the toe
of my loafer. The other patrons must have been regulars.
Instead of simply placing their orders, they insisted on
chitchatting with the girl, slowing the entire operation
down unnecessarily.

When it was my turn, I placed my order for a black
coffee and a croissant, not bothering with any additional
discussion. My order's simplicity seemed to confound her,
but with a shrug, she prepared what I had asked for before
moving on to the next customer.

Breakfast in hand, I turned from the counter to search
for a suitable place to enjoy it. With most of the customers
grabbing their orders to go, plenty of open seating availed
itself. I chose a small table for two by the front window
instead of the couches next to the counter. I could watch
the pedestrians through the window and make up stories
of my unaware victims to pass the time.

"Well, I'll be. Fancy seeing you here."

Up jerked my head at the shrill greeting. Quinn's
opposing frame towered over me. I craned my neck to look
at her. The sun haloed her from behind, and with her red
hair she looked like a ball of fire.

"Mind if I sit?" she asked.

"Yes, as a matter of fact—" Not waiting for me to
finish, she helped herself to the table's open chair.

I was about to explain my desire for solitude when she
interrupted me with a laugh.

"You're too funny. I just *hate* to eat or drink alone,

don't you? Now tell me about your date. Did you have fun? Did Rowan take good care of you? I'm sure she did. She is wicked good, isn't she? Did he ask you out for a second date?"

The stare from her intense blue eyes bored into me. She had fired the questions so fast, most whizzed by my head before I could grab them.

My chin—annoyingly—wobbled, and I blinked rapidly to ward off the tears determined to fall down my face. Again.

My battle lost, the tears poured freely.

"Oh, no." Sympathy etched Quinn's face. She drew out the last syllable and put her hands on top of mine.

"What happened? Spill it."

I teetered between my two selves, but realizing I'd already fallen to one side with my uncharacteristic display of emotion, the flood of words spilled from my mouth and onto the table.

I explained how I'd never been in love, not even in like. How I—until that prior weekend—didn't *want* any of those things. How perfectly content I was until this person, this man, this *Henry,* came barreling into my life like a freight train, messing everything up. And how he'd ruined it. The evening, my hope. All of it.

When all the words were out, I had the immediate urge to run around the shop and pick them up, to stuff them back in my mouth where they belonged. I looked at the restroom sign, my entire body itched to run in there and devour every roll.

"Sweetie." Quinn's eyes filled with sympathy, and her

freckles seemed to dance around her face as concern ticked across it.

I wanted to be somewhere, *anywhere* else, and deeply regretted my unfiltered display of emotions.

"You can't let one bad experience spoil you from love," she continued. "Love is highs and lows, and comfortable middles. But those highs and middles are worth mucking through the lows. It may not feel that's true now, but I promise you it is. It's worth every messy, awful second of it. And I speak from experience, a long history of broken hearts and nights spent crying myself to sleep."

I nodded. I heard what she was saying but couldn't fathom her words being the truth. I hadn't even gone on one date, and my body felt as if someone had dragged me by my hair over shards of glass.

Naked and exposed, both from my unintentional confession and the entire weekend, enough was enough. I thanked Quinn for her kindness and prepared to take my leave.

"I'm not letting you go that easily. I realize you may not be in search of friendship, but friendship has found you. You've opened up to me, Bev, and that's real. I'm a good read of people, and I can tell that means a lot more from you than most."

"I have a friend; his name is Bill."

"And now you have two! Let's do this again, okay? How about tomorrow, same place, same time?"

I paused, then gave into the warmth—though luke-warm—filling my chest and offered a slight nod.

She dug in her purse and pulled out her phone, fingers

hovering over the screen. "What's your cell number? I'll shoot you a text so you have mine."

My gaze dropped to my lap. "I don't have one," I mumbled.

Her entire face looked like she'd seen a ghost. Or a woman who had clearly time traveled from the past.

"I used to," I continued. "I dropped it, shattering the screen. Since no one ever called me, I didn't bother replacing it."

I could see her working very hard to control her expression. "No big deal," she said in a way that betrayed her words. It was obviously a very big deal. Yet another *thing* shining a spotlight on my differentness. "What's the best way to get in touch with you?"

"The bookshop, or we have a house phone. It's not like I'm ever anywhere else." I chuckled nervously.

"A house phone? How very vintage of you. I like it."

I recited the numbers for her, her fingers flying across a fancier phone than I'd ever even held in my hands, much less owned.

Once she was done, we said our goodbyes and were off to start our days.

Buoyed by my chance encounter with Quinn, my day flew by. The pressure weighing me down that morning lifted by the afternoon. The makings of what may be happiness tickled my skin. My anger at Henry was still very much present—he was terrible and awful and unworthy—but he wasn't consuming my mind anymore. I found a different way to rid myself of that energy-sucking negativity. No secret trips to the lavatory for a sneaky snack needed. How freeing! Quinn wanted to be my friend. No one ever wanted to be my friend, and certainly no one as fun and kind as Quinn. I promised myself I would be the very best friend I could be to her.

———

MIDAFTERNOON, a sheepish-looking Henry passed through my bookshop's entryway. Anger sharpened my words.

"What are you doing here?"

"I came to apologize, to ask for a second chance. I'll do better next time. Promise."

"Apologies aren't necessary. You proved yourself to be someone I'd prefer not to associate with. For that, I thank you."

His chin dropped to his chest, and I busied myself with rearranging papers on the desk that didn't need rearranging.

"You caught me off guard. You looked so different; it surprised me. It's no excuse. Sometimes I do stupid things like laugh when it's not what I'm meaning to do at all. I like your face without all that stuff on it, is all."

"Compliments will get you nowhere. I'm extremely busy. It was a pleasure, well no it wasn't, but we've met and now it's time to un-meet." I glanced at the door hoping he'd get the hint.

He opened his mouth as if to say something and I turned my back to him, only turning back around when the sound of the bells above the door alerted me to his departure.

I think of that day on occasion. If only Henry had

walked out of that door and never come back. What then? In my dreams I scream at the closed door. I tell him to stay away. I tell him I'm not worthy. I'm not...

Then I wake up and all the dream versions of Henry dissolve. It's too late.

Eight

A VASE FILLED with roses sat in the middle of my kitchen table. I'd never received flowers from anyone, and these were undeniably lovely. I leaned in and inhaled. The sweet scent slowly unraveled the knot of anger.

My dad sat across from me, pretending to ignore the splash of red between us.

"Do you mind if I move these so I can set the plates down?" my mom asked, her tone casual. If my parents were interested in the chain of events that brought this bouquet to our kitchen table, neither asked.

I got up, placed the roses on the counter out of the way, then returned to the table.

"I have something to say." My dad surprised us both. Being a man of few words, when they came, they hung heavier in the air.

"I'm a simple man. I don't need a lot of hubbub in my life to make it meaningful. No hobbies, no friends, no riches. I'm perfectly content with the life I've built. I'm happy. I wake up happy, I go to bed happy. But without you and your mom, I'm not so sure I'd be able to say that. Before I met your mom, I *thought* I was happy. Kind of like you, Bev. She showed me how everything I thought I knew about myself—and about life—was wrong. She showed me how much I was missing. That life could have colors, dimension. She brought out a man I had no clue existed in me, a man I wasn't even looking for. It wasn't easy for her. I'm not the most lovable man. But what I was missing, what was impossible for me, was the exact opposite for her. Your mom is warm, and caring, and thoughtful. She's never overbearing or trying to force me into a mold I would never fit in. And therefore, your mom didn't just love me, she completed me. That's a damn beautiful thing. To find someone so perfectly made for you, they fill in every missing piece with their amazing qualities."

I looked between my parents wondering where this was all coming from. My mom smiled and placed her hand on my dad's.

He cleared his throat and continued, "That person, the one meant for you, they do this without you even realizing it. Until one day, it hits you. You didn't know you had been living life as half a person, but now that you aren't one any longer, you can never go back to that state again. And when you find that person, you hang on tight, so tight your life depends on it, because it does! You step outside your comfort zone. You learn to love—in your own way—but in the important ways. Most people spend their lives hiding behind a mask of who they think they should be. And you and me, Bev, we're worse than most. The carbon fiber walls we stash our hearts and our feelings behind are nearly impossible to breach. You may meet a lot of oils to your water, but one of those tries may be the key to your lock. And the reward, I promise you, daughter, the reward is worth the journey."

The air in the room was muggy with his words. Tears filled my mom's eyes and slid down her cheeks. That may have been the most words I'd ever heard my dad say in one sitting, potentially in one day, and possibly an entire month.

My mom broke the silence, and whispered, "I love you."

"He laughed right in my face. Was tardy picking me up. If Henry is the person to fill in these supposed missing pieces, then I'm better off with them, which, by the way, I don't even believe I have these holes you speak of."

My parents exchanged a look. I fisted my hands; they didn't understand.

"Maybe he isn't, or maybe he is," my mom said. "People make mistakes, and sometimes it's okay to give them a second chance.

I chewed on their words—much preferring to be chewing on my dinner instead. Clearly, I had caused my dad to worry, which saddened me. He was advancing in age, so it was only natural he would want to secure a predecessor for his all-important role of my caretaker.

"I made a friend," I blurted out, hoping to quell his fears.

Sighing, he returned his attention to his meal.

"That's nice, dear." My mom offered a sympathetic smile before returning to her plate as well.

Satisfied with my deflection, I picked up my fork and dug into my mom's delicious food. There was even less discussion over that evening's meals. Normally this would have pleased me, however I could sense I'd said or done something to disappoint my parents. I had so few people in my life, the last thing I needed was to lose them as well.

"Sometimes I feel like an alien."

My mom, halfway standing, lowered herself to her chair.

"I know you've had your troubles fitting in Beverly, but keep trying, you're young. You'll find people who you click with."

I clasped my hands beneath the table. I shouldn't have said anything, but it was too late. I had to keep going. "No. Like an actual alien. Why else would I be so different? Think about it, my brain isn't like anyone else's brain. At least no one I've met. So maybe I have an alien brain. Like I'm some sort of experiment, sending data back to my home planet so they can study humans."

Both my parents opened their mouths to say something, then closed them and stared. I shifted under their gazes.

"It's perfectly logical. And perhaps you can't understand because you're not an alien."

My mother laughed. "Oh gosh Beverly, those books have certainly given you quite the imagination."

I chuckled to help relieve the tension in the air. My mother's shoulders relaxed, and I announced I'd be going to my room to read.

I laid on top of my bed, hands behind my head staring at the ceiling.

It seemed like a perfectly reasonable explanation to me.

Nine

THE NEXT DAY, Bill and I sat on our bench. I filled him in on the unexpected floral delivery.

"Sounds like you're making this guy really work for it, love." Bill chuckled before taking a sip of the coffee I brought him. I noticed he didn't pour any additional liquid into it.

"Work for what? I don't even understand why he's doing this. A bouquet of roses, an unannounced visit to my store, two calls to my home. I don't know him. He doesn't know me. Why doesn't he move on with his life and let me move on with mine?"

"He must see you the way I do. Perfect in every way."

I rolled my eyes. "Or he's a serial killer, and he's stalking me. Won't you feel bad when I'm found years from now buried in his backyard, nothing left to identify me by other than dental records?"

With a friendly bump of my shoulder to his, I exposed my teeth with a maniacal smile.

"I'll cry a river of tears over those teeth as they get lowered into the ground," he said.

"Ugh, I've created enough rivers of tears for the both of us lately." Sick of talking about Henry, I changed the subject. "I made a friend."

"You aren't replacing me, are you?" He laughed. "Who's this friend? Are *they* a serial killer too?"

"No, she's nice. I think you'd like her. She's not like us. She's more—" I paused, searching for the proper words to describe Quinn. "She's nice and normal. Well, actually, you wouldn't like her now that I think about it."

Bill laughed harder. "We're nice and normal too."

My face and voice sobered. "I don't think anyone would use those two words to describe either of us."

"Ah, you're probably right, as usual."

"And I'm right about you needing to go to the hospital. You still look terrible. I'm worried about you. Please, for me. I'll drive you. I'm sure I could get the day off work."

"Bev, love, you really must stop showering me with compliments. They're bound to go straight to my head." He attempted to point at his pale face but dropped his hand before it found its target.

"I'm fine. Seriously. Stop worrying over me. It stresses me out, you working yourself up like this."

I pursed my lips and considered pulling him up by the ear and dragging him to the hospital.

"I swear on our friendship. I feel great." He stood and danced a jig to drive home his point.

I'd known Bill long enough to be fully aware a continued debate would lead nowhere. "Fine. Have it your way. I'm going to go meet Quinn now. You eat that food." I said, pointing to the brown sack on the bench. "My mom slaved over it for you. You don't want to let her down, do you?"

"Never! I'll see you later, Bev."

It was Bill I was thinking about while sitting across from Quinn in the coffee shop, tuning out her repeated attempts to force me into giving Henry a second chance.

Watching her lips move, I debated whether I wanted to cup her face in my hands and thank her or slap my hand across her mouth so she'd stop talking.

"Are you even listening to me, Beverly?" she asked.

I wasn't.

"Sure, sure, I should give Henry a second chance. He didn't mean it. I'm listening."

I couldn't tell her the more pressing matter weighing on my mind. She wouldn't understand my relationship with Bill. I'd have to stop speaking to her if she said anything awful about him. I didn't want that; I was growing quite fond of her.

"You don't even have to see him again after this. But if you don't pick yourself up and move past that last awful experience, I'm afraid you're never going to date!"

The notion sounded perfect to me. I couldn't understand everyone's obsession with love and marriage. There was nothing wrong with being single. Plenty of people lived perfectly joyful lives alone. Yet another of society's rules it tried to trap its people in. I'd spent most of the prior evening awake, analyzing my alien theory, so I blame fatigue on what I said next.

"Fine. I'll give Henry another chance." I had too many things to fret over, and this would get everyone off my back.

"Oh, thank God. Now give me his phone number. I'm going to call him and explain what I expect of him this Saturday," she said.

Saturday? I was hoping to put it all off a bit longer. I agreed to the date with Henry to shut everyone up, not because I planned on falling in love with him. The whole concept left a sour taste in my mouth.

Still resolved to keep anyone from *fully* penetrating the depths of my soul.

I considered it all. A life partner—someone to share a bed and a home with—may be a logical next step. I'd always envisioned living with my parents until I was no longer in need of support and they reached an age unable to care for themselves. The only other option I'd considered had been moving into a small place of my own, one filled from floor to ceiling with bookshelves. However, this entire situation had presented a third option. With Henry being my only active suiter, I decided he would, at the very least, be good practice should the third option end up being the one I chose.

We finished our meal, and Quinn told me she would call me later after she spoke to Henry. I wanted to tell her to go on the date for me too. If she liked him so much, why didn't she marry him?

We walked to our stores and waved our goodbyes when we reached the bookshop. I sat at the counter all day with my head supported in my hand, the stolen book opened and unread, trying to figure a way out of the Henry situation. A woman came into the shop midday, clutching a young girl's hand. They browsed the children's section and brought several colorful books to the counter.

Just as I finished ringing them up, a loud banging on the window made me hop in my seat. Neither seemed fazed. Children are noisy; it made sense the mom didn't notice.

Through the enormous picture window with *Bookshop* written in large serif font across the front, Bill stood on the sidewalk waving his hand above his head, a toothless grin splitting his face. When he saw he had captured my attention, he started dancing. I laughed out loud, then stopped short when I noticed the mom looking at me with her head cocked to the side and eyes filled with concern— or was it fear? Her head turned toward Bill while I shooed him with my hands. She turned back to me with her features still pinched. No one understood Bill...or me. Oh well, their loss.

When Henry's voice filled the other end of my telephone, I explained to him I'd decided to give him a second chance. Quinn had already called him, warning him to be on his best behavior, so his mock surprise was unwarranted, and his enthusiasm grated on my nerves.

To knock him down a few pegs, I tersely explained how tardiness would not be acceptable. With this date, he should arrive on time.

The next morning, I went to the white bench, ready to use my change of heart to my advantage. I'd let Bill know I agreed to see Henry again, so he owed me and could repay me with a visit to the doctor.

When he didn't show, I hoped he'd already heeded my advice. *I should call the local hospitals to find out if he's been admitted or seen.*

Ten

Now

His chair scrapes on the cabin's wood floor while he sits and pulls the chair up to the table. At one point, scratches marring the wood would have had me lecturing him. Now I consider any marks the wood may endure like words in a book, they form the story of my home.

I fill two bowls to the rim with steaming chili, and place them on the table, joining him. We eat in silence, both clearly hungrier than we realized. Time slipped away from us on the porch, the trip into the past sucking us in and finally spitting us out. I know what comes next. It's not a trip you take with an empty belly. It's also not a trip I take very often. Though he knows bits and pieces, this is the first time I've put all together for him, beginning to end.

My only hope is that when I reach the end, he doesn't leave me like many others have. The most natural reaction is to wonder why I'm here, and not locked up...No need to go down that path. Not yet.

"How's your food?" I ask.

"Delicious," he says through a mouthful. "This cornbread. Best I've ever had. Your mom's recipe, too?"

I half-smile. "No. I stole that one from someone else."

"A thief and a heartbreaker, eh?"

"Heartbreaker?" I choke on a bite. "Hardly. I've left all hearts thoroughly intact." I avert my eyes. The words weren't a lie when they left my mouth, but now that they're out there I realize I'm not being entirely truthful. Is anyone fully truthful really? Whether from poor memory, self-preservation, or shame everyone has a reason to lie. Some more than most, including me. Not tonight though. It could be the impending storm slickening my throat so those words can free themselves. A storm whose rains will come and wash them down the mountain, sweep them away so they are no longer haunting my dreams.

"So 'I'm better off alone Beverly' gave ole Henry a second chance?"

"She did, yes." I nod, memories curving my lips into a smile.

"And was that a good decision or a bad one?"

"I suppose that depends on who you ask. Probably when you ask them, too."

He rips a piece of cornbread and uses it like a spoon to scoop his chili. "Well keep going then. I'm hooked. What happens next?"

Eleven

Before

THE SOUND of a truck engine roared outside my house, then cut off. I parted the curtain and smiled. Henry sat in his truck in our driveway fifteen minutes ahead of schedule.

Lit by the light on the garage, he flicked his wrist to check the time on his watch, then wiped his face. *It must be hot out there in that truck with no engine to power the AC.* While I could have gone outside, save him from the agony. I stood at the window watching instead.

At exactly 6:29—apparently, he is capable of following directions—he opened the truck door and strolled to the front porch, looking quite proud of himself indeed. I let him knock on the door before opening it, looking exactly like the girl he met that first day in the bookstore. We both learned our lessons the hard way, so we did have that in common.

"Henry. I see you *do* own a watch," I said.

"I sure do, and tonight I even learned to use it."

I couldn't help but smile, and I noticed he couldn't help but stand a bit straighter.

"I'm sorry again, Beverly. Really sorry. I have no idea what came over me. Like I said, sometimes I can't hold in my reactions, and a lot of times they come out all wrong."

I kept my face impassive. He hadn't proven he was worthy of full redemption yet.

He continued, "You look beautiful tonight. I'm so darn glad you gave me another chance."

"Let's get this over with." I marched to his truck with Henry in tow. Arms crossed, I stood on the passenger side. Henry's hand on the driver's door handle, he glanced through the windows across the cab, and we made eye contact. My lips pursed.

Awareness flickered across his face, his eyes widened, and he ran over to the passenger side to open the door for me. With an exaggerated sweep of his arm, he showed me the way into the vehicle. While unnecessary since I'd been getting into vehicles long enough to know the way, his efforts weren't unnoticed.

Silence, a third passenger, joined us on the ride to the restaurant. Clearly not as comfortable with quietness, he filled the void with relentless questions. My answers became shorter and shorter, and finally, he got the hint and turned on the radio.

Back stiff, I stared out the windshield. I very much disliked other people driving. The lack of control terrified me. However, Henry was a capable enough driver, putting me slightly at ease.

We pulled into the Italian restaurant's parking lot. A big fan of Italian, the choice pleased me.

"Have you ever been here before?" he asked while we walked from the parking lot.

"No, I don't eat out much."

"It's Italian; do you like Italian? If not, they have other things, like steaks too." He wiped his palms on the sides of his slacks.

"Italian is fine," I said. We had stopped on the restaurant's porch. My gaze swept the white stucco building. Ivy wound its way up two large columns. The ornate architecture made it look like it had been plucked from Italy and dropped in Newport.

"That's good. I didn't get the chance to ask you what kind of food you like, so I took a shot. Glad it was the right one." He laughed nervously.

"Bill—I mean, Henry, it's fine. Really. I'm sure I'll enjoy myself and the food. You can relax."

I stepped around Henry, opened the restaurant's door, and walked inside. I turned just in time to see him scrambling to grab the door. I tilted my head to the side. It wasn't as if I didn't give him plenty of time to grab the door. Was he second guessing himself? Did I almost just get left at the restaurant? How humiliating that would be.

Two young girls behind the podium greeted us. Henry gave them his name and let them know we had a reservation for two. One of the girls grabbed menus and napkin-rolled silverware and we followed her through the crowded restaurant.

Settled into our seats, we placed napkins in our laps. I picked up the menu and began scanning. Henry's lay abandoned on the table. I sucked in a breath, sure he was about to tell me what a horrible mistake he'd made asking me out. I looked around the room and mentally calculated how many people would be witness to my walk of shame, having to leave the restaurant before taking a single bite of my meal. While the rest of the patrons spend their evening making up stories about why the weird girl walked out without eating.

"Have you selected what you'll be ordering?" I asked. Might as well give him an out. I'd have much preferred to get it over with sooner rather than later. Leaving mid-meal would be worse, I'm sure of it.

"Who's Bill?" he asked, quite sharply too.

My mouth fell open, along with my stomach.

"Bill is my friend. I don't like talking about him," I said before returning my attention to the menu.

"You told me you don't have a boyfriend. That you don't date. If that was a lie—" My laugh cut through his words like sewing shears.

"A boyfriend? I've never even been on a date," I said, shaking my head. What a preposterous thing to say. While amusing, I wished he would shut up. Bill was none of his business.

"I'm sorry," he stuttered and tripped on his words. "I just—back there you called me. Oh, forget it. I shouldn't have brought it up."

He clearly wasn't going to let it go and allow us to move on with our evening.

"Look, Bill is my friend. My only friend before I met Quinn, and I've only just met her." I put my menu down and straightened the silverware. "He's a homeless alcoholic."

He picked up his water and took a long swig, though it didn't hide the red hue tinting his face.

"Oh geez, I'm sorry. I didn't mean to accuse you—that was wrong of me. Man, here I am apologizing to you again."

"It's becoming a pattern, isn't it?" I mumbled, turning my attention back to the menu.

I could hear him squirming in his seat but refused to look at him. Usually comfortable with silence, normally a situation like that one wouldn't bother me. However, for some reason I felt I owed Henry a bit more of an explanation. I closed the menu and met his gaze.

"I haven't had the best luck with friends. I never really fit in at school. I was picked on a lot frankly. So, I just stopped trying. Being ignored was much easier than being bullied."

"I'm sorry to hear that. Kids can be so mean, can't they?"

"Adults too." I picked the menu back up, peering over the edge I watched Henry do the same. The knot in my stomach slowly loosened.

"What are you thinking?" he asked.

"My friend Bill, the one I told you about. He's been sick lately, and I'm very worried about him."

"Oh. I actually meant for dinner. What are you thinking of ordering? But that sounds scary. I hope Bill's okay."

I sucked in a quick mouthful of air and rushed out, "I

didn't realize. Yes, of course. I'm not sure what I'm in the mood for. Have you eaten here before?"

"I've eaten here a few times. Everything is amazing. Can't go wrong with the pasta Bolognese, or if you're feeling adventurous, their lasagna is out of this world."

"Why do they call it that? Bolognese. Why not just say spaghetti with meat sauce; it's so much easier to pronounce."

"I think it's different. Like the sauce is different or something."

"Hmmm." My eyes moved down reading through the options. "I think I'll go with chicken parmesan."

"An excellent choice."

The waiter returned, and we placed our orders.

APPETIZERS CONSUMED, wine glasses on their second refill, we stared at each other waiting on our entrées.

"What do you like to do, Beverly?"

"Books. I like to read them, though I don't like to sell them much." My gaze wandered around the room. The other women looked like they belonged. So at ease, as if they did this every night. My mind on overdrive, it kept conjuring images of embarrassing things that may happen. My chair breaking and me collapsing to the floor. Food stuck in my teeth, and Henry not having the courtesy of alerting me. Walking to the bathroom—which I really needed to visit for more than one reason—and running into a server, their tray of food clattering to the floor, the entire restaurant silencing and turning to stare. Me picking up a knife and stabbing it through Henry's hand for no reason other than my body and mind were in fight-or-flight mode and my mind decided to fight.

"Ha, that's a shame you spend your days forced to sell them then, I guess." I forced my gaze on Henry and reminded myself to stay present in our conversation.

"Thankfully we don't see many customers in the book-shop, so I get to spend most of my days reading, which is nice." I remembered I should ask him questions too. That's what you were supposed to do. "What do you do for work?"

"I'm in sales. Insurance sales. Not super exciting. I don't like reviewing insurance policies in my free time like you do with your books. But it pays the bills, and I'm pretty good at it. I may even get a promotion soon. I'm hoping to get my own team one day, maybe open a broker-age. Be my own boss..."

His last sentence trailed off and he looked around the room. Did I ask the wrong question?

"It could be worse." He cocked his head and my gaze followed in the direction he'd indicated. A woman sitting in the darkest corner of the restaurant across from a man looked on the verge of tears. The man sitting across from her was leaned over the table, speaking in hushed tones with an intense look on his face. Tears began streaming down her face. I wanted to stand, march over, and scold the man for making her feel that way, and in public even. The man settled back in his chair and peered around the room, either to see if anyone else noticed or he was desperate to find a server to pay their bill and leave. He met my gaze and I refused to look away. I narrowed my eyes, wishing that alien brain of mine could telepathically tell him exactly what I thought of his behavior.

I frowned. "I guess it could be."

My bladder now screamed at me. I'd have to get up. The fear of finding a bathroom in an unfamiliar place battled with the fear of peeing myself at that table. I stood abruptly.

"I need to use the ladies' room."

"Oh, sure. Yeah, it's right over there." I followed Henry's finger with my gaze and practically sighed with relief when I spotted the sign for the restroom.

I quickly crossed the restaurant and pushed my way into the bathroom. Happy I made it without incident. In the stall, I took a square of toilet paper and let it melt on my tongue. Eyes closed, head tilted back, I let the sensation soothe my worried mind. Two women walked in chatting and my eyes popped open. I waited until they were both in their own stalls, swung the door open, washed my hands, and returned to the table.

Our conversation eased. We talked about life, our likes, dislikes. I told him about the customers who were always interrupting my reading. He laughed as I described the housewives. And then we both laughed when I came clean on my lie about never reading *The Stand*.

"Did you like it then?"

"I did." I grinned. "It's one of my favorite books."

"So, you've really never been on a date, huh?"

"No. I'd never put myself in the position where my heart could be broken. I've read enough books to know how it all works. And it's not something I care to experience first-hand."

"I mean, it doesn't always end badly. Don't you read any books with happy endings?" He asked.

"No, I prefer tragedies," I said. He laughed nervously. I most likely said something I shouldn't have. Henry had a way of making my walls weak. I could be myself around him. I think I liked it. I couldn't be sure yet, though.

The waiter arrived with our entrées, excellent timing on his part.

"The food looks amazing! And so do you. Look amazing, I mean. Not amazing, like edible, like the food. But. I mean. You look very pretty tonight, Beverly. And I'm really happy you agreed to give me a second chance. I'm not an ass, I promise. I sometimes play one on TV, though." He chuckled at his own joke.

I took a few bites of my food, though my stomach had twisted itself in so many knots, eating was the last thing I wanted to do. I'd never had a man tell me I was pretty. Was he lying? I gave him the opportunity to laugh before I responded. He stared at me, smiling, not in a mean way as I'd expected.

"This restaurant was an excellent choice. This chicken parmesan is *so* good." I allowed myself to smile, to enjoy the compliment. I was getting used to those ego-boosting things. "And I do like some happy ending books, now that I think about it."

"It looks good, mind if I try a bite?" His hand reached over the table fork inches over my plate.

I gasped. "Yes, of course I do," I said, loud enough for the people at the tables next to us to turn their heads in our direction.

He froze, eyes wide and his used fork fell on my plate.

We both stared at it, me in disgust, him in shock. I squeezed my eyes shut and fought against every instinct. Sucking in air through my nose, I opened my eyes and against all odds, relaxed. I picked up his fork and filled it with a large bite of chicken parmesan.

"Here," I said, handing him back the fork. "Try it. I'm sure you'll agree."

The tension in the air seemed to visibly dissipate. The evening continued pleasantly. Casual. Comfortable. He even made me laugh a few more times. That Henry could be very amusing.

The evening ended in my driveway. He quickly scrambled out of his seat and jogged around the truck to let me out. I grinned to myself watching him through the windshield. After walking me to the front porch, he leaned in with outstretched arms. I stiffened and took a half step back.

Quickly self-correcting, he stuck out his right hand and thanked me for a lovely evening. A handshake being more tolerable than a hug or at worse a kiss, I loosely returned his firm grip with a limp shake.

"Thank you. I had a pleasant time as well. I didn't expect to. But I did. I'm glad I agreed to let you take me out."

And with that, I walked into my house, leaving Henry on the porch for a second time. Only that time, I did not slam the door behind me. Instead, I shut the door and leaned my back on it. My skin prickled in a much different way than it ever had. I leaned my head back and let myself smile. A pleasant time indeed.

Twelve

I PACED MY KITCHEN, wringing my hands. Bill was missing. I hadn't seen him in over a week, despite going to our bench every morning and searching everywhere for him. He wasn't the most reliable friend, but I knew something was wrong. Even during his worst benders, he had never disappeared this long, and my instincts were screaming, I just knew this time was different.

I'd spent every free moment calling the local hospitals, shelters, and the police. No one had seen or heard from Bill or any unidentified man matching his description. I tried to get the police to open a missing person case, however, they didn't take a missing homeless alcoholic as seriously as I did.

Each time I called, and it was at least once a day, whoever answered the phone told me they took down my information and would call me if they located him. I didn't believe any of them. He wasn't human to them. His lack of housing, lack of job, and alcoholism made his disappearance as important as a lost pet. Not their problem. I slammed down the phone after reaching yet another dead end.

"Beverly, I'm sure he's fine. He'll show up, and everything will be okay," my mom said. She turned to me with soapy water dripping from her yellow plastic gloves. Her face didn't match her words. Worry clouded her eyes too.

"I have a date tonight," I muttered.

"Another date with Henry? That's lovely." She smiled.

I walked out of the kitchen to get ready, worry weighing my legs down, making each step harder to take than the last.

MY SECOND DATE with Henry was as enjoyable as the first, surprisingly. He had good hygiene, was well-mannered, and his *much too-ness* didn't perturb me. He found his jokes much funnier than they were, but I could forgive this much. He did make me laugh, just not that hard. He provided a distraction from my Bill hunt and a way to keep my mind occupied and diverted from images of Bill lying dead in a ditch.

I tried to be present during dinner, I really did, but I could tell Henry sensed I was distant, even for me. He offered to come in and have a cup of coffee with me when he pulled into my driveway to drop me off. I didn't want him to think my lack of attention was his fault. I genuinely enjoyed our time together and agreed to continue with our evening. Normally, I'd have found a self-invitation presumptuous and annoying, but I had been reading romance books and watching television shows to study how women being wooed acted, and attempted to emulate their ways whenever possible. Coffee in my home seemed like a very standard after-date activity.

"Hello, you two," my mother chirped from the couch upon our arrival. My stomach lurched. I had been so busy trying to decipher what the women in the books and shows would do, I hadn't thought about the inevitable meeting of my parents.

"Hello, I'm Henry." He walked right into our living room and shook my parents' hands. I died a bit inside.

"Oh, Henry, it's wonderful to finally meet you. We've heard so much about you and were wondering when Beverly would stop keeping you all to herself." My mother's face beamed as bright as the mid-day sun. My skin burned, head to toe, from its rays. I caught my dad taking a swig from his beer to hide his smirk.

"Well, honey, it's getting late. Why don't we go upstairs, I'm so tired," my mom declared, looking at my dad with raised brows.

"I'll join you after the end of—" A glare from my mom and his mouth clamped shut. He obediently turned the TV off and followed her upstairs.

"Come on, Henry," I said, leading him into the kitchen. "Have a seat, and I'll get us a pot of coffee going."

I busied myself getting the coffee ready and Henry took a seat at the kitchen table.

"What's on your mind, Beverly? Spill it. Something's bothering you; I can tell. You know you can talk to me. I'm here for you."

"It's Bill. I'm just so frustrated," I said while I watched

the brown steaming liquid fill the pot. "No one believes me. They think he's run off to go drink. But that's not true. Something is wrong. I have that feeling. You know what I mean?"

"Yeah, I do. When it's your friends, you know. I hate it for you and for him." He frowned.

When the pot finished brewing, I filled two mugs and joined him at the table.

"I believe you," he said, grabbing one of my hands. Something prickled my skin. His touch was much less revolting than prior times, almost pleasant.

"What have you tried so far?" he asked after taking a sip of his coffee.

"Well, I've gone to our usual meeting place each morning, even on the weekends when we normally don't see each other. I've done some walking around to his usual haunts. Quinn works downtown too, as you know, so she's been keeping an eye out as well. I've called hospitals, shelters, the police. The police refuse to file a missing person report, they said he couldn't be officially missing yet."

"Why wouldn't they at least file one? He's obviously missing."

"Not missing enough for them, apparently," I said, shaking my head.

"I want to help. What can I do? Just because a guy is down on his luck doesn't mean he doesn't deserve help."

I studied his face, and my feelings for him started to change. I'd like to think I would have fallen for Henry without my best friend disappearing, but I'm not sure I would have let myself. I was begging the authorities to help me find Bill, but I didn't have to beg Henry. He believed me without question. It made me trust him, made it so much easier for me to warm to him.

My eyes teared up while a strange fluttering erupted in my stomach.

"I would really appreciate that," I managed to say.

———

THE MORNING AFTER THE DATE, I stared at myself in the mirror above my dresser, going over the previous night in my head. The peeling paint of the mirror's frame, the dresser it sat upon, and the bedroom reflected behind me were all familiar. The girl staring back at me, however, was not.

Sure, the face was still the same dull face. The same brown hair and eyes. Same barely there lips. Thankfully, the same button nose. But my expression was twisting those familiar features into an unrecognizable doppelgänger. The changes—easily missed by the untrained eye —were strikingly obvious to me, the one who had lived with that face for twenty-five years, eleven months, and thirteen days. The girl in the mirror looked softer, more feminine, almost comfortable in her skin.

One potential boyfriend and two friends aren't too dangerous. Could the stranger in the mirror be convinced? My thoughts and feelings would still be mine. My secrets, well, those could never get out.

To Quinn and Henry, and of course Bill—when I found him—I would look like a normal woman, perhaps even *be* a normal woman. My parents wouldn't have to worry. My dismal future may be a bit less depressing.

The reflection started laughing. Then stopped and glared at me. "Stupid girl," it growled. I returned her stare, refusing to be scared, refusing to listen.

"Shut up you," I told that naysayer.

The empty roll of toilet paper sat on top of my dresser. My original friend. The one who had never lied, never judged, and never disappeared on me when I needed him the most, like Bill.

Reluctantly, I looked away from the interloper in my mirror and turned to leave my room. I would call both Quinn and Henry to make plans, but first, a trip to the bathroom. A few bites, and a replenished secret stash were needed.

After the bathroom visit, I sighed with relief, knowing my fruitive box was full.

I walked into a new upside-down and inside-out world. An exotic world for which I had no map. One more step and I was plunging, struggling to keep my head above the line where oxygen lives, hoping I wouldn't drown.

Quinn sounded surprised to hear from me. I was so wrapped up in Bill and Henry, the onslaught of extra humans in my life wasn't the easiest to manage, but I was trying. I had expected her to be a bit more excited, but I dismissed her lack of enthusiasm and chalked it up to her being upset I hadn't called earlier.

I hung up the phone and retrieved my previously barren day planner from my purse. On Monday, I wrote: *Quinn – Our Spot.* I had a spot—with a friend. How conventional. How delightful. I insisted on lunch that same afternoon. A new deli had opened on Main Street we were both excited to try.

Henry, my maybe-boyfriend, was meeting me after work to help search for Bill. We also had plans to see a movie Wednesday evening. He selected the movie, some comedy, which was good since I couldn't have guessed what the options were. I filled in each little box in the planner, shut the cover, and smiled at it.

I could do this, that girl in the mirror had no idea what she was talking about. But neither did I.

Thirteen

Monday morning—after Bill no-showed yet again—I was in *our* coffee shop at *our* table, perched on the end of my seat, anxiously awaiting Quinn's arrival.

I tucked my hair behind my ears and forced my lips to curve upward. This new Beverly didn't overthink. She didn't let her mind get carried away by worst-case scenarios. She had friends. Had a boyfriend, maybe. If I repeated this mantra enough, it would be true.

I fiddled with my steaming cup of black coffee. The door opened. Quinn's trademark red hair lit up the muted hues of the shop. My arm flapped above my head to wave her over.

The words forming the story of Henry and my current relationship status ready to fly out. I tapped my toes impatiently, waiting for her to collect her order and join me.

After Quinn grabbed her coffee and walked over, I was telling her about my weekend before she had the chance to sit. At least the Saturday evening portion. Nothing much happened during the other hours.

"That's wonderful! I'm wicked glad you changed your mind and gave him a second chance. Henry seems like a nice guy. For sure worth it."

I chewed on my reply. Did he feel the same about me as I did about him? This gave me something else to ponder. Could my brain process the considerable number of thoughts and competing emotions? It had never been tested in this way.

"Yes, yes. He's great, and all that. We're going to see some movie. I've never heard of it but nevertheless, I'll be seeing it Wednesday evening with Henry."

"You two should have a blast! It's great you're stepping out of your comfort zone. Doesn't it feel good?" Her hands flew about her. Quinn liked to accentuate her words with gestures. Unfortunately, it would have been most inappropriate to grab hold of them and pin them to the table.

"I suppose it does. I suppose it's not so scary. This whole dating thing," I said.

Who was this girl, sitting in a coffee shop, chatting about love interests with a girlfriend? I couldn't believe it. How far I'd come!

"Do you want me to help you two search for Bill this afternoon?" she asked.

"No!" I cried, a bit too forcefully. "No, that's a kind offer, but we'll be fine," I added, calming my voice.

"Ah, a little more alone time, I get it," she said and winked.

I wasn't ready for Quinn and Henry to meet. While her offer was a generous one, them together would cause added stress. I'd be worried they wouldn't get along. Or, worse, they would get along *too* well, and I'd be left ostracized and uncomfortable. I didn't particularly care that she'd interjected herself in our relationship earlier by calling him, because I hadn't really cared where Henry and my relationship headed at that point. Now, as I grew confident we may have a future, I much preferred a delayed introduction.

I thanked her.

"Let me know if you change your mind, I'm at your service. Still on for lunch today?"

"Yes, I'm hoping the food is as good as everyone's been saying. I swear it's all the customers talk about now. It's been an enjoyable break though, not to listen to them drone on about their favorite books or whatever silly thoughts they think I care about."

Quinn rolled her eyes and laughed. "The next thing we're going to work on is being less judgmental all the time. You may even make more friends."

"New friends. Now why would I need those when I have you?" I said matter-of-factly. I wanted to add 'and Bill,' but didn't trust myself to say his name without breaking down.

She cocked an eyebrow, then checked her phone. "Time to go. We don't want to be late."

We walked to our stores together. When we reached the bookshop, I informed her I'd swing by the boutique at twelve before she continued on.

I walked into my shop trying to decipher why Quinn would suggest I find new friends. We hadn't known each other for very long, could she be tiring of me already?

By the time I reached the counter, I'd already transported back to high school. Shy, quiet Margot moved to Newport our junior year. While I still ran into the occasional teasing, most classmates had moved on and I had disappeared, blended into the background, most importantly was finally left alone. After weeks of sharing the library during lunch, she approached my table and quietly introduced herself. Our friendship grew slowly as they do with two people who have never learned to master the ins and outs of social interactions. I grew fond of Margot, which is why I made my very bad, horrible mistake. I told her my secret.

Sitting in my room one day after school, I pulled the shoebox from beneath my bed. With shaking hands, I removed the top.

"Is that to blow your nose?" Maddie asked, genuinely confused.

I tore off two squares, keeping one for myself and handing one to her.

Without a word I opened my mouth and placed mine on my tongue. Her confusion turned to shock, then pity.

"You're eating it? Why!" she asked.

I knew I'd made a terrible mistake, immediately wishing I could take it back. Someone savvier than me would have found a way to turn the entire thing into a joke. Move on. Pretend it never happened. Instead, I ripped the square from her hand and stuffed it in my mouth.

She stood and began throwing things in her backpack, mumbling about having to get home, dinner would be soon, her mom was expecting her.

The next day at school, I went to the library to meet her for lunch. Our normal table was empty, and after wandering the shelves, I determined she hadn't come. I spent the next several months avoiding her, hoping and praying she wouldn't tell anyone about what happened in my room.

When I think back on our short friendship, I can't remember any of the good. Just that scene replaying. I try not to think about Margot. I also never made that mistake again.

AFTER A DISAPPOINTING LUNCH at the deli, disappointment due to the food not the company, and work, I met Henry downtown. We spent two hours walking the streets, checking every park, alley, and place we could think of. The homeless population in Newport was small, but we asked the few men and women we happened across. With night's long shadows giving them coverage to emerge from their hiding spots, they were easier to find. Even so, none had any helpful information.

"Don't lose hope." Henry wrapped his arm around my shoulders. We sat on Bill and my bench. It didn't feel right, but it was the last place I could think of to look.

"We'll keep looking," he assured me.

I rubbed away the tears filling my eyes. I wanted so badly to have faith, but I couldn't. I squeezed them shut and pictured a sober Bill showing up on his family's doorstep, arms wide, his wife and children falling into his embrace, and willed this image to become a reality.

I FLEW THROUGH THE WEEK, my wings only clipped whenever I'd think of Bill. Such a perplexing time. One part of my life moved in a direction I never thought possible, while at the same time, I felt as if I'd lost an appendage, my lifeline.

Henry and I spoke on the phone on days we didn't see each other. I was also meeting Quinn each morning for coffee. I still visited the white bench first, but as the days passed, the time I waited for Bill grew shorter and shorter.

I kept seeing him, though. A man in a crowd, a flash at the edge of my vision. I'd run to the spot I could swear he was in, and by the time I'd get to him, he was gone.

Where are you, Bill? I miss you. I need you.

Fourteen

On Friday, I sat across from Quinn at the coffee shop.

"What are your plans for Saturday? Would you like to get together?" I asked.

She politely declined, explaining she had a prior engagement. The rejection needled my heart.

"Well," I snapped, "if you have plans, I'll just have to find something else to do." I'd be doing nothing of the sort, there were no something elses to fill my time.

"Don't get fussy. There are plenty of other days, darling," she said, laughing.

I wasn't in the mood for her laughs or for being called 'darling.' Who were these so-called plans with? Was I not good enough to waste her weekends on?

"I'm not fussy. I just figured you'd want to spend time with me, is all. It's fine. I'll just call Henry or something." Henry had already informed me he wasn't available on Saturday, but Quinn didn't need to know that.

"I'm going to give you the benefit of the doubt and

assume this is your worry over poor Bill speaking and not you." She frowned and tried to reach for my hand. I quickly moved it under the table out of reach. Quinn puffed her cheeks and released the air slowly.

"We need to head to work." She stood. "Bev, are you okay? Are we okay?"

"Yes, Quinn, we're fine," I said. I was not fine but knew if I said anything more, she would just get angry at me, and she had no right.

I turned my head to glare out the window, unsure who I was more annoyed with: Quinn, Bill, or myself for asking the question. I was so new to friendships, a baby deer still teetering on fresh legs, and I hadn't quite figured it all out yet.

I was still a work in progress.

WITH HENRY out of town for work and Quinn's rejection, I sat around my house and pouted all weekend. There were no updates from the hospitals or the police on Bill, but I doubted they had even bothered to look.

I hid in my room, reading and attempting to smother my fear with a roll of toilet paper. Neither helped.

Sick of waiting on a phone call I knew wouldn't come, I decided to visit the police station in person. It's easy to dismiss someone when they are a faceless voice on the phone, but it would be harder to deny my request of a missing person report to my face.

My mom offered to drive me, but I had to do this on my own, for Bill. Wherever he was, I wanted him to know

I was doing everything in my power to bring him back to me.

Lost in my head, I arrived at the police station without remembering the drive that brought me there and parked in a spot marked for visitors. Ready for a fight, I walked through the glass doors and marched up to the information desk. A heavy-set man in uniform sat behind the desk.

Not taking his eyes off his phone, he asked, "How can I help you?"

"I need to speak with someone who can file a report for my missing friend."

"You that woman that's been calling?" he asked.

"I'm not sure how many women call *you*," I retorted. His uniform may have intimidated some, but I wasn't a criminal, and I was more ireful than usual.

His face snapped toward me, glowering.

"Yes, I've been calling, repeatedly. Yet, you and your colleagues continue to ignore those calls, despite my friend being missing. I won't apologize for caring, but you should apologize for your egregious incompetence."

"Homeless people disappear all the time, ma'am, especially ones with drinking problems. Nothing we can do."

"Is there someone else I can speak with? A detective?"

I could see him debating his next move, trying to figure out the easiest way to be rid of me.

"Should you even be fiddling with that?" I pointed to his phone. "Is there not a policy against using that when you're on duty?"

That did it. He pushed himself out of his chair and told me he would see if anyone was available to speak with me, explaining—rather rudely—that it was Saturday and options were limited.

"I didn't realize criminals only work Monday through Friday," I said.

With a grunt he turned and walked deeper into the building beyond my sight.

He returned a few minutes later, being led by a tall woman dressed in a well-fitting blazer and jeans. If it weren't for the large gun strapped to her waist, I wouldn't have guessed she was part of the police force.

"Come with me, ma'am. Let's talk in my office." She spoke with the precision and directness of someone in authority. Looks can be deceiving, but I felt much more satisfied in her abilities than the inept front desk officer.

I followed her through the station to her office. The station looked more like a run-down office building than a place that kept downtrodden criminals in cages, like I expected.

She looked over her shoulder and said, "I'm usually not here on the weekends, but I had some work to catch up on. Lucky for you."

Lucky is the last word I'd have used to describe what I was feeling.

She stopped at an office and indicated I should enter. I stepped in and held my purse against my chest, unsure what to do with myself. She closed the door and pointed to a chair in front of a desk covered in files and empty coffee mugs. I sat and she walked around the desk taking her own seat. She placed her forearms on the desk with her hands clasped and leaned forward, so we were eye level.

"Beverly, right? I hear you've been trying to report your friend missing."

Maybe they had been writing down my information. If I learned anything from Henry, persistence pays off.

"Yes, that's exactly what I've been attempting, but not successfully."

"Why don't you tell me about this friend you believe has gone missing."

Elated to finally have someone listen, I blathered on about Bill, providing every detail I could think of. The more she knew, the better chance we'd have of finding him. When finished, I looked at her, eyes pleading, waiting on her response.

She leaned back in her chair and crossed her heels on the desk. I was so fond of her up until that point. We weren't sitting at her home, relaxing and sharing a glass of wine. My friend was missing, not a time to put your feet on a desk like a heathen.

"I'm going to be blunt with you. There isn't much I can do. I'll file a report, but that's really all it will be, paperwork. In cases like this, where homelessness and alcoholism are already factors, it's not something we actively investigate. I know it's not what you were hoping for, but it's the best I can offer."

I puffed air through my nostrils. "That is better than I've been offered, so a report would be appreciated."

She slid a paper from a folder, and I provided all the information I could, using my address for the place of residency. I left her with my contact information and went home feeling one step closer to righting a wrong.

ELATED by the minor accomplishment I achieved in the search for Bill, I'd forgotten I was angry with Quinn and went to meet her at the coffee shop Monday morning. I was excited to tell her I finally convinced the police to file a report on Bill.

I ordered my black coffee and a croissant. The staff, now familiar with my boring order, no longer responded with confused looks. At our table—black coffee barely touched, cooling in front of me—I alternated between glancing out the window and back toward the front door. With nervous flicks of my wrist, I watched the seconds turn into minutes, then turn into a half-hour.

My blood boiled with indignation when I realized she wasn't coming. Why was it so easy for people to abandon me? Was I no better than the trash? I looked around the room and every face resembled Claire, Margot, and every other person who had given me a taste of friendship only to snatch it away. The conversations became louder, and I swear I heard my name from several of them. My gaze dropped to my coffee and my temperature rose. I had to get out of there but felt glued to my seat. Chest heaving with heavy breaths I encouraged myself in my head. Stand, head down, the door is only a few steps away. Freedom is only a few steps away

On the verge of being late for work, I squeezed my coffee mug, glad for the ceramic. A weaker material would have collapsed under my grip. Sweat trickled down my back. Finally, I popped from my seat and marched out, walking to the bookshop with pumping arms and stomping feet.

THE HOURS, and several stops in the bathroom to digest a few squares, did nothing to dampen my anger throughout the day. Anger at myself for being made the fool once again. Anger at the unfairness of it all. And also, a sadness. I couldn't understand why I was made different. Why I couldn't be someone that others liked and cared about and wanted to be around. The few customers who made the unfortunate mistake of walking into the store left without making a purchase. The books they had come for were evidently not worth dealing with the nasty girl snapping at them from behind the counter.

Quinn knew we had a standing arrangement. One I very much looked forward to each day. For her to no show without so much as a call hurt me more than it should. But after a life with nothing but rejection, I didn't know how else to react.

The old Beverly would have gone home and hidden away. Quinn had taught me that was no way to deal with things. Because of her and Henry, the stronghold I once had on my emotions had loosened.

John wouldn't know I closed early. I locked up the store, and before I knew it, I found myself standing outside her boutique, breath coming out in quick puffs of anger, making my chest rise and fall, fists clenched at my sides.

A girl I didn't recognize walked out the front door and turned to lock it. Surprised, I asked her where Quinn was.

She turned and narrowed her eyes. But then, after looking me up and down, deciding I wasn't someone to fear, she explained with a shrug that Quinn had the day off. She finished her task and walked around me, leaving me alone to stare into the darkened shop.

Confusion and irritation crackled under my skin, making it itchy. I decided there was nothing more to be done and headed home.

LATER THAT EVENING, Henry called me for what he expected to be a friendly chat.

"She left me sitting there!" I cried into the phone.

"Maybe she had an appointment. You said she wasn't at work, right? She could be sick. I'm sure she wouldn't have just not shown up if you had planned to meet. Maybe you should get a phone. It would be much easier to get ahold of you."

"Are you saying this is my fault? Because I don't have a *phone*. We always meet for morning coffee. It's our special thing. Me having a phone has nothing to do with this. And she's not sick; I called her house, and her roommate said she was out. But to where, she either wasn't willing to tell me or didn't know. You don't get it. Bill's gone, probably sick or dead, and no one cares, and now Quinn throws me away like trash on top of all of that."

"Wait, back up. Are you angry at Quinn or upset over Bill?"

I paused. It was an excellent question. I had never felt so many emotions simultaneously. I had never *let* myself feel, at least not in a long while. It was overwhelming and chaotic and confusing.

"Both. I think." I sighed. "I don't know what to do about Bill. Everything I try brings me to another dead end." I looked at the ceiling—an overwhelming need to scream washed over me.

"Here's what we're going to do. Tomorrow morning, go to the white bench and see if he shows up. You have the police report filed. Something will come of it eventually, even if he still doesn't show up. Then go to the coffee shop to meet Quinn. Don't let yourself get worked up if Quinn doesn't show. Enjoy your coffee and head to work. I'm sure everything will work out, it's just a string of unfortunate events. Total coincidences. And think about getting a phone. If anything, I'd love to be able to text you throughout the day."

"Fine, I'll think about it, and do all that."

We said our goodbyes. Henry meant well. But he wasn't fully grasping the severity of my situation. I'm sure I hadn't explained it adequately.

Fifteen

A DAY LATER, after a fruitless attempt at the white bench, I sat in the coffee shop like a fool waiting for Quinn—who apparently had better things to do with her time, again.

After sitting at the same table, watching the same front door, with the same cup of lukewarm coffee, I realized my mistake.

I was stuck in a loop, my face flushed with the heat of my embarrassment. All the conversations and laughs at the other tables were at my expense. Everyone was in on the prank. I provided a side-show to their morning coffee run. *Look at the idiot! She sits there all alone, thinking she can be one of us.*

Not able to bear their judgmental stares any longer, I stood to leave, knocking over my full cup with a loud clatter. The hot liquid filled the table and dripped to the floor. All faces shot in my direction. An audience of owls, with their eyes widened and jaws hanging loose, I was waiting for one of them to hoot.

An older woman with kind eyes materialized beside me. She placed a hand on my arm. "Are you okay dear? You look like you've seen a ghost."

I looked around the room. Time had stopped. They all stared.

"I'm so sorry," I managed to stammer. "I'll clean it up."

I wiped at the spill with a small napkin already soaked, all it managed to do was push around the liquid.

A girl in a black apron with the coffee shop logo on it joined us. She placed a hand on mine. More touching. More people. My heart raced. Sweat beaded my forehead.

"She looks like she may faint." The older woman stood next to me, yet she sounded so very far away. Under water even.

"I'm not feeling very well," I whispered. I'm not sure anyone heard me.

I blinked. Bright lights. No, ceiling lights. More people now. A man's face, that older woman. Why were they hovering over me like that?

It finally occurred to me I was on my back lying on the floor. Pushing myself up to a sitting position I rubbed the back of my head and looked around.

"You took a bit of a tumble. Do you have fainting spells?" The kind woman had her hand on my back.

I shook my head. "I don't—no. I'm sorry, I'm not sure what's come over me. Nothing like that's ever happened."

I stared at my lap, too scared to look around, knowing every eye in the building would be on me. Necks craned to get a better view.

"Should I call an ambulance?" The young girl who

normally served me my coffee stood chewing her thumb cuticle.

"No," I said too forcefully. "No, really, I'm fine. Over tired is all." I pushed myself up, and stumbled a bit, the man grabbed my elbow to help steady me. I wanted to tell them all to please stop touching me but didn't want to draw anymore unnecessary attention after the spectacle I'd already caused.

I brushed myself off and placed a hand on the back of my head where it must have taken the brunt of my fall. "I think I'll be going now."

Concerned faces met my sheepish grin.

"Really, I'm fine. I do appreciate your concern, and I apologize for the mess and disturbance."

Before anyone could protest, I pushed my way through toward the exit and walked quickly to work.

The morning sidewalk presented many obstacles— businesspeople walking to work, moms lazily pushing strollers or dragging sleepy-eyed kids by the hands, and the occasional runner out-pacing them all.

I barreled through the angry onlookers without looking up, innocent victims simply going about their daily routine. Humiliated, I passed the bookshop and kept walking until I reached the boutique.

I arrived and peered through the large glass window, spotting her immediately. The sight of her fiery hair and cheery expression sent icy anger coursing through my veins. I threw open the front door with a crash, catching the attention of Quinn—who was at the counter fussing with papers—and the two early shoppers browsing the racks.

Head still aching, and vision still blurry, I approached the counter. "How dare you."

Quinn made me hope. And hope is a poisonous emotion. Mixed with disappointment, it's combustible.

"Beverly! What's wrong?" She had the audacity to sound confused. As if she didn't know what she'd done.

"You *know* what you did," I scolded. I would not sit there and explain myself in front of those strangers. Not when she was fully aware of what had me so upset. Pretending to be my friend. Then, poof, disappearing, just like everyone had always done.

Red-faced and sweating, I stormed out without giving her the opportunity to respond. The whispers of the room crept up my back on the way out. And now I faced an entire ruined day, all thanks to Quinn.

LATER THAT EVENING, I turned into my neighborhood squeezing and unsqueezing the steering wheel. Muttering all the things I'd wished I'd said to Quinn had my anger not glued the words to my tongue.

I drove down the street slowly and the police car parked in my driveway made me forget my horrible day. *They've found Bill! The search is over. He must have been in a hospital, or somewhere without a way to reach me. Perhaps I'll be able to visit him tonight!*

I parked my car and sprinted to the front door, flinging it open with a wide smile, ready for the good news, ready to see my Bill.

My parents and a police officer holding his hat by his

side stood in the hallway. They turned. My heart dropped. My dad's arm was draped across my mom's shoulders, her eyes were red and swollen. Her cheeks shiny with tears.

My mom looked at me and said the words that could never be unsaid, "It's Bill. He had a heart attack. He's gone."

"No." My head shook. "No, I was going to see him tonight. That man"—I pointed at the police officer—"he's going to take me to see him."

"I'm so sorry, Beverly. So, so sorry." She broke into sobs.

Grief, instantaneous and all-encompassing, choked me, collapsing me with its massive weight. My knees slammed to the ground. It should have hurt. But I felt nothing. And everything. The pain in my heart pounded through every inch of my body, shattering my soul. I wanted to shriek, but there was no air to feed my voice. I grasped at my throat. My lungs wouldn't work. I was frozen in place. The world had stopped turning and now whipped around me in chaos.

It was impossible, but so was Bill's death.

Sixteen

I'D BEEN CRACKED OPEN, my skin turned inside out, every nerve exposed. Torture. The fissures in my mind finally cracked. Shattered to pieces. When your life is an endless string of tragedies, you become complacent, accepting. I could have used this to grow stronger. For years I'd been able to build a wall around my heart, if only I'd done the same for my mind. If only I'd asked for help.

In the following weeks, I was smoke, floating through life. A swipe of a hand was all it would take, and I would disintegrate.

Grief rolled into anger and back into grief. When I'd lie down, its hands wrapped around my neck, strangling me. When mobile, the air surrounding me was dense. Impossible to walk through.

My parents and I ate our meals in shocked silence. The empty thermoses burned a hole through the cabinet door they sat behind. While my parents didn't fully grasp my relationship with Bill, they knew how much he meant to me. I loved Bill. And now he was gone.

My tears dried up that first day. But my mom could have filled the ocean with her salty reserves. It's a wonder the house didn't flood. She had never met Bill, but she made him coffee and lunch every weekday morning for years. And she knew enough to know he was special.

By the time they found Bill's body, he'd long been dead. All that time, I had been searching for a ghost. The police tracked down Bill's family using an expired ID at the bottom of his backpack. They informed me the family wanted nothing to do with the service, which left me responsible for deciding how he would be laid to rest. If Bill were alive and asked how he felt about his wife and children rejecting him for a second time, he would have laughed and said he didn't blame them. But I know deep down, it would hurt him. The jokes and laughter were a shield.

My parents took over. I didn't have the capacity for such an important task. After Bill's cremation, we held a service at the funeral home. So simple and small, no match for Bill's personality at all. I had let him down. Bill deserved a proper send-off. Without my mom and dad, he may not have gotten one at all, and I'm not sure I could live with myself had that happened.

At his service I was a doll in her black mourning dress, my body stuffed with rocks, simply going through the motions.

A day later, I could barely remember the details. A blur of faces and words. Henry was there, John and his wife as well. But I don't remember talking to any of them or even seeing them. My mom happened to mention their presence at dinner later that night. I sat at the kitchen table pushing my food around my plate and she said something about it being so nice of them all to come.

I mumbled an incoherent reply and went back to bed.

Two DAYS after they cremated Bill's body, I was lying in bed staring at the urn holding the ashes and bone fragments of my dear, sweet Bill. My mom called my name. It sounded like she was underwater. I ignored her.

I barely registered the knock on my door. Mom opened it and stuck her head in.

"Beverly? Are you awake?"

Unfortunately.

"You have a friend here. It's Quinn. Come down and speak with her. It will be good for you to get out of bed."

A flash of anger flared in my chest, but I couldn't understand its cause. Morbid curiosity pulled me from my bed, and I followed my mom downstairs.

"Oh Bev, I'm so sorry." Quinn jumped up with outstretched arms. I shrank back and quickly took a seat before she could touch me.

"How are you doing?" she asked. Her blue eyes danced in their sockets, their gaze tapping my face.

"How does it look like I'm doing?"

"You're right. That was a stupid question." She bit her bottom lip while I searched my mind. I fought the urge to grab her throat. To cut her oxygen. But why such rage?

"We need to talk about what happened. I called that

night, but your mom answered and told me about Bill..." her voice trailed off.

It clicked.

"Oh yes, now I remember. You abandoned me, like Bill," I said.

She looked confused. Had I remembered wrong?

"I'm sorry you feel that way. My boyfriend broke up with me, and I was up the night before crying. I was running late and didn't have time to meet you. I should have called or stopped by the bookshop. And now, with what you're going through, it seems so insignificant and silly."

I didn't even know her boyfriend's name. What a terrible friend, no wonder everyone abandons me.

"We we need to talk about what you did," she said with a frown on her normally cheerful face.

"What are you talking about?"

"The fit you threw in my store. You could have gotten me in big trouble, maybe fired. I don't mean to pile on, you have a lot going on right now, but that wasn't okay. I'm sorry, but if you do anything like that again, we can't be friends."

"Okay, I won't." I should have asked for clarification. I hadn't a clue what she was talking about. She described a stranger's behavior, not mine. But I wanted her to leave, and I wanted my bed.

"I'll take that as an apology. Never again, though, okay?

I nodded slowly. I couldn't imagine doing it the first time much less a second time.

"Have you talked to Henry? He's worried about you

too."

I smiled despite myself. Then an exhaustion rushed over me.

"Maybe have him over? It would be good for you."

"I'm sorry Quinn, but I'm not feeling very well, I'm just so tired..."

Her face scrunched with worry. "You need to take care of yourself, Beverly. I know you're sad, but you can't sink away inside that head of yours." She stood, and I pictured the kitchen floor opening and swallowing me whole.

She titled her head to the side, an odd look on her face. I realized I had laughed out loud, highly inappropriate for the situation.

"Was just reminded of something funny Bill said once. I'll see you later. Thank you for coming."

She offered a final sympathetic smile and said goodbye before leaving.

With Quinn gone, I went back upstairs and crawled back in bed. I stared at Bill's urn, his remains mirroring my insides.

Nothing but ash and bone.

Seventeen

It had been four weeks since I'd been to work—I think. Time had lost all meaning. I also wasn't sure if I still had a job. I didn't care. There wasn't room for anything other than heartbreak. A sadness had wrapped its roots around my bones. Its grip was so tight I wanted to die.

The thought of getting out of bed was a burden. I passed my time mechanically eating my way through rolls of toilet paper. It didn't have the same soothing effect.

One night I used Bill's method of pain-numbing. I didn't bother getting dressed out of my wrinkled pajamas. Fitting, I suppose. A nice homage to my homeless friend. Me—looking homeless myself—driving to the liquor store to purchase a bottle of vodka.

I trudged into the liquor store to the section where rows of clear liquid stood waiting for me in bottles of all shapes and sizes. The only other customer became the innocent victim of my wrath. I elbowed him out of my way when he took too long to move, blocking my access to the bottle I'd wanted.

He looked at me sideways, to which I responded with my best imitation of a dog bark. His eyes almost popped out of his head, and he scurried away. The cashier shook his head and rang up my purchase as quickly as possible.

Back at home, I reached into that sad cabinet in our kitchen—the one lined with little reminders of Bill—and took out a thermos. I filled the entire thing with vodka, before returning to my room.

I sat on my bed and drank and drank and drank. Once properly drunk, I cried.

What a terrible idea. I cursed Bill for his bad influence. And then cried some more, knowing how hard he would laugh at me sitting in my room drunk, mad, and blaming him for the state I'd gotten myself in. With puffy eyes and all the salty liquid drained from my body, I collapsed into my bed and lost consciousness, wishing I could sit on our white bench and tell him about it.

I WOKE up the next day with a hangover and regrets. It must have been mid-afternoon because the blinding sun filled my entire room; a room that reeked of Bill. My head hurt too bad to feel any effects of the nostalgic stench. The room spun, and pure vodka seeped from my pores.

Stumbling to the bathroom, I vomited up my poor decisions.

I plopped to the floor, arms draped on the toilet seat,

head leaning through the hole, praying to join Bill, when my mom called me to the kitchen.

Head pounding, I walked downstairs on shaky legs, gulping back stomach acid. Henry sat at our kitchen table with his worry creased on his forehead. Mom placed a mug down for me. I collapsed into a chair and watched his head multiply and float off his neck in a fuzzy haze.

My hair and teeth unbrushed, my tattered T-shirt and worn sweatpants marked by countless days and nights of sleep, my pounding head took up too much space to feel shamed by my appearance. Henry placed his hands over mine. I shook my head and blinked rapidly to bring his face into focus, watching his moving lips, yet unable to make sense of the words they formed.

"Beverly. Did you hear me? Beverly?"

I looked at Henry with lazy eyes. An ice pick hammered into the back of my right eye, and my brain moved too slowly to manage the basic functions my body required.

"I'm sorry, what? I have no idea what we're talking about," I slurred.

"I'd like to get you out of the house. It's terrible what happened. Awful. I understand why you're so sad. But you can't wither away in here. Bill wouldn't want that. I'm worried about you." His eyebrows knitted together, and his eyes pleaded with me. I felt guilty for worrying him, especially when my biggest issue at that moment was a terrible hangover.

"What day is it?" I asked.

"It's Saturday. Why don't you go up and get showered, put on some fresh clothes? We can go out. Walk around the park. Stroll downtown. Get some lunch. Anything. It will make you feel better. I promise, it really will."

My dad's words tumbled back about finding your person. The block of ice freezing my life in place melted in Henry's presence. It occurred to me that Henry may be my person. He could lead me—if I let him—back to the land of the living.

"I can understand why it feels like it's going to be this way forever. Like the pain won't ever end. It will. You're a bird, trapped in a cage of pain; I want to open the cage for you. I want to let you out so you can fly again. Do you trust me? Will you try?"

I nodded and shuffled out of the kitchen, letting him know I would return shortly, with a tiny voice calling from somewhere far, far away, telling me to take his hand and let him lead me, that he would set me free.

Eighteen

Now

I SWIPE under my eyes to dry the few tears that have snuck out. I don't talk about Bill much anymore. Think about him, that's a different story. He's with me always, when I'm awake and in my dreams. Those times are happier, though. I prefer to focus on our time together, and not the fact that he's gone.

"I'm so sorry about your friend," he says, tears shining his eyes as well. Bill has that effect on people, even those who have never met him. You can't say that about many people now can you.

"He was a wonderful man. It's a shame that more people weren't able to meet the real him. You can't blame his family or anyone for that, really. Bill wouldn't want that blame on anyone but himself. Alcohol is no different than a disease such as cancer. If untreated it will kill you.

But unlike cancer it will also kill everything you touch, your relationships, career, life."

"My mom was an alcoholic, did I ever tell you that?"

I shake my head.

"Drank herself to death. Liver disease. The day of her funeral, I was young, fifteen. I stood over her grave and thanked God he took her. She wasn't a good mom. I was the oldest, so most days the only reason my siblings ate was because I cooked or attempted to cook. I did the grocery shopping, kept the house clean, tried to do right by my brother and sister. A fifteen-year-old boy can only do so much, though. Now that I'm older I realize it wasn't her fault, not entirely. It was the disease. I've forgiven my mom, I'll never forgive the disease."

I reach out a hand and give his a squeeze. "I understand. You remind me of Bill. Have I ever told you that?"

"Those are some big shoes to fill."

We've finished our meal, so I stand and collect our plates. I stand at the sink and gaze out the window. The first rain band has arrived.

"So you and Henry grew closer."

I nod still watching the rain. "I suppose that's one good thing that came of Bill's death. Though I hate to put it that way. If you consider Henry and I good. There was a lot of good. But the Universe has its way of balancing things out. Which reminds me, I never answered your question. Henry once told me the reason why he didn't walk out of that bookshop and run as far away from me, as we both know most people would have. He said he saw something special in me. Silly really. That was a different time for me. I didn't like myself much at all, so it was hard to imagine what he or anyone could see in me that was special." I shrug. "But that's how he would describe it. 'There was something more to you, I was sure of it, and I wanted be the one to discover it.'"

"He's a smart man. And right."

I laugh. "I mean, people want what they can't have. Henry could have just been saying that to be romantic. That's a very Henry thing to do."

"Nah, I don't believe that. Henry doesn't seem like the type to blow smoke up your ass for no reason."

"You're probably right. He's a good man."

I wipe another stray tear. This one from regret.

Nineteen

Before

ENERGY SURGED THROUGH MY VEINS. I paced my bedroom and caught my reflection in the mirror. She cocked an eyebrow, arms crossed across her chest. I told her to take her judgement elsewhere. It felt like I'd spent years in bed, and I was ready to fly. A Bird. Just like Henry said.

I stood under the hot stream of water in the shower and watched it swirl down the drain, taking with it my grief, and anger, and hopelessness. I'd read about the stages of grief. Sure I'd reached the acceptance phase, I was further buoyed. The worst was over. I survived.

I pulled on a pair of jeans, and they practically fell off. New clothes. That's what I needed. I found my mother downstairs and kissed her on the cheek. She looked shocked but relieved.

"Headed out to do some shopping," I called on my way out the front door.

First order of business was to get myself one of those fancy phones that no one used to talk on the phone with. I drove to the mall and circled the parking lot. Normally I'd avoided the mall. So many people. So many opportunities to embarrass myself. As I parked and walked in, I kept waiting for my usual anxieties to take over and send me running back to my car.

"Well Bill, it looks like I'm a brand-new woman." I laughed and caught the eye of two teens passing. I lifted a hand and waved. "Hello!" I called. They looked at each other and quickened their pace. *Friendliness is a lost art.*

I stood at the store entrance marveling at the widgets and gadgets lining the tables. People milled about, speaking with store employees, or playing with the various devices and their colorful screens.

"Can I help you?"

I jumped and turned a friendly staff member stood waiting my response. He looked to be still in high school, but it may have been the messy hair sticking up all over the place making him look younger. "Oh, yes, hello! I'm here for a phone. Not one that plugs into the house."

He laughed and I joined in, though I wasn't sure what we were laughing about. After clearing his throat, he continued, "Right. Do you know which model you want?"

My gaze scanned the store and landed on one that looked similar to Henry's, "One like that will do."

An hour later I had my fancy new phone and very detailed instructions on how to use it. Not only did that little device allow me to search the internet and play games, I could read books on it too. When he learned I was an avid reader, he showed me the larger tablets and how wonderful they were for reading. I purchased one of those as well. I left feeling both elated about my new purchases, but also silly for not trying these things out sooner.

After the phone store, I visited several clothing establishments. I'd lost so much weight a new wardrobe was needed. Feeling adventurous, I even purchased several pairs of jeans with holes in them. I no longer had a job, and the shopping trip wiped my bank account clear out, but I didn't care. I felt new, refreshed, ready to dive back into life.

Back in the parking lot I programmed Henry and Quinn's numbers into the phone and sent them both a text: *Hello! Look who has a new phone. Sincerely, Beverly.*

Henry texted back right away: *Woot! Welcome to the twenty-first century*

Quinn's response was very Quinn: *Thank God* followed by several laughing faces.

I grinned at my phone then placed it in my purse. Many things had changed, but I would not be one of those drivers on their phone putting everyone's lives at risk around them.

A HAND gently laid on my shoulder from behind makes me snap back to reality. I'm sitting on my front porch with no recollection of how I've gotten there.

"Bev?"

I turned and looked up at my mom. My smile widens. "I'm so glad you're back, you'll never believe what I got today, one of those smart phones, and jeans, with holes in the knees." I chuckled. "Such a silly trend don't you think? Buying clothes with holes already—"

I can't fully read her expression, but it's enough to make me stop talking. Worry. Fear. Something.

I'm immediately transferred back to that night, standing in the hallway hearing about Bill's death. I jump up. "What is it? Is it dad? Henry? Why are you looking at me like that."

She gripped my upper arms and searched my face with her eyes. "Why don't we go inside?"

She's talking to me like I'm fragile. Why? I'd had such a productive day. I'm better. Stage acceptance had been reached.

She sat me on the couch and took the seat next to me.

"What's going on, Beverly?"

"I'm not sure what you're asking. I had a lovely day at the mall, my new phone. Here let me show you it."

I go to stand but she placed a hand on my leg, indicating I should stay.

That voice returned, the one she'd use on a child. "Do you want new furniture too?"

I'm utterly perplexed and have no idea why we'd be talking about furniture.

"No. My furniture is just fine."

Her head nods slowly.

"I'm just curious why'd you'd move your entire bedroom set into the hallway."

She may have well been speaking a foreign language, one in which I had no grasp of.

This time she let me stand, and I carefully made my way up the stairs, gasping when I reached the top step. The hallway, no longer passable, was filled with the entire contents of my bedroom.

My parents, too deep in conversation, didn't notice the groan of the stair trying to alert them to my eavesdropping. I tiptoed down to the bottom step and sat, straining to hear.

"I think we should take her to see someone," my mom said.

"You said she showered, got out of the house today. Those have to be good signs. Don't they?" My dad's final question didn't sound like he believed what he was saying.

"If you could have seen it. And I don't think she remembers doing it either." My mom's worry turned into a cloud, bloating full of rain and filling the entire house. "She said she wanted a fresh clean room to go with her new life. But I don't know..."

"She's up and seems to be coming out of her funk. Why don't we keep an eye on her and see how she does. I don't' want to set her back by doing anything drastic."

A silence as bloated as her worry filled the house along with it.

Finally my mom agreed. They would wait and see.

I tiptoed back to my, now put back together, room, and pulled out the shoebox of toilet paper.

I felt better than I had, maybe ever. I didn't think there was anything wrong with me. But our minds are the worst liars of them all. Especially when they have something to hide.

Twenty

UNEXPECTED WAVES of sadness still came. A smell or a sound would bring a forgotten memory swimming to the surface. On most occasions it was gentle, like a breeze tickling my face. Other times, it came more forcefully. These reminders knocked the wind from my chest before crushing my heart. I had a support system that I learned to lean on. I didn't have to be alone, I had Quinn and Henry, and my parents of course.

Soon, these painful reminders came less frequently, with their impact less powerful.

Henry and I lazed on his couch one Saturday evening, a movie played in the background that we were too focused on each other to pay attention. He still made me laugh, and not just a chuckle, laughs that shook my body and made me feel whole. My dad was right, I did have holes to fill. I didn't think anyone could make me laugh the way Bill had, but Henry's brand of humor grew on me. Or perhaps he wasn't trying so hard.

It was like I had unzipped my skin and a brand-new Beverly stepped out. As if she had been sleeping quietly below the surface, waiting for her prince to come wake her with a kiss. And once I had my taste of that first kiss, I couldn't get enough. I'd steal soft pecks and longer, deeper ones whenever I had the chance.

I leaned into the crevice beneath his draped arm, a spot I fit in perfectly. I lifted my face toward him. He tilted his and our lips connected for five blissful seconds. My stomach still fluttered at his touch.

"I was thinking," he said once we disconnected, "we could ask our parents about getting both families together for Thanksgiving. I'm sure my mom would love to have you and your parents over here."

The only extended family I had was an aunt on my mother's side. Her grown children were married with their own kids, so we hadn't seen each other on the major holidays in years.

"That would be lovely. I must speak with my parents, but we don't have any big plans; I'm sure they would be thrilled."

We turned back to the movie. I still couldn't get my head wrapped around how happy I was. I had never been so alive. I was in love; it was beautiful. I couldn't understand why I had run from this thing for so long. It wasn't love that was scary and awful. The scary and awful part was that I'd almost missed out on it.

As expected, my parents accepted the invitation with enthusiasm. The next two weeks flew by. Preparations and communications distracted me from having to think much about the actual event and its importance. Blending the families for the first time. A practice-run for a possible future.

Until the morning of.

The significance of the day punched me in the stomach the moment I woke.

I had done well the last month, pretending to be this new Beverly, but my old anxious self had been crouching in a corner, waiting for the right moment to reemerge. I got out of bed and began pacing my room and chewing my fingernails down to nubs.

I leaned in nose to nose with my reflection and the girl laughed and laughed and laughed.

Silly Beverly. You think you're one of them now.

Books always describe women in love as so caught up in the bliss of it all that the world could collapse around them, and they'd sigh, hand in their chin, and smile while thinking of their lover. This always seemed trite and ridiculous to me. Nothing could be so absorbing. Real people didn't react like that. Oblivious to their surroundings all because one person showed them a bit of attention.

How could I have been so foolish? So enamored by Henry, I had become one of those women I had rolled my eyes at so many times. I was about to walk through a minefield where every step could set off the devastating explosion to end my life and this relationship. The heartbreak fused to the end of every relationship. A million things could go wrong with this day. So many people together in one room; the lack of control racked my nerves. A million seconds spread out in opportunities for arguments, embarrassment, or offense.

I snatched my box from under my bed and collapsed

on the floor of my closet, knees bent to my chest. While each square of toilet paper melted on my tongue, I wrapped my arms around my knees, body rocking and head slamming into the wall behind me. I turned my wrist, checked my watch, then got up to get dressed. I couldn't control much that day, but I could control my punctuality. I picked out my outfit with shaking hands, a pair of slender black slacks, olive V-neck sweater, and ballet flats.

My mom called me from the bottom of the stairs. Somehow, after managing to get myself ready, I took a long, steadying breath before heading down to join them.

"You look lovely, Beverly." My mom's warm smile did nothing to soften the anxiety crawling under my skin.

"You too, Mom," I said, trying to hide the quiver from my voice.

Dad looked confused. "You okay? You look terrified."

My mom hit his arm, shushing him.

"She does not. It's a big day." She looked back at me. "Being nervous is normal. I remember the first time all your grandparents got together. I was a bundle of nerves myself. It will be fine, don't worry."

"I'll try my best." I forced a smile.

"Enough of this, let's go. The faster we get there, the faster we eat." My dad grabbed his jacket off the hallway hook and the keys from the bowl on the credenza.

Mom hooked her arm his, and I followed them out to the car.

I sat in the back seat chewing the side of my thumb, trying to push away all the ill-fated scenarios flashing through my mind.

Twenty One

AFTER ONE KNOCK on Henry's front door, it flew open, Henry's form filling the doorway, beaming proudly.

I lifted my hand in a timid wave. "Hi Henry."

Henry's mom nudged him out of the way and opened the door wider. "Come in, come in. Bev, so good to see you." She pulled me into a warm embrace.

"You must be Debbie?" his mom said to mine. "Joyce." She introduced herself before giving my mom the same hug.

The two moms hit it off instantly and the rest of us settled into the living room, while the two newly best friends disappeared into the kitchen to finish preparing the meal.

I sat rigid on the couch; a forced smile stretched across my face.

"Bev, you may want to slow down on the wine a bit." Henry laughed, glancing around the room. The dads watched television in silence. The floats from the Macy's

Day Parade filled the New York streets with colorful holiday cheer.

I took the final swig of my third glass of wine and whipped my head Henry's way. The daggers shooting from my eyes impaled his face. Without a word, he got up and refilled my glass. Henry was normally good at understanding my needs. We'd spent enough time together, I'd expected him to realize how utterly uncomfortable I was. The wine helped.

"Ready!" Joyce called from the dining room, as Henry handed me a freshly topped wine glass.

We hauled ourselves from our chairs with watering mouths, the entire house filled with the scent of what was sure to be a feast.

I stumbled slightly when I stood, red wine sloshing on Joyce's cream carpet. My eyes followed Henry's to the fresh stain. If I'd been in my right mind, I'd have panicked. Unfortunately, my wine-softened brain couldn't conjure the proper reaction. Henry grabbed my elbow to help steady me. I jerked my arm away, scolding him with an expression. There was no need to bring attention to it.

Once settled into our seats, Joyce explained their Thanksgiving tradition of going around the table, each person giving thanks for something or someone.

She started, telling us she was thankful for Henry and his dad. "Her answer has been the same, every year for as long as I can remember," Henry said, chuckling.

"Well it's true, it's what I'm most thankful for," Joyce protested with a grin.

Henry's dad was thankful for naps. Something I could relate to. My mom's answer mirrored Joyce's, thankful for her family and good health. My dad nodded, and proclaimed he was thankful for the same. Henry looked at me and said how thankful he was for finding me. So kind and sweet, the moms sung a chorus of awws.

And then it was my turn.

I held up my glass, and in slightly slurred speech, proclaimed, "I'm thankful Henry turned out to be less of an idiot than I believed him to be when we first met." I giggled, no doubt thinking I was the funniest person in all America.

Everyone laughed nervously. Except Joyce, who silently glared at me from the head of the table. It should have been enough to shut me up. If I hadn't been over-served and out of control, it would have been.

"Well, that's something to be thankful for," Joyce said flatly. "Let's eat."

The scraping of silverware on plates and spoons in serving bowls quickly replaced the silence along with the 'please pass me's', and 'thank you's'.

"Tastes great, Ma!" Henry said between bites.

Everyone around the table agreed.

Over the course of the meal—while the rest of the attendees got drunk on turkey, gravy, mashed potatoes, stuffing, green bean and sweet potato casserole, homemade macaroni and cheese, and cranberry sauce—I continued to get drunk on wine.

"You know," I slurred, with glazed eyes, "Henry could still be an idiot, and I'm simply too inexperienced with men to realize." I chuckled to myself, swirling the wine in my glass.

"Enough," Henry said. He'd never raised his voice to me. The drunk Beverly train kept barreling forward.

"Well, it's true, Henry. You're my first boyfriend. I mean, you were my first date, for heaven's sake." I attempted to make my face serious, but the alcohol made it hard to control my expression.

My mom cleared her throat, "That's right, dear, and we're all so happy you two found each other. You seem so happy. Both of you."

"Put down the booze, Beverly, you're drunk and making an ass of yourself," my dad said.

"Oh Dad, I'm not saying Henry isn't the *best*. We're all fully aware he's much nicer than I am, obviously. I mean, he made *me*—the girl who hates *everyone*—fall in love with him. All I'm saying is that his mental capacity is still an uncertainty. You'd have to be an idiot to want to be with me, after all." Still thinking I was being hilarious, I was now the only one at the table laughing.

"I suppose it doesn't matter though, does it, Henny?" I asked, looking at Henry, miscalculating the turn and falling into him. He righted me back into my seat.

"Henny? What exactly *doesn't matter*, Beverly?" Henry replied through gritted teeth. If only drunk Beverly could have read the room, I would have noticed the daggers Henry now shot toward me with his eyes.

"Everyone at this table knows that *this"*—I flapped my hand between us—"has about a five percent chance of survival. I mean, it's quite apparent I'm not good enough for you, or you're not good enough for me. Or you'll cheat. Or I'll get bored. Whatever the cause of our demise, it's coming. I'd bet money on it. If I had a job and an income with money, I mean."

"All right. Time to go. Beverly, get up and get in the car." My dad stood, sending his chair scraping back. He walked over and dragged me up and toward the front door by my elbow.

I heard my mom say, "I'm so sorry. She's usually not like this. I'm not sure what's gotten into her."

I looked over my shoulder, Joyce stood and put her arm around my mom's shoulders, whispering in her ear as she walked her to the door.

"What a shit show," Henry's dad said, laughing. He took a swig of beer and focused his attention back on his meal.

The ride home sobered me, when we pulled into the driveway the rational part of my mind began to grasp what I'd done.

"Go to your room," my dad demanded.

There would be no argument from me.

Twenty Two

So. Many. Regrets.

But I couldn't tend to them that morning, as I was too busy hugging my toilet, vomiting wine and shame into the porcelain bowl.

All.

Day.

Long.

Twenty Three

"I screwed up."

Two days later—when my humiliation was far enough in the past, I could re-enter the world of the living without wanting to die—I scheduled an emergency lunch with Quinn.

"Yeah, you did, babe. Henry called me and told me what happened."

My body felt like static prickled beneath my skin. I was no longer sitting at the table, instead I stood off to the side watching Quinn and I like a movie.

"Did you learn nothing from me, love?"

I turned my head to Bill. He shouldn't have been there, I shouldn't have been watching myself from besides the table, but it all seemed so normal.

"I do prefer to learn my lessons the hard way it seems," I said.

"Don't we all, love. Don't we all."

A blink and I'm back at the table with Quinn and

remember what she'd said. A small flash of annoyance flared in my chest. Annoyance and jealousy. I didn't understand why Henry thought it was appropriate to gossip about our private matters. I also didn't like how close the two of them appeared to be getting. It was great that everyone got along, but I preferred to compartmentalize my relationships. I was in no position to have opinions on anyone's behavior, so I bit my tongue to avoid further digging myself deeper in the grave I already stood in.

"What do I do? I'm so embarrassed. Do I call his parents and him to apologize? Do I walk away and move on with my life?"

"Apologies are a good place to start. You owe Henry and his parents that much, at least. What possessed you to get so drunk?"

"I have absolutely no clue! My nerves, I started drinking wine to take the edge off and didn't stop. My mom is mortified, my dad thinks I'm an ass, and Henry's parents hate me. Who can blame them?" I buried my face in my hands.

"Well, it sounded like Henry has calmed down enough to at least hear what you have to say. So, I would start there."

Quinn then told me she had finally saved up enough money to enroll in classes at the University of Rhode Island to get a degree in business, with hopes of a career in marketing. It was a hike across the bridges, but she was excited.

"Only problem is, I'll have to move back into my parents' house. No offense."

I knew what was expected of me, so I told her how happy I was for her. But silently, I panicked, Quinn would be at a big school meeting new friends and with a new busy schedule. Would she even have time for me?

We finished our lunch and hugged goodbye. I practiced my Henry apology speech the entire ride home, and by the time I pulled into the driveway, I still didn't feel ready at all. But I couldn't put it off any longer.

"I'm sorry," I said. I could hear him take a deep breath and release it slowly through his nose.

"Are you aware the first time you told me you loved me was in a drunken ramble while simultaneously questioning my intelligence?"

I groaned. "Well, if I'm being honest, I don't remember my words exactly. Unfortunately, I don't remember saying that, or much of anything."

"Well, it was!" His voice pierced my ear. I held the phone at arm's length, I should have texted.

I placed the phone back up to my ear and continued, wishing he would calm down and listen. "It was wrong. I was wrong. And if you remember, you were wrong once too, and I gave you a second chance."

"Throwing my mistakes into an apology isn't the best tactic."

"Fine, you're correct. But it had to be said—"

"No, Beverly. It didn't need to be said. Not everything *needs* to be said all the time. Especially not the mean and hateful things."

"I'm sorry, Henry. I hope you can accept my apology, and we can move on. I will also formally apologize to your parents. I messed up. I'll mess up again, not with alcohol though, as I think I've learned my lesson in that respect. But I will try to be better. And that's all I can offer. If you will give me a second chance."

I held my breath, anticipating his reply. I couldn't imagine leaving him and his family with that dinner as their lasting impression of me. I could already feel the holes beginning to form without having Henry in my life. I pictured my bed and considered crawling into it and never getting out.

"All right, Bev. I may regret this, but let's get together and talk it out."

Another one of life's decisions. This time it being Henry's. Another step down the path that led us to where we ended up. While I know where the path led, I still don't know if it was worth it.

Twenty Four

AFTER A FEW STRAINED MEETINGS, Henry warmed to me again, and thank goodness for that. He made me work very hard for it, too. I never imagined myself forced to work for affection. I hated affection, feelings, attention. To now be in a position where I was desperately chasing them, well, it was both confusing and exhilarating. I was on my best behavior. Compliments, laughing very heartedly at all his jokes, responsible alcohol consumption, and finally, we fell back into our routine and back in love. I understood what all the fuss was about. The lows *were* terrible, but the highs made it worth it.

I just had to make sure I didn't mess it all up again.

With no job, I started to get restless. Unemployment did have its advantages, with no pesky customers to deal with and no manual labor, it left me with a lot of time to spend with myself, searching for things to do. My whole life, I'd dreamed of being able to sit around, doing nothing else but read, but even that began to bore me. The thought of losing my love of books terrified me, maybe even more than the thought of losing Henry. No, no. That's not true. But a very close second for sure. The remaining holidays—Christmas and New Year's—passed much more peacefully than Thanksgiving.

Henry's parents were kind enough to forgive and forget, and the two families gathered for Christmas day. Maybe it was the comfort of it taking place within my territory—my house—or maybe I had learned my lesson. But there were no drunken outbursts. His parents trusted me again, and I hoped they didn't hate me. If they did, they were too gracious to say or act on it. I was sure the next year would be my year. The year of Beverly. But first, I had to figure out what to do with my life.

"Henry, hi, it's Beverly," I said into the phone. Quinn had tried to explain that now that I had a smartphone, it wasn't necessary to talk on the phone all the time. Not when you could text. I disagreed. There was no point in carrying around a phone, able to make a call from wherever I was, if all I was going to use it for was texting.

"You don't have to say whose calling, I can see it on the screen." He laughed. "But this is the third time you've called today. I'm at work. You have to stop." Henry wasn't too fond of my aversion to texting either. "Go for a walk, read a book, or get a job. I love you, but I'm hanging up now. I have gobs of work. Sorry babe."

I ended the call, put the phone down, crossed my arms, and glared at the phone. *Well, maybe Quinn will be happier to hear from me.*

I threw on my coat and drove downtown. I parked farther away than necessary. The air was chilly, but there was no snow on the ground. Christmas decorations blanketed downtown instead. They weren't as beautiful as they were at night, but I still enjoyed the splashes of red and green marking the small streets.

Quinn was helping a customer when I walked in. She didn't look pleased at my appearance, but not letting that deter me from my need for social interaction, I pretended to browse the racks and patiently waited for her to finish.

After the customer left without making a purchase, she joined me. "Beverly, what are you doing here? We've talked about this, darling. You can't just keep showing up here unannounced all the time. I know you're bored, but I'm working."

"Everyone is so busy all the time, I'm bored and going crazy at home," I whined.

"You literally just described your perfect life. Alone, no one to bother you. My little girl is all grown up now. A true people person." She laughed and patted my head.

"Stop it. I just wanted to say hi. I guess I'll leave," I said, turning around.

"Stop pouting. I have a break coming up. Let me grab Beth from the back and make sure she can watch the store. We can grab a coffee."

My heart lifted, I resisted the urge to clap my hands.

"Wipe that smile off your face. This is the last time. Next time you call first. And not multiple times a day. Or text, for the love of technology. Okay?"

"Yes, fine. I will *call*. Those are the rules," I said. She rolled her eyes and disappeared behind the door marked *Staff*, before returning with her jacket and a frowning Beth.

We walked to the coffee shop, ordered, and slid into the chairs at our usual table.

"You're looking so much better, Beverly. How are you doing?" Quinn asked before taking a sip of her cappuccino. I never understood the point of them. Why not just leave coffee alone? It was already perfect as is. Now you have to layer a bunch of stuff in, blow some air in it, add some tasteless white fluffiness to the top. Did people feel fancier drinking a posh-looking drink? And each sip leaves you with a cappuccino mustache, so they don't look fancy at all, in fact, they look like a child drinking milk. Quinn dabbed away her white mustache with a napkin and laughed. I managed a courtesy chuckle and bit my tongue.

"I'm fine. Bored, but fine." I sighed.

"And how's Henry? Everything good with you two?" she asked.

"Oh yes, he's wonderful."

"Well, since you asked, I'm doing great as well," she said and laughed. I arched an eyebrow. An odd way of continuing our conversation, but okay. "What are you two doing for Valentine's Day?"

"Valentine's Day is such a cliché holiday, invented by the greeting card manufacturers, candy factories, and florists. It is nonsense disguised in meaning for the sole purpose of driving commerce. But of course, Henry being Henry, insists we do something nice and made reservations at a fancy restaurant. A steakhouse, I believe. I don't know, I'd much prefer to stay home and watch a movie."

"Sorry I asked," she teased. "You just said you were bored, and now you want to stay home? You don't know what you want, sweetheart."

"That's because every time I think I want something, I get something else and realize I wanted the wrong thing all along. It's quite frustrating. I've given up on guessing what it is I actually want. Turns out I am terrible at making life plans. I am the new *adventurous* Beverly."

"Whoa, watch out world," Quinn said, laughing and shaking her head.

We finished our coffee and Quinn had to get back to work, I decided to stop at the white bench. I'd attempted a few times, but always stopped short once it was in sight. It didn't seem right to sit there alone.

I turned the corner and there it was. And as luck would have it the square was empty. I took a deep breath of cold air and took several steps toward it.

Come sit with me, love. I miss you. The wind whispered, but it sounded an awful lot like Bill.

"I miss you too."

Chin up, shoulders back, I crossed the square and settled into the bench.

"There's a lot of change, Bill. It scares me."

I closed my eyes and when I opened them, he was there, next to me. I sucked in a deep breath through my nose and inhaled his musky scent. With a shaking hand I reached out and cupped his face. The stubble on his face pricking my palm.

I gulped back tears and thought of all the things I needed to say. All the things I needed to hear. When I opened them again, he was gone.

Twenty Five

HUSHED MUMMERS of love and adoration filled the dark room, broken by the occasional tinkle of laughter. Happiness coursed through me—not fake, forced-smile happy, but actual calm, relaxed, feeling comfortable in my own skin, not needing to run to the bathroom and stuff toilet paper in my mouth, happy.

The lobster was bathed in a sherry cream sauce. Each bite melted in my mouth. Wine fogged my mind—but not too much.

"Aren't you glad I convinced you to come out tonight?" Henry asked.

"I am. This lobster is delicious. Want to try a bite?" I held out my fork with a butter-doused lump. Henry leaned in and ate it.

"Ah, so good," he agreed.

"I still don't believe in Valentine's Day, so don't think you've converted me or anything. But this restaurant was a great choice," I said. "Are you not feeling well?"

"I'm fine. Why?" Henry dabbed his forehead with a napkin.

"You look. I don't know, all sweaty and sickly," I replied.

He laughed nervously. A pit formed in my stomach. He was about to break up with me. I frantically searched the room for the nearest bathroom.

"I need to use the lavatory," I said, shooting out of my seat and scurrying away.

In the stall, I gulped in air from my spot on the toilet seat. I reached down and unrolled the toilet paper and dabbed my eyes before taking several bites. I couldn't imagine what I had done. I should have known this would happen. *'Heartache and hurt'* that's what Bill used to say. He was the smartest person I've ever met, and the second he died, I forgot all his wise words.

"Ma'am? Are you okay?" A knock sounded on the stall door. I swallowed the wad of toilet paper I had been melting on my tongue.

"Yes. Fine, thank you," I said with my voice entirely too high.

"Um, your husband—"

"I don't have a husband. You must be looking for someone else."

"Sorry, I mean your boyfriend, the man you came with, he's worried about you, you've been in here for some time, and he asked me to check on you."

I looked below the stall and noticed the shiny black shoes that the entire waitstaff wore. I opened the door to our waitress, who looked both worried and uncomfortable.

"I'm fine, sorry. A sour stomach is all. I wanted to

make sure it would pass before returning to the table." I walked around her to the sink with a tight smile where I concentrated on washing my hands. When I looked up in the mirror, she was still behind me, her reflection stared back. "I said I'm fine. You can go now."

She walked briskly to the door and mumbled an apology. "Thank you," I called to the closing door, hoping she heard it and didn't think me rude, she wasn't the one about to break up with me. I splashed my face with water and tried to remember how to stuff my feelings deep in the caverns of my belly. I lifted my chin, straightened my back, and returned to our table.

Henry stood abruptly upon my return, knocking his chair over and causing several couples to stop talking and look our way. His hands wrung his napkin. At least he felt bad about what he was about to do.

"You okay? You were in there forever," he said as I took my seat.

"Yes, I'm fine. I wish everyone would stop asking me that," I replied. I placed my napkin on my lap and turned my head from Henry. Out of the corner of my vision, I watched him drop to the ground. "My word," I said with my hand covering my mouth. "Are you sure you aren't sick, Henry?"

"Beverly, you are amazing. Everything about you. I love it. All of it. Your dry humor, your odd yet extraordinary view on life. You make me laugh and feel ways I never thought I would feel—"

I slumped down in my chair, but there was no hiding. "What are you doing? Get up here this instant. Everyone is staring at us."

"Beverly, my beautiful Birdie, will you marry me?"

I sat up straight in my chair. Those were the last words I expected to hear. At a complete loss, my jaw hung loose.

"I—What? Is this a joke? Are you playing a trick on me?" I whispered.

"Of course not, I love you, you love me, let's get married," he said.

I couldn't make my voice work, so I just bobbed my head up and down.

"Is that a yes?" His smile widened. "It's a yes," he shouted, standing. "It's a yes!" His voice grew louder with each proclamation. Every person in the restaurant had turned in their seats watching us, craning their necks to be a part of the action.

He scooped me into his arms and swung me around. We leaned our foreheads together, and both cried tears of joy. I felt like a bird. Because of Henry, my wings had finally grown. I was ready to fly. The entire restaurant erupted in cheers.

Finally able to compose ourselves, we settled back into our chairs. I held out my hand so he could slip the perfect diamond ring onto my slender finger. I twisted my hand and delighted in the sparkle that danced in the diamond when it reflected the light. It reminded me of Henry's bright smile.

"It's perfect. This is perfect. *You're* perfect. Thank you."

Twenty Six

I NEVER STOPPED WORRYING that the day would come when Henry's mom would finally change her mind and realize I wasn't good enough for her son. When she called, a pit formed in my stomach. The scene I caused at Thanksgiving played out behind my eyes.

"Beverly? It's Joyce."

I swallowed and braced myself for what was inevitably to come.

"I'm calling about the wedding."

I unclenched the phone.

"Your mom and I have been chatting, and we're concerned no plans have been made. Not even a date. Now I know it's only been two months, but I'm not sure if you realize how much planning these things require. Do you need help, dear?"

"Yes!" I calmed my voice, removing the desperation from my delivery. "Yes, I'm not sure where to start. So, well, I haven't started."

I looked down at the diamond sparkling on my ring finger. I still gasped sometimes when it caught the light. It seemed like a dream—a very long and detailed dream—where any moment I would wake up and resume my lonely existence.

"I've tried discussing it with Henry, but he is apparently as lost as you are. Ask your mother if she is free for lunch today. The three of us can meet and begin planning."

The last time my mom had to step in and plan an event for me was Bill's funeral. A lump formed in my throat; it still did that sometimes when I thought about him. I swallowed it down.

"Do you mind if I invite my friend along?"

"It's your wedding, dear, invite who you want."

I promised to call her back, and after confirming both Quinn and my mom were available, I hurried to get ready.

I still couldn't believe that I, the girl who was so sure solitude suited her best, was getting married.

PLEASANTRIES EXCHANGED, orders placed, we huddled together in a booth at Brick Alley Pub.

I studied the room through the crowd. Artifacts of Newport's history hung from every space on its bricked walls. I could spend a day in there, examining each item, imagining the life it had before ending up in the pub. The other diners appeared too engaged in their meals and conversations to notice. Such a shame. The world was filled with so many fascinating and beautiful things, but people were too wrapped up in people most of the time to experience it all.

"I'm sorry, what?" I asked when I noticed all three of them staring at me.

"The date, silly, when do you want the wedding to be?" Quinn asked.

"Sometime next month?" I shrugged and took a sip of water.

"Next month!" my mom squeaked, expressing what they were all apparently thinking because six eyes practically popped out of three heads.

"Is that too far? Should I do it sooner?" I asked.

"These things take time to plan. I'm not even sure we could find a place available on such short notice," Henry's mom said.

"I don't want a big thing. You have a nice backyard. Can we have it there?" I asked.

The women looked horrified. It was as if I had stood up on top of the table and screamed, rather than simply suggested a backyard wedding. Elopement sounded nice. I liked the sound of the word too. I imagined rolling it around in my mouth like a cherry lifesaver. Eh, loh, and a pop with the p.

"It's your wedding, not ours," Joyce replied, plastering a smile on her face, "and if our backyard is what you want, then our backyard is what you'll get."

"Perfect, so that was easy. Wedding is planned. And you all had me worried." I laughed and returned to eating.

"Ey yi yi, Beverly," Quinn said.

"What?" I asked.

"It's fine, honey," my mom said. "We'll take care of the

rest." She and Joyce exchanged a glance. Fine by me. Less work for me to do on things I couldn't care less about.

I was very wrong about the amount of labor the wedding would require of me. Despite me telling them multiple times, 'I don't care, just pick,' they all insisted on making me a part of every decision. Flowers, décor, food, chairs. Who cares which chairs we rented? Did they have four legs, a seat, and a back? Great, then those are the chairs I wanted. Invitations, so many fonts, colors, embossed, not embossed. There were way too many choices for items I'd have preferred not to concern myself with.

Despite my lack of enthusiasm, Quinn, Joyce, and my mom dragged me through the wedding planning process, and we made it through unscathed, a date set, and a wedding planned. It would be in a little over a month, the backyard no-frills wedding they decided didn't need that much time. Turns out I did know a thing or two about weddings.

Twenty Seven

WE WERE BLESSED with a cloudless day in May for our wedding. A slight breeze tickled our faces, the type with perfect timing, that shows up right when you start to feel the sun's heat. Joyce's peonies were in full bloom, filling the backyard with their intoxicating perfume. I can't stand the smell of peonies now. The sweet smell transports me back to that day, what used to be my favorite day. A painful reminder of what should have been. And how happy I was to wed Henry and become Beverly Bonnefinche.

"Stop fussing," Quinn said. She grabbed my lower chin—much too tightly—and touched up my lip gloss. "Now, you're perfect." She took a step back and spun me around so I could view myself in the full-length mirror in Henry's parents' room.

I'd opted for a simple dress. I was draped in white cotton to my feet and a shelf of lace hung from my shoulders. Quinn found it, of course. Left to my own devices, I would have shown up in my favorite gray pleated skirt, not appropriate, according to her. Rowan did my hair and makeup, but we chose a more subtle look. She felt horrible about what happened the last time; thankfully it all worked out in the end.

"Oh, Beverly," my mom gasped from the doorway. "You look beautiful." Her hands pressed together at her lips. She was already crying.

"Let me get a look at my girl," my dad said. He stepped around my mom and grabbed my hands before taking a step back. "Stunning." He pulled me into a hug. The smell of Polo cologne pricked my eyes with tears.

"I have something for you," my mom said, reaching into her purse. She pulled out a small bottle and handed it to me.

"What is this?" I asked. I turned it over and realized it was a tiny bottle of vodka. My piece of Bill. I took a moment, rolling the bottle around my palm. Bill's goofy smile materialized in my mind. If only he could have been there. He would have been so proud of me.

"I miss him so much it hurts," I said, my mom blurry from the tears filling my eyes.

"I know you do, Bev," my mom said, squeezing my hand.

"Thank you for this," I said. "It's perfect." I tucked the bottle into my bouquet, so Bill could walk me down the aisle with my dad.

"You ready to do this?" my dad asked. "You can still make a run for it."

"You stop." My mom smacked him on the arm. "Quinn, want to walk down with me and grab a seat?"

"Yes, let's get this party started," she said. She pecked me on the cheek before following my mom out of the room.

"I'm proud of you, Bev. Really proud of you. Henry is a good man, and I'm so proud of the woman you've become."

"I love you, dad."

He held out his elbow, I threaded my arm through, and grabbed my bouquet.

"Let's do this," I said.

"Let's do this," he replied.

When I stepped through the sliding glass door, I gasped. I understood why it took so much planning. The entire yard was transformed. Our guests, mostly Henry's friends and co-workers, were all seated in neat rows of white chairs. I suppose plain metal ones wouldn't have fit and chair type *did* matter. White gossamer fabric was draped in lazy loops connecting the outside of the rows, connected to the chairs with bouquets of daisies. Henry stood at the head of the white runner beneath an archway of more daisies. The second he laid eyes on me, tears poured down his cheeks.

Everyone turned in their seats, watching me and smiling. I looked down at the ground, not sure what to do with my face.

"Just look at Henry, Bev, you're doing fine," my dad whispered in my ear.

I looked up and locked eyes with him. I couldn't control the smile splashed across my face. A smile that reached my eyes.

Henry was the key who had unlocked my life. The life

I was meant to live clicked into place, turned, and opened for me. He brought forward a girl who I never knew existed, softening my jagged edges, making me yearn for things I had so steadfastly rejected out of fear.

I remained quiet and reserved, uncomfortable with people, but with Henry around, that was okay. I could blend into the background and let him take the lead. He knew how to include me without forcing me into actions that unnerved me. A quick smile. A hand squeeze. A 'Beverly, do you agree?' I could nod and smile at, taking part without having to take part.

After a brief ceremony, when the I do's were sealed with a kiss, we enjoyed a delicious barbeque. Burgers and hot dogs his dad grilled to perfection. Plates piled high with homemade potato salad and macaroni and cheese, courtesy of Henry's mom. Finished with cupcakes, courtesy of mine. It wasn't a lavish affair but a perfect one. I wouldn't change a thing.

Well, except for everything that happened after it.

Part Two

Twenty Eight

Our house that would become our home was the first one we looked at. We had lived with Henry's parents for the first nine months of our marriage, but we had overstayed our welcome, and we needed a place of our own. Not that I wasn't grateful for Henry's parents' hospitality.

"You are just going to love this one," Lynda, our real estate said as we pulled into the cracked driveway in her massive SUV.

I stepped out and gazed at the quaint, two-story colonial nestled in the crook of a cul-de-sac. White siding with black trim and shutters. The front windows were adorned with flower boxes, adding a splash of color.

Lynda came and stood beside me. "We don't need to spend too much time inside, most folks are buying these for the lots." She swooped her arms like a circus conductor introducing the next act. "Think of this like your blank canvas."

"What a prosperous thing to say." I looked at her aghast.

Her hands dropped to her sides and her face fell.

"Why would anyone want to tear down such a lovely home?" I shook my head and walked to the front door, where I stood waiting for her to catch up and enter the code so I could wander what I knew would be my forever home.

Inside the front door the narrow stairs to the second floor stood before us, the living room stretched the length of the house to the right, but to the left...

I circled the perimeter, a single hand grazing along the built-in glass-front cabinets. Henry joined me with his hands in his pockets.

"Think of all the wonderful things I can fill these with."

"I figured you'd just fill then with books."

I spun in a circle and nodded. "Those too."

I walked further back into the kitchen. A large spacious room, with windows facing the backyard that bathed the entire space in natural light. A kitchen that inspired culinary creations.

I stood in the breakfast nook. "Henry, look at this. We can put our table right here. Imagine. Every morning we can sit here and drink our coffee and look out into that backyard."

The backyard featured a concrete patio: the ideal spot for relaxing or reading and a mature oak whose branches filled the space, offering shade on hot summer days and its beauty on all others.

Henry kissed the side of my forehead then walked into the living room.

"Jeez, would you look at this. You could fit three couches in here."

I followed the sound of his voice. The threadbare carpet revealed the room's secrets. That space was where most of the living in the home took place.

I didn't have to see the larger owner's suite and two smaller rooms, or even the bathrooms to decide.

"We'll take it!"

Lynda beamed. "Great, let me show you the mudroom, I think that's the door you'll use most. We exited through the long wooden room the length of the house next to the kitchen that would come to serve as the main entrance we'd use.

While my life had improved and I had shed much of my bitterness and judgment, I was not so successful at shedding my tether. My anchor. My calming, self-prescribed medicine for the anxiety that still gurgled beneath my skin. I spent many hours in that bathroom eating my toilet paper. And hating myself for it.

So far, I had been able to hide my secret from my husband. It had been easy. His parents' house had more hiding spots, and the rooms were filled with more people to distract from my sudden disappearances. Perhaps they all believed I had some sort of gastrointestinal issue. A sensitive topic keeping their questions at bay. The thought of my secret being revealed both shamed and horrified me. But not enough to stop.

Henry was doing very well at work. Well enough that a second income from any menial work I could drum up was not worth the effort. So instead, after moving into our new home a few weeks later, I slid comfortably into the shoes my mom had worn her entire life. I became a housewife. How unexpected.

"It will make it easier when we start a family. No sense in getting a job and having to quit right away," Henry had said.

A family. Babies. I hadn't ever considered becoming a mother, but the idea didn't send me screaming from him, running as fast as I could back to my parents' house. The more I thought about it the more it didn't sound so entirely awful. It would require more contemplation.

I insisted on a tidy home. Therefore laundry, dusting, dishes, mopping, and other essential housework were the tasks with which I occupied my mornings. I spent my afternoons reading and contemplating my boredom. I longed for the days when I had customers to break up the monotony. Those same customers I used to pray wouldn't interrupt my solitude were the very thing I now wished for. The grass, as they say, is always greener.

With a slow and heavy book I was attempting to trudge through sprawled on my lap, I sat in the living room, rocking lazily in the chair Henry usually filled in the evenings. My mind wandered, seeking some other form of entertainment. In my head, I had already burned the house down around me. My charred skin melted into the chair's brown upholstery. Then a carbon monoxide leak quietly pulled me into a forever sleep. A bomb had also already dropped, decimating the entire house into a smoking pile of ash. I was running out of ideas.

With nothing to do with my time I felt myself become more and more lethargic during the afternoons. I could feel the sadness calling me from a distance. My life was perfect in every way, but too much free time can be a dangerous thing for a mind like mine. When I wasn't picturing my demise, I'd reminisce about every embarrassing or horrible thing I did or that happened to me, then I'd walk upstairs and stand over my bed. It was becoming harder each day to resist the urge to crawl under the comfortable covers and go back to sleep.

Bill would come to me during these times. Standing on the other side of the bed shaking his head and wagging a finger.

I needed a reprieve from my boredom. Tempted to call Quinn for the second time that day, I resisted, remembering the important lesson from our first and only quarrel. Friends are still friends, even if they don't spend all their free time with you. I also learned friends will have other friends. And that doesn't mean your friendship is less meaningful or important. The second part was confusing to me. With Bill being gone, I didn't have any other friends. In my mind, when Quinn and I weren't together or talking on the phone, she became immobile—a collapsed marionette, waiting for me to pull the strings and bring her back to life.

Regardless of my opinions on the matter, I was fully acquainted with the rules now. I slipped up occasionally, but I was getting much more proficient at being a friend.

About to give in and knowingly break those social rules, I was saved by the doorbell, sending me leaping from the chair in an unusual show of enthusiasm. My boredom made even a delivery a welcomed reprieve. I'd grown so sick of talking to myself in my head.

Almost at a run, I took long strides toward the front door, cutting the time from the chair to the front entrance in half. I whipped open the door to a face I didn't recognize.

A woman filled my front step, clutching a plate over-flowing with cellophane-topped brownies. I had to strain my neck to meet her eyes.

"Oh! Hello!" Her raspy voice was scuffed from years of chain smoking. A habit that had long since gone out of style, but this woman didn't seem the type to care. "How rude of us ladies to wait so long to introduce ourselves."

I looked beyond her round form in search of the ladies she was referring to.

"They aren't here right now. I was just saying. Anyway, I'm Bonnie. Same side, two doors down." She pulsed her thumb in the direction of her house. "Any-who. We had our weekly book club last night, and we were all aghast when we realized our blunder. You and your old man have been here a whole month. And not one of us has welcomed you. You must think us terribly uncouth. I stayed up all night baking my Gramma's famous brownies hoping to rectify the situation."

She passed the large plate of brownies to me. I scram-bled to take them before they crashed to the ground.

"I'm Beverly. I wasn't expecting anyone to welcome us, so no worries."

"Bonnie and Beverly! What a nice ring that has. Say listen, Beverly, the gals and I get together for book club once a week. Why don't you join us next week and you can meet everyone?"

"I'm not sure..." I said, thinking maybe I shouldn't have answered the door.

"Don't worry if you don't like to read. It's really just a cover to complain about our husbands and get tipsy on a school night. Come on, the ladies would love to meet you," she said, leaning toward me.

I took a step back. "No, I love to read. I just. What night? Where?"

"Oh, perfect, are you a fast reader? I can text you the book and you can catch up. I'll come scoop you Wednesday evening, seven p.m. We get together after dinner so all the mommas can get their littles in bed, and the husbands are fat and happy. No grumpy men to interrupt our good time. Do you have any kids?" She peered around me.

I shook my head. She pulled out her phone and saved my number to her contacts.

"Great, Wednesday, seven. I'll see you then. Or around. Great to meet you, Beverly." Before I could decline, she was side-stepping her way back down my front steps and waving her goodbyes.

With a deep sigh, I stepped back into my house, shutting the door with my foot.

I groaned internally. I placed the brownies on the kitchen counter, side-eyeing them—they were tempting. Eating from strangers' kitchens always made me uneasy. You could never be too careful. Did they wash their hands? Share their kitchen with shedding animals? People are filthy. Even the ones who look hygienic can deceive you. Which I understand is quite the contradiction coming from a woman who consumes toilet paper.

Lifting a corner of the cellophane, I bent to take a whiff. The chocolaty smell made my mouth water. Throwing caution to the wind, I got myself a glass of milk and enjoyed one of the most delectable brownies I'd ever had.

If they had been full of poison, I'd have died happy.

Twenty Nine

LATER THAT NIGHT, Henry—as Bonnie would say—was fat and happy, and enjoying the comfort of his recliner. I was in the kitchen, leaning against the counter talking to Quinn on the phone.

"Yes, I suppose she seems nice enough. I mean not my cup of tea, but nice enough. She makes good brownies."

"Let's be honest. No one is your cup of tea. You don't even like tea, you like coffee, and all people, to you, are tea!"

Her assessment should have offended me, but it was accurate, so I let it slide.

"What have I gotten myself into?" I groaned.

"Go buy the damn book and put on a nice outfit. One that makes you look like you're a respectable member of society and not some squatter. Smile, and you go and meet your neighbors. And stop having such a sourpuss attitude about it. You may have a good time, but if you don't go, you'll never find out."

"You should come with me." I straightened my spine, excited at the excellent idea I had come up with.

"No, ma'am. I'm not coming. I'm pushing my little birdy out of the nest. Other enjoyable people are inhabiting this world besides Henry and me. I set the bar high. But regardless—"

"Ugh, fine. But if it goes horribly, it's all your fault, and I'm allowed an entire evening of my choice out with you. One which I can spend complaining—uninterrupted."

"Fair enough, darling. Now you keep me posted. I gotta jump off. Big kisses. Proud of you."

"Birdie," Henry called from the living room. A name he'd started calling me since our engagement dinner. I kind of liked it. "Could you grab me a beer on the way in here?"

I rolled my eyes. As if getting up and walking the extremely short distance was too much for him. My mother's advice sounded in my head: 'marriage is loving someone for their flaws, not despite them.' And by comparison, Henry had a lot more flaws to find a way to love than I did. I grabbed a beer from the fridge, then placed the bottle on the end table next to his chair where the empty one he'd finished was also sitting. One that would most likely still be there the next morning, waiting for me to pick it up.

"Thanks," he said, smiling. "What's this about the neighbors? Did you make some new friends?"

I sat on the couch and sighed. "Yes, fortunately, or unfortunately, I'm not sure yet."

"What are they like?" he asked, taking a sip of his beer.

"I only met the one. Her name is Bonnie." I pictured

Bonnie's towering form, searching for the words to describe her. "She was—large."

Henry laughed. "That's not very nice, Bev."

"No, I don't mean her size. I mean, well, that was large, too. But that's not what I meant. She was loud, abrasive. She and the other women in the neighborhood have a weekly book club they invited me to. I guess I'll meet some of the other neighbors, too."

"A book club! Perfect, it sounds like your kind of people."

"I'm pretty sure they will hate me. Or think I'm weird."

"You are weird. But that's what makes you so lovable." He winked.

"Thanks for the endorsement. I'll be sure to lead with that when I meet them all," I replied, laughing.

I was a bit jealous of Henry's social skills. Without him or Quinn there to lean on, I would have to find the strength to converse with strangers—an entire evening of small talk. If I ran upstairs and locked myself in the bathroom, Henry may become suspicious. I didn't want to look antsy, but I couldn't stop my wringing hands. The roll of toilet paper called to me from upstairs. I couldn't take it any longer. Finally, I stood and announced I was taking a shower and getting ready for bed.

Without taking his eyes from the TV, Henry wished me goodnight.

Upstairs in the bathroom, the seat and toilet lid were both flipped up, of course. After slamming them shut, I collapsed onto the top, then unraveled the roll. With closed eyes, I nibbled my tension away, square by square.

Thirty

THE NIGHT OF BOOK CLUB, no amount of toilet paper could console me. Quinn's words echoed in my ears. Every outfit I tried on *did* make me look like a squatter. That thought reminded me of Bill, so then I was nervous *and* sad.

I plopped on the bed surrounded by discarded clothes, ready to give up. I was an imposter putting on a disguise. And not even a good one. Henry found me sitting on our bed, head in my hands.

"You gotta stop worrying yourself over this. They will love you. And if they don't, you don't need them."

I appreciated his kind words. However, they did nothing to calm the storm brewing beneath my skin. It wasn't the overarching evening. It was the details. Like where would I sit? What if I picked the wrong seat and had to move under the glares of everyone in the room? What if Bonnie didn't remember inviting me and forgot to come get me? What if I walked to her house, and she opened the door then asked who I was? The possibilities were endless.

"Come on, stand up, Birdie. I'll help you get ready. You'll go out and have a fun time. It's books. You know more about books than anyone. You'll be in your element."

Henry dug through the pile of discarded outfits on the bed and picked a cream sweater. He then pulled a black pair of slacks I'd forgotten I owned from our closet. He always knew exactly what I needed—well, most of the time.

"Now, here. This will look great on you. Go ahead and get dressed."

Thanking him, I pulled myself together enough to change. I walked to the bathroom and locked the door behind me. I leaned on the counter and took deep breaths, trying to push thoughts of a room full of women laughing at me from my head. I unrolled the paper and ripped off enough to quiet my rolling stomach. After, as I was splashing my face with water, I looked up. The girl in the mirror's grin widened, stretching until it took up the entire bottom portion of her face. I was about to tell her to go away, I couldn't deal with her that night, when the door-bell rang. I turned off the light leaving her smiling her grotesque smile at no one.

I grabbed the book from my nightstand and heard Bonnie's voice from downstairs.

"There she is," she called when she noticed me coming down. "I was just gabbing your old man's ear off. Ready?"

No.

Henry gave me a kiss goodbye and an extra tight hug.

Bonnie kept talking the entire way, but my mind too full of anxieties couldn't process a word she said. Sure we'd walk into a room of twenty chattering women, they'd all turn and stare at me with unwelcomed scowls.

"Here we are," she said stopping at the bottom of a driveway. The front lawn littered with various toys. "This one's mine. We switch off where we meet each week."

"Is there assigned seating?" I asked.

"Assigned what?" She laughed then wagged a finger at me. "You're a funny one. You'll fit right in. Tonight's at my house, so you will miss out on Kat fussing over coasters."

Coasters? Does she collect them like fridge magnets or shot glasses? I'd never met anyone who had a passion for those. I hadn't met many people, though.

I held my breath when she opened the door, then released it when two women stood and smiled upon our entrance. Three was a palatable number. I could handle three.

Katherine, or Kat as she went by, lived in the house between Bonnie's and mine. Kat resembled the women who were always smiling back at you from advertisements, trying to sell you a new stove or cleaning invention of some sort. The envy of the entire PTA——of which she was the president, naturally. Kat's entire world revolved around her husband and two children. A boy and a girl twelve and thirteen years old. Unlike Bonnie's perpetual messy bun, a hair misplaced on Kat's head would be as shocking as a hoard of zombies walking down the street. Her hair was cut in a severe bob, which she blow-dried to perfection every morning. I imagined her carefully styling each strand, one at a time. I'm sure this isn't the amount of labor the look required, but I couldn't fathom how she got that result any other way.

As one would expect from her outward appearance, her home was immaculate. While keeping her home and appearances perfect, she also found time to prepare three courses for every meal and be the first to volunteer for every school function and fundraiser. All this I would come to learn, as each meeting took place at a different home each week. I grew exhausted just thinking about how much she accomplished each day. Other women may have gazed upon her with jealousy and awe, fighting for her approval and acceptance, but I found the entire notion of her life and daily routine tiring.

Even the thought of Jeanine's name makes me smile. She was the newest member of the club and neighborhood prior to my arrival. Also, the newest of the women to enter motherhood, with a nine-month-old baby girl, Charlotte, Charlie for short. Her very strait-laced husband had swooped in and saved her from what I learned is called van-life. She'd been living out of an RV, becoming one with nature as she described it. And thank goodness for that. What a life. Permanently camping. No thank you.

I would sometimes catch her with a far-off look in her eyes, that old life tugging the edges of her lips into a smile. It was enough to create a vivid picture in my mind of Jeanine twirling around a field of flowers, her long dirty-blonde hair billowing around her in waves, her skirt flaring out, revealing bare feet adorned in jingling anklets.

The Jeanine of the past and the present exuded every-thing expected of the lovechildren of the 70s; she was born in the wrong era. Peace, love, and happiness—an intoxicating aura, dispelling all prior notions I had of these types of people. She was my antithesis. The embodiment of everything I despised. But as much as I wanted to hate her, I couldn't. From the second I met her, I loved everything about her. It was impossible not to.

When Jeanine listened to you, no matter how mundane the topic, she *heard* you. She took the time to understand the meaning behind the words you were offering her. And always had a thoughtful response to reward you with. Through my interactions with Jeanine, I developed a better understanding of why I loathed small talk. With her, talk was never small. I despised people who ask questions only to hear themselves answer those very questions, not caring one bit what your answer would be. Yet, they ask it, as it opens up the opportunity for them to talk about what they care most about—themselves. But when Jeanine asked a question, it was because she wanted to hear the answer; *your* answer.

Bonnie's blunt and messy nature annoyed Kat, who was constantly hushing and cleaning up after her. That amused Bonnie, who would place a drink down next to a coaster—which she did not in fact collect, she did, however, prefer glasses be placed on them—and smile slyly, waiting for Kat's disapproval. Jeanine was the group's mediator. Swooping in any time Bonnie and Kat's game of cat and mouse proved too intense. That dynamic allowed me to slip easily into the folds of the group. Where my idiosyncrasies would typically shine blindingly bright, among these women I could hide behind theirs.

My earlier fears of a cool reception were proven unnecessary that first night. They welcomed me with open arms. My confidence swelled. I could do this. I really could be normal. And not just with Henry and Quinn, but with other people, too. I could have multiple friends.

After a few Wednesday evenings—and a few much better book selections—I found my voice and was able to interact. My role became the one who took the book discussion portion of the evening most seriously. I would find myself deep within an insightful analysis of the current book's plot, or an interesting character when Bonnie would groan, cut me off, and try to move the discussion to a complaint, gossip, or her immediate need for a refill of that evening's alcohol of choice. Kat would scold her for gossip or her lack of a coaster. And Jeanine would grin sweetly and admit she had either not started the book or was so far behind the chances of catching up near impossible. But she always showed her appreciation of my analysis, letting me know if she *had* read the book, she would agree. Jeanine's compliments and kindness dampened any annoyance at Kat and Bonnie's rudeness.

These were my Wednesday nights. And other than the occasional get-togethers with Quinn, or date nights with Henry, I lived a quiet and reserved life. But like my wedding, it was perfect. Before meeting Henry and Quinn, I hadn't actually hoped for anything other than finding my next great read. This wasn't the life I had dreamed of, or the life I wanted. But it turned out to be the life I needed. I should have known it wasn't my forever, but complacency hides in comfort.

Thirty One

THE FIRST WEDNESDAY of November had plunged New England into a deep freeze. The kind of cold that steals your breath and makes you angry, then enraged because you have nobody to take your anger out on. Weather couldn't be bothered by your misery. It couldn't care less. I wrapped myself in my thickest jacket and braced myself for the icy air, before sprinting to Bonnie's house.

Snot and tears streaming down my face, Bonnie opened the door and quickly shooed me in.

"God, I feel awful," I said, collapsing on her couch.

"I have to be honest with you, you look like shit. Have you caught a cold or something? Hopefully not the flu. I hear it's a bad one this year."

"I'm not sure. I must have eaten something that didn't agree with me. My stomach isn't feeling well, and I'm so tired. You don't happen to have a ginger ale, do you?"

"I think I do. Let me go check."

The ginger ale soothed, at least a little. I sipped the

bubbly drink, praying the nausea I'd been feeling since waking up that morning would release my stomach from the evil it was inflicting upon it. I never got sick. I liked to think it was because of my cleanliness and well-balanced diet, but it was most likely luck and good genes.

Thousands of fatal diseases were potentially eating away at my insides. Stomach cancer, internal hemorrhage, some rare disorder I'd never heard of. It could be anything, really. Or it could be food poisoning.

"I don't know what's—" an ocean of warm saliva flooded my mouth, cutting off my words. I ran to the bathroom, hoping I could make it before my dinner made a second appearance all over Bonnie's carpet.

After violently emptying the contents of my stomach, I splashed water on my face, inspecting my reflection in the mirror above the sink. My skin looked pale, almost gray, and my cheeks more sunken than usual. I stole a few squares of toilet paper for good measure and stared at the floral pattern of her wallpaper, trying to steady myself and my stomach. When the flowers stopped moving, I returned to the living room where Jeanine and Kat had joined Bonnie.

The conversation halted at my entrance, making it obvious I was the topic of their hushed whispers. Bonnie looked sympathetic, Kat looked like I had the plague and she wished she had chosen a hazmat suit instead of the emerald V-neck sweater she wore, and Jeanine looked deep in thought.

"Oh, my God!" Jeanine squealed.

I jumped at her outburst, despite my weakened muscles. I shuffled to the couch, desperate to sit.

"What are you on about Jeanine? She's sick or ate something rotten." Bonnie rolled her eyes. "You and Kat need to calm your britches. She's not dying, for the love of God."

I was grateful for Bonnie and the plate of Saltines she passed me with my ginger ale.

Kat, still looking like she may be sick herself, spat, "I don't want to be insensitive, Beverly, but if you have a stomach virus, I can't be around you. I have the annual bake sale to prepare for and oversee next week. It's a big deal for the school. Not something I can miss."

Jeanine shushed her in an uncharacteristic act of defiance. Frustrated by the realization she was outnumbered, Kat slumped back into the couch with her arms crossed and a sour look on her face.

Turning back to me, Jeanine asked, "What other symptoms have you had?"

I thought for a moment. "I suppose my stomach has been a tad off, and I've been a bit worn out maybe," I replied. Although I'm not sure fatigue was a symptom, as that was a part of my normal existence, sometimes it was there, sometimes it wasn't.

Jeanine smiled, and asked, "When was the last time you got your period?"

Eyes big as saucers, understanding smacked me in the face. "Oh my, no! It can't be *that*." Of course, physically I knew it could be what they were implying. I understood how reproductive science worked. We hadn't been trying; however, we hadn't been practicing any preventative methods either. My mind just simply could not process the idea. I had simply assumed I wasn't meant to be a mom so nature wouldn't allow it.

"Unless old Henry is more boring than I thought, it most certainly can be," Bonnie said. She heaved herself off the couch. "And I'm always prepared for this exact situation."

Nausea gave way to a light head. I could feel myself about to float away like a balloon filled with helium. I picked up a cracker and nibbled the edge, hoping it would keep me from passing out under Jeanine and Kat's scrutiny.

Bonnie came bounding back into the room, gripping a long plastic item. It looked like the tampon I desperately wished I needed right then. "All right, Bevie, up up up." She waved the stick up and down to demonstrate what she wanted from me. "Now bring your drink, in case you need help peeing when you get in there. To the bathroom with you, let's go."

I staggered back to the bathroom, trying to hide my horror, grabbing the pregnancy test on my way. Henry wanted children, and while I wasn't opposed to the idea, I just assumed nature wouldn't allow me to. Still, we had conversations about how many, and when. Now was not aligned with the timeline we had agreed upon to try. Why hadn't we been more responsible? There were a million different versions of birth control available.

Worried the vomiting had dehydrated me, I really didn't want to be sitting on the toilet gripping the stick beneath me forever, but the urine flowed easily, covering the test and the hand holding it. I gagged, mostly because

I'd urinated all over myself, but also from the nerves at what the results would be.

I allowed myself one small bite of paper before wrapping the pregnancy test in it. I placed the bundle on the side of the sink and washed my hands. Once done, I looked down at the wad of paper wrapped around my fate. Not sure how long it was supposed to take, I grabbed it and returned to the ladies with my precious package clutched to my chest.

"All right, enough of this. It's like a band-aid. You gotta look and get on with your day. One way or the other." Bonnie snatched the test from my hand and plopped it down on the coffee table. Our heads were drawn to it like magnets. My stomach plummeted to my feet.

And there it was. Two distinguishable lines. Funny how such a tiny little extra line can hold so much meaning. Bring with it so much upheaval. All the eyes in the room were on me, anticipating my reaction. My mind short-circuited. There was no reaction to give. I picked up the test, thanked Bonnie for her hospitality, and numbly walked back to my house—the freezing air not bothering me one bit.

Back at home, I made it as far as the kitchen table, my knees buckled, and I dropped into a chair, the life-changing bundle discarded on the table. Bizarre how a room could look so *normal* when everything was so completely and irreversibly changed.

I was positive Henry could hear my heart pounding from the other room. My breaths came out in short, hurried gasps and my entire body shook. I couldn't bring myself to call to him. Once he knew, there would be no turning back.

"Bev? That you? What are you doing home so early?"

He didn't understand the gravity of the situation. The earthquake that, without warning, folded and crumbled the core of our lives. I called to him in my mind, told him to come to me. That I needed him. But I couldn't command my voice to rise above a whisper. His chair creaked, and the hard thudding of his steps carried him toward me.

I looked up and Bill sat in a seat across from me. *"I don't know about this, love. You're amazing and wonderful, but a mother? You can barely care for—"*

Henry walked in and Bill disappeared. "What the—sweetheart, are you okay? My gosh, you look like you've seen a ghost! Do you not feel well? Want me to help you upstairs?"

I looked up at him with a face surely unreadable save for the tears in my eyes, threatening to spill over. I needed him to look down. To see the test for himself so I didn't have to say the words out loud. He was taking too long to catch up.

Why does he have to be so damn slow sometimes! Look down, dammit! Fear hissed these harsh words in my head. But I didn't have the capacity to push it away. I moved my hand to the test, hoping it would be enough for him. He looked down, and without saying a word, sat and picked it up.

"Is this...?" he whispered, his own eyes filling with tears. Only his tears spilled more freely down his face than mine.

"Oh my God, Bev. Oh my God!" He picked it up and held it an inch from his face. He looked as joy-filled as he did on our wedding day. "I'm going to be a dad! A dad!"

Henry ripped me out of my chair and pulled me into a tight embrace, spinning the two of us around in the center of the kitchen. The motion threatened to induce a second round of vomiting.

"Oh no, oh, I have to be careful with you now. You've got precious cargo in there." He gently released me, patted my belly, and stepped back. His unfiltered glee was splashed clear across his face.

I wished I could melt his joy and drink it up. But too frozen with terror, I was unable to match his enthusiasm. Was it the weight of the responsibility of keeping another human alive? Or the burden of having to care for a child? All day, all night, every day. Miniature little vampires. They drained the life from the very people who gave them theirs.

"I haven't felt very well," I whispered.

"That little whippersnapper, already sucking his momma's energy."

Did he read my mind?

"Let's get you in your PJs and into bed, get you off your feet. I'll take care of everything. Don't you worry."

He scooped me into another tight hug. Not caring if I puked on him.

"We're going to be parents. My gosh, what a thought," he said, face buried into my hair.

Normally, Henry could fill up my half-empty glass with his unwavering optimism. But his presence wasn't having the same magical effect.

I convinced him with a laugh that I was more than capable of getting myself ready for bed. In the bathroom it was me and my reflection alone again. Only this time she didn't look like she was mocking me or judging me. She looked sad, devastated. What did she know that I didn't'?

Thirty Two

SIXTEEN WEEKS PREGNANT, almost half-way there. The morning sickness had finally passed. My belly's flat sameness made it easy to ignore the inevitable, to stick my head in the sand like an ostrich. My routine continued—housework, cooking, book club on Wednesdays, and the occasional date night with Henry and coffee with Quinn.

Henry had changed, though. He treated me like an invalid. Always wanting to do everything for me or talk about the baby. Whether it was a girl or a boy, baby names, ideas for the nursery. Some days I wanted to scream at him to shut up and get out from under my feet.

I can get my own water, no, my feet aren't sore, I'm not too hot, not too cold.

Maybe it was the hormones twisting me into an evil witch. Or maybe he was annoying.

Desperate for a break from the house, I made plans with Quinn. I sat across from her, complaining over a giant plate of spaghetti, fighting the urge to dig my face into it and inhale the entire thing in one breath. She interrupted my grumbling with an announcement.

"I have a new boyfriend!"

I held my eyes steady, keeping them from rolling into the back of my head. The man at the table next to us caught my stare. He looked up to no good, with shifty eyes. Perhaps he had a body in his trunk. My gaze found the couple on our other side. The woman at the table looked up through insanely long lashes at the man she was with. She was undressing him with her eyes while she licked her injected lips. Definitely the other woman. His poor wife at home slaving over his laundry while he enjoyed a meal with his mistress.

Quinn snapped her fingers in front of my face. I frowned at her, wishing I could bite them.

"Hello, are you listening?"

"Yes, Quinn, that's great news."

"Could you be any less excited?" She pouted, picking at her salad.

"I'm sorry, it's these hormones, I think. I'm a disaster. Every silly thing burrows under my skin, making me feel like if I don't run I'm going to die. It's like a constant panic attack. Tell me about him. Where'd you two meet? What's he do?"

"He's a musician." The effort to keep my eyes on her and not in the back of my head was now taking all my willpower. "We met at one of his shows. Brian, that's his name."

"Maybe Brian will be the one who sticks around, and you can get married and be pregnant with me. Misery does love company."

"I'm going to ignore the sarcasm and give you a pass for those hormones." She rolled her eyes. Unfair, I at least controlled myself and my eyes. "Once you feel the baby move, it will be real, and I think you'll be a lot less grumpy. At least I hope so for mine and Henry's sake!"

"Ugh, yes, you're right. He's doing everything he should. It's *too* perfect, *too* much. We wanted kids, but I didn't want one so soon." I stopped and pinched the bridge of my nose. "What an awful thing to say. It's just that I'm still trying to wrap my head around it all. Some days it feels like he's forcing me into the whole situation. Smothering me. Like hands are wrapped around my throat, and every time he's around, they squeeze tighter. God, I sound like a horrible person. I should hush."

"Nah, let it flow. It's better than holding it in. You'll explode with it all."

I sighed and changed the subject.

After lunch, I decided to drive to the beach. It was still freezing outside, so I knew I'd have the place to myself. I parked and enjoyed the feeling of my feet sinking into the sand. Wind whipped my hair in my face, I closed my eyes and enjoyed the sting of it.

I wasn't fully honest with Quinn. Not only were my nerves perpetually on edge, but I also constantly felt a deep fear. I had tried meditation apps, and reading, and everything I could find on the internet, but nothing worked.

When I was in my house, I'd swear I could hear someone breaking in. When driving, I just knew a car was seconds away from hitting me head on. Normal, the internet said, all part of mom adjusting to this exciting transition in her life, that mixed with hormones, it was nothing to fret over.

It didn't *feel* normal. It felt *more*. It felt different. I was so sick and tired of always being different.

"Why?" I screamed at the rolling sea. "I just want a normal brain. Why does it have to act like this? Why can't I just be!"

I promised myself I'd ask my doctor about it at my next appointment. I'd be honest with someone for once in my life. I'd admit I needed help.

The doctor appointment came and after performing her exam she helped me up and asked if I had any questions or concerns. I shifted on the cold examining table, the paper gown and paper table cover crunching in response.

"No," I said with a forced smile on my face. "Everything is great. Wonderful even. Can't wait to meet this little one."

Another path. Another decision. Another wrong turn.

Thirty Three

THANKFULLY QUINN DID GET one thing right. I was sitting in Henry's chair one afternoon with my belly just starting to show when a fish fluttered through it. Not sure if I was feeling the baby or lunch digesting, I stilled, waiting to see if the fish would return. They did. I could picture their little tail swishing back and forth, and I knew. It was the baby.

It was real. A moving, breathing creature. A tiny part of me was growing right there under that slight curve beneath my belly button. I had been so miserable since seeing those two lines, I couldn't remember the last time I had laughed a genuine laugh, not one forced as a courtesy.

But I laughed out loud.

I rubbed my belly, coaxing the little one to move again. My feelings about the pregnancy transformed in an instant. I hummed and talked to the baby. I talked about everything and anything, sure whoever that baby was, they heard.

I fell in love that day. Head over heels, completely and madly in love. I had no idea it was possible to love someone so deeply and fully—especially someone with no face or name. So different from the feelings I had for Henry. I understood why Kat sacrificed her entire world for her children, why Jeanine still glowed even after an entire evening of being woken up every two hours, why Bonnie didn't go absolutely mad from the chaos reigning her house, and why my mom had always accepted me—weirdness, sharp edges, and all.

By the time Henry came home, I hadn't moved, not for food or even for a square of toilet paper. I sat in that chair all day rocking my baby. Talking and happily humming. An unfamiliar strength coursed through me. I was invincible. Anything was possible, even ditching my strange secret habit.

Henry walked in to find me grinning like an idiot. His shoulders dropped, I hadn't noticed the tension holding them up, that had assuredly been there for months. He kissed me on the forehead and placed a hand on my belly.

I smiled and told him how I spent my day.

"Come on, Henry, what's taking so long?" I called up the stairs.

"I'm ready, I'm ready," he said, hopping down the stairs.

"Here, I have your jacket for you," I said and handed him his winter jacket. "It's a bit chilly outside, winter just won't leave this year, will it?"

"Thanks, Birdie." He leaned down to kiss me on the cheek while he slid his arms into the sleeves.

We had purchased a few things for the baby here and there, but today was going to be the first day we would go all out. Crib, changing table, stroller. All the things you need to bring a baby home from the hospital.

"My mom said we shouldn't buy anything at all," I said as we walked out the door.

Henry locked the door and turned around. "Really? Why's that?"

"She said you're supposed to wait until you have your baby shower, see what people buy you, and purchase anything you didn't receive as a gift."

"Seems kind of presumptuous, doesn't it?"

"I thought the same thing," I exclaimed. "To rely on friends to buy things for our child. Besides, I don't think I have enough friends to get everything the baby needs."

"Quality is always more important than quantity when it comes to friends."

"You make an excellent point," I said before climbing into the truck. When Henry got in, I intertwined my fingers with his. "I think I may want to have the shower after the baby is born. What do you think of that? Everyone can meet the baby. We can have it in the backyard."

"Whatever you want is what I want," he said and gave my hand a squeeze, not releasing it until we pulled into the parking lot of the store.

We wandered around aimlessly up and down the aisles for a bit.

"There's so much stuff," I said. "Where do we even start?"

"I'm as lost as you."

"I suppose we could look at furniture first. That's something we need for sure. A crib and a changing table. Maybe we can start with the basics and come back another day for all the rest."

I stopped, and Henry, not paying attention, ran into my back.

"Wha—Bev, you okay?" he asked, panicked.

"Henry shush, shush." I grabbed his hand and grinned at him. "Do you feel it?" After a few seconds, his entire face lit up.

"Was that the baby?"

"Yes, isn't it amazing?"

"Oh wow," Henry said. "Just flying around in there like my mini baby Birdie."

Another pregnant woman waddled by and smiled. "First time?" she asked, nodding toward Henry's hands still on my much flatter belly.

"Yes," he exclaimed.

"Aw, that's so exciting. There will be plenty more where that came from too. Congrats, you two."

We both muttered thank you but were too busy looking down at my stomach, waiting to see if the baby would do any more kicking for her daddy. I'd decided it was a girl. A boy wouldn't be disappointing, but I just had a feeling. It drove me mad not knowing the gender, but Henry was so excited by the idea of being surprised I relented. And despite my best effort at studying the ultrasounds, I couldn't tell one way or the other.

He took his hands from my belly and rubbed the sides of his face. "Wow, it feels so real now. We better get moving on that crib and changing table, huh?"

I laughed. "Yes, we better."

We picked out a white set. The crib and matching dresser and changing table were unadorned. Some of the pieces seemed better fit for a palace with their intricate details and pricey costs. The set we picked out was simple but in a precious way.

After checking out, Henry pulled the truck up to the front of the store, and one of the employees helped him load the furniture in the bed.

"If this baby turns out to be a boy, he's just going to have to live with white furniture. Once I put all that together," he pointed his thumb to the back, "I'm not taking it apart."

"Furniture color isn't gender specific, that's silly. Regardless, I think it's a girl. Don't you think white will make the room bright and cheery? A white and yellow room. Like the summer or like the daisies at our wedding."

"What about Daisy for a name? That's a cute one?"

I wrinkled my nose. "Oh no, I don't like that. Keep thinking."

He laughed and drove us home.

Thankfully, the rocking chair we purchased came assembled. It gave me a place to sit while Henry struggled through building the furniture. A grueling three-hour battle.

"Are you sure you don't want help?" I crossed my fingers. The work looked awful and nothing I wanted a part of. Poor Henry was sweating and muttering to himself, so I felt inclined to be polite and offer. He shook his head, and I finally rocked myself to sleep.

"Alright, done," Henry announced, waking me. He scrambled up from the floor and wiped his hands on his jeans. I opened my eyes, not sure how long I'd been dozing.

"I love it." I stood and wrapped my arms around his waist. "It's perfect." He leaned down and kissed me. My whole body tingled, and the baby somersaulted in response. "Why don't you go grab a shower, and I'll reward your hard work with some dinner."

After he left, I slowly spun in circles in the center of the room, drinking it all in, picturing a wiggling baby in the crib. Tears pricked my eyes, and I wasn't even bothered by them. My cheeks hurt from smiling; it was still hard to fathom what had become of my small yet beautiful life.

Thirty Four

THE CASHIER at the grocery store scanned my items too slowly. Other drivers were incapable of following simple traffic laws. Henry could do nothing right. I was big, bloated, and miserable. Pregnancy was a nightmare.

And the obnoxious girl at the bookstore was smacking her gum like a drunk cow while ringing up that month's book club selection. A book, like most of Bonnie's selections, I had no interest in reading. Bonnie in her laziness, went along with what every other book club in the world was reading. To make matters worse, the book was about a million pages long. I would suffer through the entire novel, knowing that none of the other ladies would have the patience to make it to the end.

Pointless suffering.

If she couldn't be bothered to do research, I wished she would let someone else pick. If it was my choice, I'd give them something to talk about. I'd go dark, real dark, some old school horror, *A Clockwork Orange*, perhaps. We could actually spend book club talking about books. I realized I was laughing out loud when the obnoxious chomping stopped. The girl stared at me, one eyebrow cocked. I resisted the urge to bark at her or do something else bizarre enough to warrant her judgment. Instead, I chose to complete my purchase and leave.

My hatred of people was growing as fast as my belly and swelling ankles, to the point where I could barely stand to be around anyone, including myself. My old self began to take over, pushing that new, pleasant, sociable Beverly back to a place too far to reach.

Furthermore, my obsession with cleanliness had gone far beyond obsession. A single speck of dust had me running to the kitchen for my cleaning supplies. And Henry seemed to be purposefully taunting me with his clutter.

I stomped into the living room one evening when it all became too much. "I can't live like this any longer."

Without taking his eyes off the TV, he said, "Not too much longer, have a seat, put your feet up."

I grabbed the remote and smashed the off button.

"Hey, I was watching the game."

I stood over him, hands on hips. "This place is a disaster. Every day I clean, and every night you come home and mess it all up. Look at this..." I picked up the shoes laying haphazardly next to his chair. "These belong in the mudroom, on the shoe holder. And this"—I dropped the shoes and picked up the empty beer bottle sitting next to the full one—"would it be so hard to take this one with you and throw it away when you get a new one?" I put the beer down. "And don't get me started on the dishes. We paid good money for that brand-new dishwasher. Yet you just pile your dishes in the sink like some dish fairy is going to come clean them for you. This house is full of dust, and clutter, and filth. I can't take it!"

Henry's mouth hung open.

His bad habits certainly hadn't increased since we'd gotten married, and certainly not since I had gotten pregnant. But the sudden rise in blood pressure and the hot flashes of anger fueled by pregnancy hormones were unstoppable. They took over my ability to think for myself and immediately changed thoughts of baby fingers, toes, and giggles into murderous schemes.

Henry stood and collected his shoes and the empty beer bottle. I started crying and flopped to the floor.

"I'm sorry," I said. "I don't know what's wrong with me."

He put everything down and sat down next to me, I lowered my head into his lap and he ran his fingers through my hair. "Please don't apologize. You're pregnant. I'm the one who should be apologizing. It's my job to make your life easier right now and I'm clearly doing a terrible job of it."

His kindness made me cry more. Damn those hormones.

Poor, sweet Henry. How did such a kind and thoughtful man get stuck with me?

That week's book club meeting was at Kat's house. I waddled next door on feet that must have been covered in bruises, a back that had to be collapsing in on itself, and skin that could tear open at any moment, pouring blood and intestines onto the sidewalk that connected Kat's driveway to mine.

Kat opened the door, her figure accentuated by her designer dress. Hair and makeup flawless. Her perfectness highlighted my flaws and incensed me. I followed her through her immaculate home and took a seat on the uncomfortable couch. The vines of snarky remarks were twisting their way up my throat. I wouldn't be able to control them much longer.

The couch was the tipping point. A couch has one purpose, to provide comfort. It is an affront to its entire reason for being when for the sake of optics, it doesn't serve that purpose.

"You look tense, Beverly. Everything okay?" Kat stared at me like I was about to burgle her fine china and silver— or stain her furniture.

"I'm fine. Just very, very pregnant." I was proud of myself for keeping my thoughts of her offensive couch to myself. The doorbell interrupted us, saving me from any potential slips of the tongue.

Kat returned with Bonnie and Jeanine at each elbow.

"Can we get this over with?" I heaved a sigh, regretting my decision to attend that evening's meeting.

"Okay, Beverly, but no need to be nasty. We get it, you're uncomfortable. We've all been there and can sympathize. But don't take it out on us." Bonnie's lecture bristled my nerves. But I pursed my lips and stayed quiet.

Jeanine sat next to me and whispered, "Don't worry,

it's awful at the end. But it will be over before you know it."

My face attempted a smile, but all I could muster was a grimace. Even Jeanine's presence didn't soothe me. I shouldn't have gone. My comfortable bed and my silent house called to me from next door.

On the one hand, I worried I'd ruin the few friendships I'd scraped together. On the other hand, I didn't care. Set those bridges afire and dance in the ashes.

Once everyone found their seats, the drinks and snacks were passed around. After taking her first sip of wine, Bonnie placed her glass down on the coffee table precisely one inch to the right of the provided coaster. Kat, wanting to keep the peace but not wanting her coffee table to suffer a ring, picked Bonnie's glass up and placed it on a coaster for her.

Bonnie opened her mouth to speak.

"Just shut up, Bonnie," I snapped. "Kat's entire sense of self-worth is built on her unmarked furniture. Use a damn coaster, so we don't have to suffer through another fight over it."

The room went uncomfortably still. A child laughed from upstairs. Bonnie's mouth formed an *oh*, Kat clutched her pearls, and Jeanine's mouth curved down.

I suddenly doubled over as far as my protruding belly allowed. My baby had—against all laws of nature—obtained a knife and used that knife to slash my insides. The room liquified. We were no longer on land—we were on a ship being churned by nine-foot swells. Sweat poured down my face and back. My breathing was ragged and heavy.

Jolted into action, the women swarmed around me.

"What's wrong? Are you okay? Is it time?" Whoever was speaking sounded like they were under water. Their voice garbled and far, far away. My mind could only grasp onto one thing; the searing pain shooting through my stomach. A pain so intense I didn't have time to realize it should scare me.

I sat up and rubbed my eyes. "I'm fine. I still have six weeks." I waved them off and smiled through clenched teeth. "The doctor warned me this would happen toward the end. False labor. That must be it." They nodded.

"Yes, I remember that," Jeanine said. "I went to the hospital so many times thinking that for sure it was time, only to be sent right home."

The ladies nodded and mmmhmmd.

Another sharp pain made my temperature rise. I closed my eyes and tried to breathe through it.

"I dunno Bevie," Bonnie said. "Maybe you should go in, just in case. Better to be safe than sorry, ya know."

I waved a hand dismissively. "I'm sure I'm fine," I managed through clenched teeth. With one hand gripping my belly and the other the couch, I tried to picture my pain as a ball, if I could just mentally throw it away, I'd be fine. "Maybe I should go home and lay down."

"I don't like this," Jeanine said. "We should call Henry."

"No, please don't. He's at an important work dinner. I really don't want to disturb him."

The women looked at each other, clearly not sure what to do.

The waves of pain seemed to have lessened, so I pushed myself up and waddled to the front door.

Kat jumped up. "Are you sure you don't need help. Why don't I walk you home."

"It's right next door, I'm sure I can manage." She didn't look convinced. "I'll call if it gets worse, I promise." That seemed to make her feel better.

"Okay, I don't like this, you going home alone. If you change your mind, one of us will drive you in."

Somehow, I got from Kat's house to my bathroom floor, where I was lying down curled in a ball, writhing in pain. I must have done a good enough job covering the severity of my agony since I was lying there alone and none of the ladies had followed me. Waves of misery rolled through my stomach, morphing between hot slices and intense cramping, getting more intense and soon with no relief. Fear turned the blood running through my veins to ice. I'd left my purse with my phone downstairs. By the time I realized something was very wrong and I needed to go to the hospital, it was too late, I couldn't move.

"No, no, no, no," my scream echoed through the empty house, "it's too early."

That was the last thought I had before hot sticky liquid ran down my legs and black ink poured over my vision.

Thirty Five

"BEVERLY? Can you hear me? You're in the hospital. But you'll be alright." Henry's lies dripped so easily from his mouth.

I blinked the unfamiliar room slowly into focus. Were my eyes covered in Vaseline? My mouth felt like I drank acid, my body like I'd been thrown from a cliff. My foggy brain tried to piece together where I was and how I got there. Flashes of horror flickered like the reel of an old film in my mind. A frantic Henry running into our bathroom. Him panicking. Trying to figure out how long I'd been there. So much red. An ocean of it. An entire bathroom of it. Drowning in it. Ambulance. No, too slow. Did he say this or did I? *Who knows...who cares.* My body tossed and turned in the backseat of a car driving too fast. The blinding light of a hospital room, masked doctors and nurses, their calming words not matching their rounded eyes.

The operating room. The tugging behind the sheet

separating me from my baby. The silence that should have been pierced by the wail of a newborn.

The deep still of nothingness.

"Where is she?" I croaked, my dry throat struggling. I was desperately searching Henry's face for answers, but for once, it gave nothing away. He sat beside my bed, gripping my hand. The purple bruises painting dark moons beneath his red-rimmed eyes told me what I wasn't ready to accept. But I needed to hear the words spoken out loud.

"I'm so sorry. She's gone. The baby ... didn't make it."

Those ten tiny words, words if in a different order, under any other context, could have been so insignificant. But not there, not in that hospital bed. Not in that room smelling of antiseptic, with the beeping of the tubes binding me to machines.

In that room, those words were boulders, rolling from Henry's mouth and crushing me.

Someone screamed, and if I could form sounds, I would screech back at them, tell them to shut up. *Don't you know what is happening here?* Before I could say this to them, nurses surrounded me. My head lolled to the left. I watched one insert a needle into the tube feeding me liquid through another needle that disappeared into the crook of my arm. She depressed the syringe, the contents traveled down the tube, merging with the IV drip, and disappeared into my arm. Within seconds my body melted into the bed, and a great fog rolled in, filling my head.

My eyes became too heavy to hold open, and it dawned on me, the screaming woman was me.

THE SECOND TIME I gained consciousness, they didn't need to sedate me. I was already gone, a pile of skin and bones and blood and organs lying in the bed next to a haggard-looking Henry. He cradled his head in his hands, and his shoulders heaved to the beat of his muffled cries. I knew he had suffered a loss too, but I had no pity for him. I had no feelings. There was nothing left to live for. Another tragedy. I should have known. I wasn't meant to have happiness. Only taste it so I knew what I was missing.

My daughter was gone and with her my life, my feelings, my soul. I loved her so deeply, and I never even got the chance to meet her. What a cruel and vengeful world to show me a mother's love, only to rip it away before giving me the full experience of it. I tried to remember my love for Henry, to ease the agony of my loss, it was impossible. Every cell in my body was coated in grief, I could feel nothing else.

Henry, clearly sensing my wakefulness, was looking at me and speaking, I watched his mouth moving, staring through him. My mind was too tired to interpret the meaning of his sounds.

He hauled himself out of the chair. He looked like he had aged ten years since we'd entered that house of horrors, then he walked out of the room. He must have finally come to his senses; he was done with me.

That was okay. I was done with me, too.

I squeezed my eyes shut and begged to reenter the world of dreams. A world where pain and sadness couldn't reach me. The door opened. Henry—a glutton for punishment—had not given up and walked in with an older gentleman.

"Beverly, I'm Doctor Moore. It's nice to meet you, though I wish it were under less somber circumstances. How are you feeling?"

I bit back the urge to snap at him. My perfect daughter had been ripped from the world, not even given a chance to taste air. How the *fuck* did he think I was feeling? But the exhaustion overtaking me was greater than my anger, so instead, I turned my head away and stared out the window.

"You suffered placental abruption. This means your placenta separated from the womb. This cut off oxygen to your fetus. It can be a very serious condition for both mom and baby. Do you remember how long you were in the bathroom before your husband found you?"

"You're lucky to be alive Beverly, I was so scared I'd lose both of you," Henry interjected.

"How long? Are you saying—is this my fault?"

"Or course not!" Henry said. "This is not your fault, doctor, tell her it's not her—"

"Stop speaking. Henry, you need to call our parents. Please leave me alone. Both of you." I closed my eyes and willed myself to sleep. Of the millions of words I'd read in thousands of books, there were none worthy of those feelings.

"Henry?" He rushed to my side and leaned down. When he placed his ear next to my mouth, I whispered, "Make sure they name her Daisy."

Thirty Six

Now

THE STORM HAS INTENSIFIED along with my story.

"It's getting bad out there," I say.

"I had no idea."

"That I lost a child? No, I don't like talking about her much. It's too hard."

He simply nods and stands, walking to the window. "I hope the electric stays on. But there are worse things than losing electricity, aren't there?"

"There certainly are."

He turns and tilts his head at the table. "Ah, this is why you keep a vase of daisies on your kitchen table."

I nod. "She's always with me. Bill too. When I think about all the horrible things I've done, they remind me of the good. They keep me going."

"Do you feel like not going on some days?"

I retreat into my head and think about how to answer. "Some days are certainly harder than others."

"You've had a lot of trauma in your life, too much for one person. But why this guilt? All these things that have happened to you, they aren't your fault. Sure, you were a bit prickly to Henry at the beginning, and you weren't the easiest person to get along with. It doesn't seem like the punishment you've sentenced yourself with fits the crime."

"You may feel differently when I've finished. You have this impression of me based on who I am today. I haven't always been this person, though. It may change your mind. I wouldn't blame you if it did."

"I'm a pretty forgiving guy. I also believe people can change."

"Interesting you say that. It's a concept I often find myself pondering when alone with my thoughts."

"And here I thought your mind spun up disasters and murders when left alone." He winks.

"It still does that, too. Some things never change." I smile into my glass and take a sip of water. "Back to what you were saying, about people changing. I mean really changing. It's hard for me to separate who I was from who I am. It scares me even. There have been so many moments in my life when things were looking up. Like I'd finally shed my skin and could be someone who I wanted to be. Then bam, I'd be knocked right back to where I'd started. But what if I'd never truly changed in those good moments? What if it was all a very good act? A trick of the mind. As you see, my mind is very good at lying to me. This person you're sitting with, who cooked you dinner, who you call a friend, what if it's all a lie? The real me is in here, waiting for the next excuse to wake and take over."

"Emotions are a strange thing. Jealousy, hurt, fear."

"My issues go much deeper than emotions though. My brain isn't made like other brains."

"No personality is the same. We're all different. And now we've circled back to where we started."

"Which is precisely what I fear the most."

Thirty Seven

Before

HENRY BROUGHT A SHEATH OF SKIN, empty, no longer his wife.

When he found me on that bathroom floor, the river of blood that flowed from me carried with it everything that made me, me. He led me upstairs and tucked me gently in bed with a kiss on my forehead. I had finally spread my wings, finally learned to fly, and I was caged again. Only this time was much worse than when I lost Bill. The chances of him finding me again and pulling me back was much smaller.

Both Henry and I battled internal demons, his fear and guilt of the decisions he'd made, to not call an ambulance. Mine to lay down and not call him. Were there early signs we'd missed? Did we do enough? These thoughts would silently haunt us forever.

Henry's purpose became two-fold: keep me alive and

collect casseroles. The casseroles became a convenient tool in the first mission. I refused any visitors. I could picture the ladies standing on our front porch, hands outstretched holding the pre-made meals, Henry mumbling his thanks, before sending them and their sympathetic looks away.

My mom, not giving up, came to the house at least once a week, walked upstairs, and asked me to come down and sit with her. Each time I told her not today, rolled over, and shut my eyes to the room and my family.

They begged me to go see someone, a therapist, a doctor. I refused.

Henry dragged himself through his daily routine while I stayed in bed, floating between life and death. Bills don't care about your personal life. They demand payment regardless of circumstance, so back to work he went. His days spent in the office doing whatever he did there, his nights spent trying to coax me back to him.

The more time crawled on the more I withered away, like a puddle shining in the midday sun after a spring shower, slowly shrinking within itself. Henry tried to force me to eat. Quinn, my mom, and Henry tried to make me get out of bed. Nothing worked. I couldn't even try. I had no desire to.

In bed, on my back, I didn't hear the door creak open over the sound of a lawn mower outside. The smell of roses filled my nose, and I looked up at Jeanine's small frame standing next to my bed. She took a seat and placed her cool hand on my arm.

"Hey, Bev. I'm not going to ask how you're feeling, because I already know the answer. We're having our neighborhood barbeque for Fourth of July, and I wanted to see if you felt up to coming. We'd love to see you there, all of us."

Her face swam in and out of focus. The mere thought of leaving my bed and facing the entire neighborhood exhausted me. But I didn't want to disappoint Jeanine. The concern on her face was enough to make me agree to go. Smart of them to send Jeanine and not the others.

Bill stood watching us from the corner of the room. He no longer spoke to me. Just stared looking sad and disappointed. His head tilted to the side, his eyes pleading with me to fight.

I turned my attention from him to Jeanine. "Yes, I'll go. I'm sorry, but can you please leave now?"

She looked shocked by my acceptance or maybe because I had kicked her out of my room, perhaps both.

"Sure, honey. No problem. I'll see you in a few days, okay?"

She placed a soothing hand on my shoulder and walked out of the room before casting one final worried glance over her shoulder.

My body hitched with dry sobs. It had run out of tears many days before. I rolled myself up to a sitting position. My head was dizzy from too much lying down. I made my way to the bathroom on my weakened legs and stuffed myself full of toilet paper, thinking about everything I did wrong. If only I had gone home and immediately called for help. Or driven straight to the hospital. Or what if, what if, what if...

HENRY CAME INTO THE HOUSE, sweaty and stinking, to find me sitting at the kitchen table, hands folded in a tight fist in my lap, staring out the window. My hair was a knotted mess. I stank too. I turned my head slowly and met Henry's shocked face with dead eyes.

"I told Jeanine I would go to the barbeque. Did she tell you about it?" I asked, voice hoarse from lack of use.

"She did," Henry said while he washed his hands at the sink.

He shut off the water and stared at me intently. "Want anything? Lunch? Coffee?"

"No, I think I'm going to sit in the living room for a bit and read."

"Good. That's good."

I may have changed locations physically, but emotionally I remained in purgatory. Still dead inside. My back hurt, and I was sick of staring at the same spot on the ceiling. That was all. I walked into the living room and found the book I had been reading before the incident. I opened it to the page where I'd left off and stared at the same sentence for an hour before going back upstairs and back to bed.

THREE DAYS LATER, Henry came into the bedroom to wake me up for the *big event*. I regretted the acceptance. My eyes squinted against the searing light he let in the room after pulling back all the curtains.

"What are you *doing*?" I asked, pulling a pillow over my face.

"It's the barbeque, remember? We should leave in about thirty."

The pungent scent of cologne filled the room. My head throbbed. He always insisted on drowning himself in that junk for any occasion he deemed worthy. It was usually tolerable, but between the sun and the smell I oscillated between wanting to murder him and needing to puke.

"Get out. I'll meet you downstairs." I wasn't in the mood to temper my words. It would take enough of my strength to make it through that day.

I stood in front of my closet, staring at my clothing. This would have been a stressful decision for the old me. But when you've lost the ability to feel, you no longer care about simple things like what to wear. I looked down at myself, gave a half shrug, and walked downstairs in the same outfit I woke up in.

My hand got stuck in my knotted hair when I ran my fingers through it. I looked down at my stained shirt and sweatpants, I should have been appalled, but I wasn't.

"Ready?" I asked.

"Are you? Maybe you should jump in the shower, change—"

"Nope, I'm good. Let's go." I ignored his creased forehead and pinched eyebrows, walked to the door, and opened it, assuming he was coming.

When we reached Kat's house, we followed the noise to the backyard. Adults stood in small groups clasping alcoholic beverages, while flashes of red, white, and blue blurred amongst their legs from the gleeful children adorned in their Fourth of July outfits chasing each other.

Smoking charcoal mixed with honeysuckle saturated the air.

One by one, the adults took notice of our arrival. A hush fell over the yard. All heads twisted toward us, frowning faces stared back at me over their wine glasses and beers.

The tittering of beetles, or possibly cicadas, thousands of them, sounded like they were miles away but creeping closer. They scrambled over each other, tiny legs tapping on hard bodies. The sound got louder. I realized it was the whispers of everyone who stared at me. Indiscernible whispers, so close I could feel their breath tickling my neck. I grabbed my head in my hands and squeezed my eyes shut.

"Beverly?"

I flinched.

Kat stood next to me, gripping my arm. How long had she been saying my name?

"I should take her home. I think this is too much too soon," Henry said over my head.

"I think you're right," Kat said. I could barely hear her muffled voice over the whispering in my ears.

"Beverly?" Kat asked again. I looked at her, eyes squinted and strained to hear. "I think you should go home. Join us for book club instead. Fewer people."

"Yes, you're right. This was a terrible idea," I replied. "Henry, you stay." He tried to protest. "No really, I can get myself home. It's fine. I'll be fine."

I left Henry there to discuss his crazy wife with the gossiping neighbors to return to my bed, too numb to be embarrassed.

Back in my house I pulled myself by the railing up the seemingly unending staircase. The door to the nursery stood slightly open. I hadn't been in there since I'd lost her. Every step through the room felt like a step through quicksand. I stood over the empty crib picturing her rolling around, grabbing her feet, smiling, and cooing at me. A teddy bear sat on top of the dresser. I reached for it before laying down in the center of the room on my side, curling myself around the bear. Silent tears wet the top of the bear's fur as I laid there picturing the life that was stolen from me.

Thirty Eight

DESPITE MY DISASTROUS first attempt at rejoining the land of the living, I didn't give up. Henry didn't give up. My mom didn't give up. And neither did my friends. I cried through most of July, mostly while in bed. August was easier. I started taking guests again, one at a time and not every day. I began showering, brushing my teeth and hair, putting on real clothes, and leaving my room.

Once again, I leaned on the people around me to crawl my way out of a hole. Only this hole was much deeper, its walls much more slippery.

"Beverly, I have something to tell you," Quinn said, one August afternoon as she sat across from me at my kitchen table.

"I'm pregnant, due in December." She held her breath, eyes refusing to meet mine, waiting for my reply.

"Pregnant?" I whispered. I looked over her head out the window, deciding what to say next. "That's. Well, that's shocking. Who's the father?"

225

"Oh my God, Beverly. If I didn't love you, I'd be totally offended. It's Brian, you remember Brian?"

I didn't remember Brian.

"Did you get married?" I had more questions.

"No 'course not. I'd never get married without you there. Just because we're not married doesn't mean we can't have a baby. I thought we'd finally pulled you from ancient times. Guess we still have some work to do." She laughed, and looked down at her coffee, fiddling with the cup. Usually, I was the one who didn't know what to do with my hands.

"I guess that's nice. No, I'm happy for you. Don't listen to me. This is lovely. Just because of what happened to me doesn't mean you should be ashamed that you'll get what I wanted."

I grimaced. It finally dawned on me—Brian, the musician.

Quinn explained she and Brian were going to wait for the baby before getting married. Sometime next year they'd have a small wedding like ours. I gasped when she told me she quit her job at the boutique. Did she really think they could support three people on an unknown musician's salary?

"I don't have much longer left of school. It will be a lot easier to just focus on school and the baby," she explained.

I thought she loved working at the boutique; I guess you can never really know anyone completely.

She looked at her phone.

"Oh shoot, I have to go. I have a doctor's appointment. I'm going to be late."

She stood. I stared at her belly, imagining what it would look like big and rounded.

Processing Quinn's pregnancy took some effort and several squares of toilet paper. It was so unfair. *Why did everything always come so easy for everyone else?*

"Quinn is pregnant," I said to Henry later that night while we sat in the living room watching TV.

His face changed quickly from a smile to a frown. "How do you feel about that?"

"I don't know. I'm happy, angry, jealous. A lot of things. But it's better than feeling nothing, I suppose. Or maybe it's not. Maybe nothing is better than feeling bad feelings."

He waited a while to answer, I figured the conversation was over, and we had gone back to ignoring each other and staring at the TV.

"No, I'm not sure that's true," he said.

"Not sure what's true?"

"What you just said, about nothing being better than bad feelings. I know it's hard to remember what it felt like to be happy, but try. You don't want to feel nothing. That's no way to live."

"I wish it were so easy, just to snap my finger and go back. I hate being like this. I hate all of it. I don't know how to fix it. It's hard, too, learning that my best friend is pregnant so soon after I was supposed to be welcoming my little girl into the world. I want so badly to be happy for her, to share these moments with her."

Henry stood and sat next to me on the couch. He put his arm around me and pulled me in close. It felt nostalgic, like a song that brings you back, not to a time, but to a feeling. It was so close. Happiness. Curled under Henry's arm, I could almost see the possibilities, sprawled out in front of me like an empty highway with nowhere to go but forward. I could feel again I told myself. I could be happy again. I could survive this.

Thirty Nine

ON A SEPTEMBER AFTERNOON, Henry was at work, and I had no plans for the day. I was getting out of bed each day but not accomplishing very much else, the bare minimum at most. Once again, going through the motions of a mundane, gray life. The faces on the TV were a blur. I barely paid attention. After several hours, I realized I should use the bathroom. My body still had the standard human demands. I pulled myself off the couch—still weak from the little food I'd consumed—and shuffled to the bathroom.

Once there, I stifled a scream. The partially open closet door revealed a child's face. She was smiling at me from the dark. Had my daughter returned? Was my love too strong to snap the thread binding us together?

I thrust open the door, ready to save her from the dark closet, and gather her in my arms. With the door fully open, the bathroom light illuminated the space. It revealed the source of the cherub's face that had so cruelly deceived me. It wasn't my baby girl; instead, I looked down at the image of some other, more fortunate mother's child, smiling beneath the scripted letters *Angel Soft*. The drawn-on wings a coffin nail pounded in, reminding me, in case I'd forgotten, that my child was dead.

I stared at that brand new package of toilet paper while hot tears burned my cheeks. A fit of anger stormed within me. I was angry at that mother, who didn't realize how lucky she was. If only she knew how thin the fabric was separating her fate from mine. A few weeks, a placenta with a firmer grip, and I could have been her. I was also angry at Quinn, who would soon have her own cherub-faced baby to hold and to love. I was angry at every woman who wasn't standing in a bathroom with an empty womb, staring at the face of someone else's happiness.

I snatched the unopened package from the closet and dragged it back to the living room, where I furiously ripped off the plastic. I tore that smiling face into bits and stuffed them into the bottom of the trash can. After stomping back to the couch, I began stuffing my mouth with paper, choking on each bite.

That was how Henry found me, surrounded by a heap of empty toilet paper rolls, their brown cardboard innards discarded around me, gagging on the toilet paper stuffed in my mouth. I'd hoped it would choke the life out of me, and Henry would have instead come home to a corpse. He'd find my empty body, but the real me would be transported to whatever world held my daughter captive.

Three quick strides, and Henry crossed the room to me. He then slammed my back with one hand, folding my chest to my knees, and ripped the paper free from my mouth with the other hand. I vomited, sending a wave of stomach acid and pulp over his shoes and the carpet.

"What are you *doing?*" he yelled.

I lifted my chin, snot dripped from my nose, and puke covered my face. I replied, "dying."

Forty

APPARENTLY, being found choking to death on toilet paper is enough to warrant a trip to the psychiatrist. An emergency trip, to be exact. My greatest enemy, my mind, had finally shown its true colors. The demons who had haunted me for years in the form of my own reflection and my best friend had won. I could no longer hide how broken I truly was. In the waiting room I could sense them there with me, laughing and celebrating their victory.

I sat on the doctor's plush couch with my wrists resting on my lap, palms facing to the sky, wondering how much it would hurt to slice the thin veins snaking up my forearms. Would I have the strength to break the skin? Or the courage to cut through the second wrist after I'd slit the first? Would I be able to sit idly by and watch my blood drain out onto the expensive-looking couch and the area rug between it and the armchair the doctor was sitting in?

Probably not.

"Beverly, why don't you tell me why you're here today?" the doctor asked me.

I paused and tried to determine which answer would get the appointment over with as quickly as possible.

"My husband made me come."

Her red lips turned down in a frown.

I'm sure she was qualified enough. But she was so shiny she hurt my eyes. I wondered if it would be weird to grab my sunglasses from my purse and put them on.

Icy blue eyes poised for judgment stared at me. She ran a hand tipped with red lacquered nails through her glossy black hair. Her cream cashmere sweater, black slacks, and expensive-looking beige heels screamed money and comfort. How could someone so posh and put together fathom what I'd been through? If she couldn't relate, how could she possibly help me? The most catastrophic event that had ever marked her life was most likely a broken nail.

I was attempting to read the spines of the textbooks lining the bookshelves, then glanced at the walls lined with muted paintings of flowers and scenic images depicting faraway oceans and villages. A room decorated with the goal of relaxing its inhabitants so they would vomit their feelings on to her eager lap.

"Your husband is very worried about you, Beverly. Losing a child, especially losing one in such a traumatic way, can make us do things we may not normally do, think things we wouldn't normally think. Is that why you tried to kill yourself with the toilet paper?"

Her words made my focus snap back to her. "I was mad at the baby and its mother."

"The baby? You were mad at your baby? You were mad at yourself? Why were you mad at yourself and your baby, Beverly?" she asked with a single arched eyebrow.

I couldn't stand the way she kept saying my name. Some stupid technique she picked up in school to establish trust and intimacy with her patients, I'm sure. It came across as phony.

"No. I'm not mad at *myself*. I was mad at the mother of the actual baby. The one on the toilet paper packaging." I sighed. My skin itched. I hated that room, that woman, and Henry for forcing me there.

"Hmmm, interesting." She changed the cross of her legs and jotted something in the leather folio opened across her lap. I wanted to rip the pages out, then stab her in the ear with her pen.

"It's not interesting. None of this is *interesting*. I gave birth to a dead baby. It's pretty fucking terrible as a matter of fact." I was losing my patience and with it my control.

"Yes, it is *pretty fucking terrible*. And I'd like to help you learn how to cope, Beverly. Do you feel like hurting yourself or others?"

I shook my head.

She continued down a line of questions, reading them like she was reading a grocery list. She almost sounded bored. Like we weren't paying her almost $300 to ask me a list of questions I could have gotten from the internet.

"Not only are you traumatized from your loss, but I also believe you are suffering from the baby blues."

"I'm sorry, but did you say the *baby blues?*"

"Have you talked to your OBGYN about your feelings? Pregnancy can wreak havoc on our hormones. What you're feeling is common. Nothing to be embarrassed about."

"Common..." The gall of this woman. I'd lost a child, and she called what I was feeling *common*.

"Yes." She nodded enthusiastically. "But that's good news. It means it's treatable. You'll be feeling like your old self in no time. Speaking of time, it looks like ours is up."

Had this woman listened to a word I'd been saying?

I popped up from the chair, ready to flee when she stopped me.

"One more thing, Beverly. I'd like to give you a few prescriptions. I think they will help you feel better."

She walked over to her large mahogany desk, its clean surface free from clutter except for a few small silver photo frames which I guessed held faces of children that— if I laid eyes on them—would make me hate her more, a gold-plated stand holding a fountain pen most likely for show, and a large calendar blotter. She pulled out a key from her right pocket, and one of the desk drawers scraped open.

Back in her chair, she scratched out a prescription on the pad. Once done, she ripped the paper off with the practiced efficiency of someone proficient in dolling out pills as cures for whatever mental issues graced her couch. She handed the small square to me, tapping it with one of her red talons.

"One of these, Prozac, in the morning." She quickly scribbled out the next sheet and passed it over. "This one, the Valium, is for at night. Take it thirty minutes prior to bed. It should help you sleep."

I snorted. She'd confirmed my guess. Sleep was about

the only thing I wasn't having trouble with. But I took them without a word, and she was off the clock. The source of my amusement was no longer her problem.

"Let's make an appointment for next week to check in and see how you're doing. I'm confident with time and work, we'll get through this together." The red lips smiled at me as if those two small squares of paper were the antidote that would cure me of my incurable state. I'd tried paper enough times to know it didn't hold the cure.

I walked out the heavy door into the room where Henry awaited me. On the way out, we passed her next victim, a woman who was hiding her crazy much better than myself with her brushed hair and unwrinkled clothes. She had even put makeup on.

Henry was more annoying than his usual obnoxious self on the ride home. The love I had for him was currently mixed with ash in an urn, and I was resisting the urge to rip the steering wheel from his grip and give it a hard jerk to the right, plowing us headfirst into oncoming traffic.

"So. How did it go?" His voice was two octaves too high. It's the new way he spoke to me those days. High-pitched and slowly. Like he was talking to a paper doll. A little girl cutout that a slight drizzle of rain or puff of air could ruin. The careful handling was for my protection, but it still made me wish his high-pitched tone would shatter my body into a million pieces too small for the human eye to decipher my elbow from my knee.

I sighed and watched the landmarks of our tiny suburb passing by, my forehead pressed against the passenger window. We whizzed past purposefully planted trees, houses, and typical people. Mothers with their children, oblivious to the fact these mundane moments are the most critical of them all, clueless to how a single flash could turn their worlds upside down, ripping everything they took for granted out of their stupid manicured hands.

"It was fine, Henry. She was fine. She gave me these prescriptions." I waved the papers in his direction. "Said I have to take one in the morning and the other at night. It will be the magical cure for all that ails me. We should stop by the pharmacy on the way home."

Not sensing my lack of faith in the magical pills, his face brightened with hope. I caught a shadow of that face-filling smile from the Henry of the past. Anyone else would miss it. Someone who didn't know him like I did. That hope and smile had brought out something inside me once before. Maybe it would rip me home from the nothing existence I was floating in again.

"I have a good feeling about this doctor, she has great reviews online."

"She didn't ask the right questions."

He glanced at me, the smile gone as quickly as it came. "Is there something else you needed to tell her? Or me?"

The demons cackled. "I'm just sick of this stupid brain. It's never worked right. It's not fair. I want to be normal, to not need stupid pills."

"Some people need pills for allergies, some need pills for their mind. It's no big deal. Nothing to be embarrassed about."

Tell him, tell him, tell him. Bill's voice came at me, insistent and urgent. I couldn't trust him anymore. He wasn't my Bill; he was some evil version of him my lying mind had contrived to fool me.

"Shut up," I whispered.

"What? Why would—" Henry looked appalled.

"No, not you. I'm sorry. Sometimes I replay conversations in my head. I'm tired, that slipped out." I cursed Bill for making it harder to keep my inside thoughts in.

Henry sobered. "If there is something else you're not telling me I need you to be honest. We can't help you if you hide things."

I put my hand on his leg. "I promise. I am feeling better and I'm hopeful these pills will help. If they don't, and I still feel bad I will let you know. Full honesty, nothing else."

I could practically see the gears in his mind whirring, trying to decide whether to believe me. He nodded once. "Okay. That's good. We'll drop them off on the way home and I'll grab them as soon as they're ready."

We drove in silence for a bit longer. "Quinn has been trying to reach you. Maybe you could give her a call when you get home. Talking to her may help."

I loved Quinn—more than any person who I wasn't related to by blood or by marriage—but facing her in person, seeing her full belly growing with a healthy child she would get to hug, and smell, and kiss; who could stand that?

"She understands you may not be ready to see her in person." Henry's mind-reading ability had always shocked yet endeared me to him.

"She wants to hear your voice. She wants you to hear hers. I met her for lunch the other day and she's going out of her mind wanting to help and not knowing how to go about it."

"Do *not* do that again." The venom behind my words must have surprised him. "And keep your eyes on the road. Are you trying to kill us?"

"Okay. Sure. But I'm going to need a little help here. What exactly is it I'm not supposed to be doing?"

"Going to lunch with Quinn! She's *mine. You can't have her.*"

The red crept from his collar to his face, and the knuckles he gripped the steering wheel with turned white. It was two blocks of silence so thick you could eat it before he found what he was looking for and pulled into an abandoned parking lot of a nameless, boarded-up store.

He pulled into a parking spot, shifted the truck into park, and turned the key to cut the engine. Hands still gripped on the steering wheel, he stared straight ahead. Resolute in the rules I had laid down, I stared straight ahead along with him, not willing to be the first to break the silence. Especially since I hadn't a clue what he was so worked up about. It was a simple rule. It's not like I had demanded he cut off one of *his* actual friends.

He turned to face me. A gnarled expression contorted his features.

"People aren't *yours,* Beverly. Quinn, me, anyone you feel worthy of your affections and attention—that doesn't make them yours. I put up with a lot from you. We all have faults, and with yours, I don't love you despite them, I love you for them." My mom's words being used against me made me flinch. Henry continued, unfazed, "Because that's what love is. Loving all of someone, not just the good bits." He shook his head. "But sometimes, and more often than not these days, you've taken your shit too far. You spent the end of your pregnancy lashing out at the people surrounding you, the people who did nothing, *nothing*, but try to make you comfortable and cater to your ever-growing needs. Then all those same people who you treated like shit were the very ones who helped you heal. Ready to drop anything for you at any time."

I flattened my back against my door, too dumbfounded by Henry's fury to speak.

"*I lost her too!*" he screamed. I slammed my hands over my ears. The sound reverberated through my skull, so loud I was sure my eardrums would explode and fill my head with blood. He leaned over with his red face streaked with tears until he was inches from my own, his stormy eyes bored into mine.

Then he slumped back into his seat and buried his head in his hands repeating, softer now, "She was mine too, you're not the only one who lost her, and now I'm losing you too."

I clutched my hands in my lap and squeezed them together to keep them from ripping the door open, so I could run. Run for home. Run directionless until I couldn't run any farther.

Run into traffic and end it all.

The wave of emotions engulfing the truck began receding out to sea, leaving the cab in a hushed gutted silence. I dug deep, clawed my way past the anger, past the jealousy, and the grief. I dug until I found what I needed. My arm weighed forty pounds more than it should. I lifted it and gripped Henry's hand with my own. My limbs were weak, but I squeezed as tight as my atrophied muscles would allow.

I had no words, but I pleaded with him with my eyes. Pleaded for him to see the girl he fell in love with, pleaded for patience, for him to know how much I cared about him. I *knew* his pain. I knew it better than any other person in the entire world. And I pleaded for more time because I knew what he needed—on some level, I knew what I needed, too. I simply couldn't provide it yet.

He took his hand back, sighed and wiped his face, then turned the truck back on.

"I know, Bev. I know. Let's go to the pharmacy and get you back home. It's been a day."

Forty One

My assessment of Dr. Red—I couldn't remember her name, so that's who she became to me—was that she was incompetent. A pill-pushing drug dealer who took the easy way out. I took her pills diligently, though. Once again, I became the compliant wife cleaning the house, cooking the dinners, and, now, popping my pills. Mother's little helpers.

Perhaps if she had asked the right questions, or listened to any of my answers, she would have understood my situation, and developed a more effective treatment plan. But she didn't. No one was listening.

Or maybe I wasn't speaking. At least not loud enough.

The benefit of being pumped full of pharmaceuticals is they leave you comatose. Vegetables can't feel, and I was too numb and too doped to be annoyed by her inadequate doctoring, by Henry, or more importantly, to feel grief. That could have been the point. But without sadness, there is no happiness either. I simply *was*.

Her cookie-cutter approach to pill-popping her patients back to health may have worked for some of her less dire cases. Unfortunately, I was not a typical case. And we were running out of time.

"Mom?"

"What is it Bev, you sound out of breath. Everything alright over there?"

"Are you busy? I need you to come over. It's an emergency."

"I'm calling Henry. If this is an emergency, call an ambulance, right now—"

I'd forgotten people's perceptions of me had been drastically altered by my current state. I reminded myself to choose my words more carefully. "No, mom. Not that kind of emergency. I need to show you something. Are you busy? If you could come over that would be much appreciated."

"Are you sure?"

"Yes mom, I promise. Just come over, please?"

She sighed. "You scared me half to death. Let me get my things together and I'll be right over."

I thanked her and put my phone down next to my laptop and re-read the screen.

Twenty minutes later, I heard her car pull into the driveway. I jumped from the chair and scurried to the mudroom to meet her with an open door.

"Come in, come in," I called to her.

She reached the top of the stairs and searched my face, looking like she wanted to say something but choosing instead to walk through the open door and into the kitchen. She turned and asked me what this was all about.

I walked past her and flipped open the laptop. "This." I pointed to the screen. "Sit. Read this."

She approached the table and slowly lowered herself into the chair and began reading.

"Don't you see?" I asked, my voice rising.

"I—Beverly, I'm not sure I understand. What am I supposed to be reading? It's just a bunch of information about your medication."

Frustrated I huffed air out. "No. *This* part." I jabbed my finger at the screen again, then began pacing the kitchen. She followed me with her gaze instead of turning her attention back to the article.

"That medicine that so called doctor has me on can cause depression and suicidal thoughts. *Suicidal* thoughts, Mom! What kind of doctor puts a suicidal person on a pill that can create the very thing they are seeing them for. Don't you get it? She's trying to kill me!"

She gasped and pulled her purse tighter. "I think we should call Henry."

I froze. Realization smacking me in the face. "What if he's in on it?"

Another emergency visit to the psychiatrist. No, I didn't believe she was trying to kill me or that my husband was, either. Yes, I was confused and paranoid and acting irrationally. No, I don't still believe all those things. Yes, I'll continue to take my medication as prescribed. And finally, yes, I understand those side effects only affect a small number of people who take them.

Back to my routine, clean, cook, another pill down the hatch, ignore the demons, sleep, repeat.

WITH ONLY DAYS away from her due date, Quinn called and begged me to meet her for lunch. It had been three months of Dr. Red's—who turned out to have an actual name, Dr. Clarke—regiment. Take the pills, answer benign questions once a week, go about my life. Most patients get moved to a once monthly schedule, but after my little incident no one was ready to give me that much freedom.

I hated how the drugs made me feel—or not feel. Sometimes I would catch Henry looking at me with a peculiar expression on his face, having no recollection of what I did to make him look that way. It was better than grief, I suppose, but I wasn't sure how long I could go on like this. I later learned this wasn't normal, only a few people experience this zombie-like state. And even less don't adjust after a few weeks. Who was to blame? Me for not advocating for myself or Dr. Clarke for not seeing what had been staring her right in the face, sitting in her office weekly. Then there was of course the much larger thing we all missed.

I asked Henry to go with me, and we drove to the restaurant to have lunch with a very pregnant Quinn.

She was already at the table waiting for us when we arrived and waved us over. I gasped when she rose from her seat to greet us. Her belly had doubled in size. Henry and Quinn hugged their hellos while I pulled out a chair and quickly collapsed into it. The thought of touching that life-filled bulge proved too much to bear. She sat and pulled her chair as close to the table as possible in a failed effort to conceal her belly. It was too late. I could feel my heartbeat echoing through the empty cavern of my empty uterus.

"Bev, I've missed your face." She knew not to give me the sympathetic smile everyone else forced on me those days.

I looked around for the waiter to come save me from myself. I wanted to jump up and hug her, let her unwavering love and devotion pull me from the fissure I'd fallen into yet again. But everything had changed, our paths had curved sharply in two different directions.

I couldn't drain them anymore, Henry and Quinn. I'd already exhausted their resources. The two people—besides my parents and Bill—who had done so much for me. Too much. I didn't deserve them.

I never had.

"How are you?" I asked.

"I'm okay. Brian and I broke up. But this baby is coming any day now. It is what it is." She shrugged.

"Oh, no. I'm so sorry. You're still going to keep the baby then?"

"Of course she is, Beverly. What a question," Henry answered for her.

I pushed away the quick spark of annoyance and explained myself. "Well, I was only wondering. Babies are hard, I figured I'd ask."

I should have left him at home.

I bit my lip, and we sat in an uncomfortable silence.

"It's fine, Henry. I've known Beverly long enough now not to take offense," Quinn said, laughing. Then turning back to me, she continued. "Yes. You're right. It *will* be hard. It'll be worth it, don't you think?"

"I do. It would be nice if we were doing it together," I said, inspecting my lap as if the answers to all these complicated questions lived there.

"I know, sweetie. I'm so sorry. Will you two try again?" Quinn asked.

"No, Bev's psychiatrist said she isn't ready." Henry answered.

How did he know, and more importantly how did she know whether or not I was ready? Further, I had never observed him speaking with Dr. Clarke alone. Perhaps it was from one of his secret conversations. Henry—once the open book—seemed to have a lot more secrets those days.

"Oh, I see. Later then. I would love for you to help me with my little one if you're up to it. You'll make a great auntie."

"Yes. That would be nice," I said, wanting to change the subject.

We finished our meal talking about everything else but babies. Quinn was still in school and had moved back in with her parents. She still hoped to get a job in marketing when she was done.

Apart from Henry's annoying little truth bomb, I thought lunch went well. It wasn't exactly like old times. But close enough.

Forty Two

I STOOD in the kitchen with an empty casserole dish in my hands, but no recollection of how I got there. I looked around. Raw chicken melted onto the counter and a tired looking Bill sat at the kitchen table watching. He was present more often than not those days and he no longer spoke. He simply sat or stood and stared, leaving me to guess what he tried to communicate. Some days I thought he was my Bill, and his presence brought me comfort, others I was sure he was a demon wearing Bill's skin, not to be trusted.

My hazy mind realized I was preparing a meal. I squeezed my eyes shut, trying to imagine the steps it would take to turn the raw slab of meat into an edible dish.

"Any suggestions?" I asked.

Bill stared.

"Thanks for nothing."

The best I could come up with was to turn the oven on. I walked over to it and was happy my fingers remembered the process to set the temperature to three hundred and fifty degrees. With the empty casserole dish on top of the stove, I braced myself on it while it preheated.

Why was time moving so slow? Why couldn't my eyes stay open and focused? And why wouldn't Bill talk to me anymore?

The oven dinged, announcing its task completed. I grasped the handle and pulled the door open, releasing a burst of scorching air. The wave of heat hypnotized me. Desperate to move closer, I leaned in, and the rush of torrid air consumed my face. Unfortunately, it wasn't hot enough to do any damage, but it felt nice to feel something.

To the innocent observer, I may have looked like a typical housewife, cleaning her stove, attending to her wifely duties. Not that a man wasn't capable of cleaning a stove, but unfortunately, mine hadn't learned that skill yet. But I was not a typical housewife, I was a broken woman, with her head in the oven, searching for the least painful way to die. Once the kitchen's cool mixed with the sweltering air of the oven, turning it into a tepid, bearable temperature, I pulled my head out and straightened, grabbed the raw chicken, threw it in the casserole dish naked and unseasoned, then slid the dish in before slamming the door shut.

"Looks like I'll live to see another day." I thought I caught a hint of a smile on Bill's haggard face.

An hour later, I pulled out two charred chicken breasts and slapped them on two plates with a side of potato chips. It wasn't the finest dining experience, but it would have to do. Henry came home to me at the kitchen table with plates of a cold dinner in front of our usual seats.

"Beverly, you cooked. Dinner looks delicious!"

An excellent liar.

He kissed my forehead and scraped the chair across from me back to take his seat. With a knife in one hand and fork in the other, I studied his movements while he pretended to enjoy his dinner. We were both world-class actors. It occurred to me that my husband would eat anything. Next time, I'd season our chicken with arsenic. We could go to bed quietly and never wake up.

"So? What do you think? Are you up for it?"

I'd tuned him out again. I paused, waiting to see if he'd offer more context so I could pretend I was engaged in our conversation and not plotting our deaths in my head. He didn't, and instead stared, waiting for my response.

"Up for what?" I asked.

"You have an appointment Friday with Dr. Clarke. I took the day off work to bring you. Thought we could grab lunch after?"

"She told me I didn't have to see her for another week the last time I saw her, that we'd be changing to every other week. Why are we going so soon?"

"You haven't been getting better. In fact, you've gotten worse. We couldn't wait another week, so I called her and moved up your appointment."

He stood and rinsed his plate in the sink, as if he had casually delivered a weather report. But it wasn't a casual remark. It was presumptuous and controlling.

"You could have at least conferred with me before making a decision on *my* healthcare," I snapped.

"You're right, I could have, but you can't be trusted to contribute to these decisions right now." With that, he left me alone to pick my jaw up off the table and stew on the unfairness of it all.

"Fine, I'll go see Dr. Clarke Friday—" I tried calling out to him, but my phone's ringing interrupted my thought.

"Hello, Beverly? This is Quinn's mom. I've been trying to get ahold of you all day. So glad I finally caught you. We're at the hospital, and she had the baby. A Christmas baby, can you believe it? Both her and Jacob are fine and being released tonight."

"Who's Jake?" I asked. I had forgotten it was Christmas. My parents were on a cruise somewhere in the Caribbean, and Henry's parents were visiting family out of town. We hadn't bothered celebrating.

"Oh no, not Jake, *Jacob*. She doesn't want anyone shortening his name. She was very particular about that." I listened while she chuckled and wondered if she was going to answer my question, "Jacob is the baby. That's what she's named him. It's a nice sturdy name, don't you think?"

"That's wonderful news. Yes, it's a nice name. Thank you for calling."

"She told me to let you know that she would love for you and Henry to come visit. Tomorrow, if you're free."

"Yes, we would like that very much. Tell her congratulations. From both of us."

"What are you smiling about?" Henry asked, re-entering the kitchen.

"Quinn had the baby. A boy, she's named him Jacob. They are both doing very well."

"That's great news. Can we go meet him?"

"I was going to stop by tomorrow—"

"Excellent, I'll leave work early and drive you. I want to meet the little guy, too."

My possession of Quinn flared. I wished he would stop talking about her. I also wished I could have visited her and the baby by myself. Apparently, like decisions about my medical care, the decision wasn't mine to make.

"You'll be so busy with work. If you would prefer, I could go by myself."

"Nonsense, I'll be fine. I'm sure I'll be able to sneak out early for this."

"Wonderful." I tried to look pleased; it was nice that he cared about my friends. But I realized how much I missed Quinn and wanted some time alone with her.

Something sparked within me. Something I'd feared I'd lost forever: joy. Little baby Jacob. My best friend was a mother.

Forty Three

I woke up with the lead gone from my limbs, and the mist cleared from my head. Henry chose to skip work for the day so we could spend more time at Quinn's. I had been terrified to meet the baby, but that morning I was eager to hold Jacob and see Quinn.

The hot water from the shower poured over me, turning my skin pink. Steam rose from my skin when I stepped out of the shower. I wrapped myself in a towel and stepped up to the sink. A swipe of the mirror cleared its fog. My reflection stared back at me through the streak in the condensation, drops of water slithered down, distorting my face like a funhouse mirror.

I looked gaunt, but I looked like me. Mourning had stolen my heart and my face. Sunken cheeks, deep purple half-moons beneath my eyes, and my pale skin looked gray. I smiled at myself and my reflection smiled back. I licked my teeth. Perhaps I would grow fangs and suck the life out of everyone around me. Lips closing around their neck, teeth penetrating the jugular, a meal of blood to fill my empty stomach. Then they would understand how it felt being forced to live with nothing to sustain their act of living.

A soft rap on the door interrupted my bloody thoughts.

"You alright in there?"

Henry was always worrying about me. No one should have to worry about someone else so much, and no one should have someone worrying over them like that.

"Yes, totally fine. Just getting myself presentable."

I dressed, even applied some makeup to cover the bruising beneath my eyes. By the time I finished, the steam had lifted from the bathroom, the mirror was now providing a clear reflection. Pleased with my results, I was ready. Hand on the door, I paused.

Just a few quick bites before I go.

"You SEEM to be in a better mood today," Henry observed from behind the wheel.

"Yes, I suppose I am." I turned and smiled at his profile.

"That's great, Birdie, really great." I watched the tension he'd been holding in his muscles melt. It made me happy to see him less stressed. He worried about me too much. It wasn't good for him. It made me fear for his heart; I had already lost one man I loved to a hard life, and I couldn't stand to lose another.

I leaned my forehead against the cool window and

watched the houses pass by. I imagined the families filling them.

I had ruined so much, and Henry deserved better. He was good and kind. It wasn't fair he gave his heart to a broken ghost.

"Are you excited to see Quinn? I know she misses you and is really looking forward to seeing you."

"I am. I've missed her too. I can't stand myself for being jealous."

"You're doing fine. You'll be fine."

We pulled into Quinn's driveway. Henry turned the truck off and looked over at me. I could tell he had something to say. Instead, he looked back at the house and said, "Let's go."

I could feel the words spoken behind my back dancing in the air outside Quinn's house. Everyone wondering if I'd snap once I laid eyes on the baby. If I'd ask to hold him and then throw the baby across the room or shake him out of anger and jealousy. I planned to do none of that. I had decided I was happy for my friend. It wasn't her fault the world rejected my daughter.

Henry knocked on the front door. I turned my back to it, closing my eyes and tilting my face to the sun, enjoying its light on my face, a juxtaposition to the frigid December air smothering me. I reminded myself how lucky I was, to be thankful for all that I had, and not to lament on all I had lost. I turned back to the house at the sound of the door opening. Not wanting to cause any more concern, I figured I had better behave like a normal person. I brushed invisible lint from the front of my shirt and stitched a smile to my face.

"Henry, Beverly, hello! Come in, Quinn is right in here with Jacob. He's eating. That's about all he does with his days, eat, poop, and sleep." She chuckled to herself while corralling us through her entryway and into the room where Quinn was on the couch, surrounded by presents, some half-opened, some already opened.

An explosion of blue and baby. My breath hitched when my gaze fell on her and the tiniest, most perfect head with a splash of red attached to her right breast. Despite the red hair piled on her head, naked face, and eyes heavy from lack of sleep, she looked beautiful. Natural. I wanted to reach out and trace her freckles with the pads of my fingers. Her sole purpose of motherhood had come to fruition. I doubted if fate had afforded me the opportunity to be in Quinn's place—sitting on my own couch, feeding my own baby—I would look as natural.

She smiled, motioning us to take a seat.

"He's been at it for a while. I'm sure he'll be full soon. I'm so glad to see you both. Beverly, I've missed you. How are you feeling?"

That question again. I was sick to death of people asking it. I lost a baby, I had been sad, but I wasn't anymore. Everyone wanted me to get over it, and now that I had, they needed to heed their own advice. I ignored the question.

"You look great. How are *you* feeling? Look at that red hair! He's going to look just like his mom. Getting any sleep?" I asked.

"Not at all." She laughed. "But I don't mind. I could just stare at him forever. Even if it's just the top of his fire engine head. He's a pig."

"Like his dad," I said.

Quinn snorted. "Exactly. That asshole hasn't even seen him, hasn't asked to either. My mom called him, and he just said thanks. Can you believe it?" She shook her head in disbelief.

She detached Jacob from her nipple. A trickle of milk dribbled from the corner of his mouth, and his eyes fluttered behind his closed lids. I had the decency to look away while Quinn adjusted herself. Henry did not; I could smack the dopey smile off his face.

"Do you mind if I hold him?" he asked. My eyes narrowed.

"Why don't we let Beverly go first? He's been so excited to meet his auntie."

I had never held a baby, and what had always looked like such a simple task, suddenly had me very nervous. But I wanted to, desperately. I *needed* to hold that baby. To smell him, to feel his soft skin, and explore every inch.

I got up and sat next to Quinn to make the hand-over easier, but also in case I needed to hand him right back.

"Here you go. Just make sure you support his head." She placed the sleeping Jacob carefully in my arms. "There you go now. You're a natural."

I was the opposite of natural. He was so tiny, so breakable. My mind was in overdrive, drumming up scenarios of all that could go wrong. The moment was impossible to enjoy. I imagined my arm slipping out from under his head, snapping his neck back. Or perhaps a noise would startle me, and I'd drop him. His soft skull, not yet fused, would collapse in on itself. Or, I would stand up, walk into the kitchen, place the baby in the microwave and turn it on.

My thoughts horrified me, but I couldn't control them. Jacob must have sensed the wrongness of my mind because he woke up and let out a blood-curdling scream. I panicked. Were babies born with a second sense that us fully grown humans didn't possess? Was he aware of the several versions of his death that had just invaded my thoughts? His cry for safety intensified and his face turned the color of the sprout of hair sticking up off the top of his head.

"He probably just needs to burp," Quinn said. She reached over for a white cloth and draped it over my shoulder. "Hold him up like this and pat his back gently." She demonstrated using an imaginary baby, then helped me adjust Jacob on my shoulder.

I patted his back a few times. The sour smell of rotten milk followed his muffled burp. I couldn't help myself when I gagged.

Quinn giggled and reached over to relieve me. "Henry, how about you? Want to give him a hold?"

"Yes, absolutely." He nodded enthusiastically, already standing and reaching for Jacob.

Henry and I shuffled around each other so he could sit next to Quinn.

My stomach clenched. Henry cradled Jacob in the crook of his arm, cooing and whispering to him. Jacob fell, almost immediately, back into a milk-induced coma. The visit made me absolutely sure of two things. I did not want children, ever. And that was something I could never tell Henry.

Quinn's mom walked in and asked if we needed anything. This interruption broke the spell Jacob had placed on Henry and Quinn. They both looked up.

"I'd love a coffee, Mom, if you don't mind. Henry, Beverly?"

"Coffee would be great," Henry said. He didn't look up, too hypnotized by Jacob.

"Yes. Coffee, please. Black," I managed. The rush of emotions roared in my ears.

"Lovely. I'll be back."

Quinn turned her attention to me, relaxing back into the couch, tucking her legs under a blanket, and fluffing a pillow behind her back.

"How's everything else? Still doing book club?"

"Yes, every Wednesday." I smiled.

"That's great. I can't wait for winter to be over and get out of this house. Won't it be fun to take Jacob to the beach?"

Gasping, I replied, "Doesn't that scare you?"

"What do you mean?" She looked confused.

"There are so many things that could go wrong. A riptide pulling him under the water, an unexpected wave smothering him. A kidnapper lurking among the sunbathers."

"Oh my gosh, Beverly. You have *got* to stop reading all those books. You can't live your life scared, always thinking of every worst-case scenario."

I looked at Henry for support, but he was too enamored by Jacob's sleeping face to offer any.

"I mean, yes, those are the extremes. But you can never be too careful, can you?" I asked.

"I have to admit, ever since having him"—Quinn tilted her head toward Henry and Jacob—"I think I finally understand how your mind works. I keep randomly finding myself panicking for no reason. Then looking around whatever room I'm in and picturing all the potential catastrophes."

"That's perfectly normal," Quinn's mom interrupted. She balanced a tray of steaming mugs and walked around the room distributing beverages. "It's the hormones tricking your mind. All new moms go through it."

"Well, that's how my mind has always worked. So, I can't imagine what it would do with these hormones you speak of."

The weight of my words sent a hush over the room.

Henry cleared his throat. "You're just more creative than the rest of us, Birdie."

"Perhaps. Or perhaps I'm just a bit mad." I laughed. After a shocked beat everyone else joined me.

Quinn and I settled back into our banter. She described the gory details of birth, the pain, the messiness. For half a second, I was grateful to have avoided the whole ordeal but then felt horribly guilty for thinking that way. Henry held Jacob the entire time we were there—barely looking up from him. A few times I caught a sadness wash over his face, pulling his smile down at the corners. I could finally feel for Henry, my own loss forgotten enough to recognize his.

When it was time to leave, I was ready for a nap. We said our goodbyes, and Quinn made me promise to call her more. An interesting turn of events since I was used to getting chastised for calling too much. Nevertheless, I agreed.

After leaning my head back on the truck's headrest, I fell asleep the second my eyes closed and woke up to Henry nudging me in our driveway.

"We're home. Time to get up."

It took me a second to recalibrate and realize where I was. I opened my eyes. My memory worked much slower than my sight. I mumbled something incoherent even to me and maneuvered out of the truck.

Henry didn't follow me in, yelling at my back that he had some yard work to tend to. I took my time walking into the house. Afraid that the emptiness of it would scream at me from every hollow room. I stepped into the kitchen and held my breath, preparing for the overwhelming emotions to come. They didn't.

Was I really healed? I felt the scrape of hope's flint on my bones, its sparks flashing. I sucked in a deep breath and released it slowly, using my oxygen to ignite the flame.

Forty Four

I HAD A BIG PROBLEM. I paced my room, wracking my brain for a solution. There was none. It was an unsolvable problem. Unless—

"It's time to go. Come on, we're going to be late." Henry interrupted my thoughts.

I rolled my eyes. "Dr. Clarke will survive if we're a few minutes late."

"Our bank account won't. She charges an arm and a leg in fees for missed appointments and showing up late. She explained all this the first day, don't you remember?"

"Of course, she does."

Dr. Clarke was just the kind of person I would expect to charge for tardiness. On the other hand, I could respect our shared aversion to it. I finally found something I liked about her.

"All right, all right, I'm ready."

Henry was agitated for some reason and remained quiet during the drive to my appointment.

He pulled into the small parking lot, and we walked into the old home that had been converted into Dr. Clarke's office. Henry held the door open for me, and we entered and sat in the small waiting room.

After a few minutes, Dr. Clarke materialized from the door to her treatment room. I sat up straighter and put a smile on my face, hoping it was enough to show her how much better I was doing.

"Hello, Henry. Beverly, you can come with me now." She turned to walk back into the room. I slumped down; she didn't compliment my efforts. It was going to take more work than I anticipated.

"Have a seat wherever you'd like," Dr. Clarke said. Yet, she gestured to the couch. She wanted me to feel like I was in control, but she and I both knew who held the power. I was a pawn on her chessboard, and she was moving me right to her navy-blue couch.

"How are you feeling today, Beverly?"

I renamed myself in my head, Bethany, Mary, Laura, I would be any other name if it meant I never had to hear Dr. Clarke say it again.

"I'm fine. Actually, better than fine. I can say with absolute certainty I'm improving. You were correct in your assessment and treatment plan. Do you think we might be able to increase the dosage? I think it would be exactly what I need for a speedier recovery."

"I don't see why not? If the medication is helping, you're not at the maximum dosage allowed per day yet." She retrieved the pad from her desk and wrote the prescriptions. "Keep taking your morning dose, and you can add one at lunch. I increased the Valium dosage, so you don't need to take any additional pills."

Smiling, I took the piece of paper from her hand and said, "thank you."

Bill leaned in the corner, back against the wall, arms crossed. We made eye contact and he grinned.

It's time, he whispered.

Forty Five

Now

"THAT EVENING really became the beginning of the end. You'd think Bill's death, or Daisey's would be, but no, it was that night." I shiver remembering.

"It's so sad, all that happened to you. I can't imagine one person dealing with all of it."

I wave my hand shooing away his statement. "Oh please. Everyone has tragedy in their life. The news is filled with it. Kidnappings, murders, illness. I was simply too selfish to see I wasn't the only person in the world suffering. Mental illness does that to you though, you're so lost in your mind you can't be bothered to pay attention to anyone but yourself."

"A mental illness is not your fault, though. You're being a bit harsh on yourself."

"Just realistic. I've forgiven myself. It's taken many years, but I have. Part of that forgiveness came with finally opening my eyes and really seeing how I treated the people closest to me. That forgiveness eventually came, not only for the really bad things I did, which I'll get to, but the small things, too."

The lights flicker and a crack of thunder reverberates through my small home.

He looks across the kitchen in the direction of the TV room. "Should we head in there and make ourselves comfortable?"

I stand and begin walking, he follows.

Once settled, I fill my lungs with air and blow it out slowly.

"We got home after that appointment and poor Henry had no idea anything was amiss. I went upstairs and he settled himself in his recliner with a beer. Where he eventually fell asleep. You have to put yourself in his shoes. My mood had never been the most predictable, but after Daisey...he was tired. And who can blame him? On the surface, it appeared I was getting better. Henry knew me better than anyone; he knew something brewed beneath the surface. But as I said, he was tired. He didn't have the energy to dig for whatever that brewing thing was. He said he woke up hours later, he flipped off the TV and the house was too quiet. He described it as the kind of quiet after a scream. Chilling visual, yes?

"He got up and stood at the bottom of the stairs, right hand on the banister. He said he couldn't shake the strange feeling. He tried to convince himself he simply hadn't fully woken yet. He finally walked up the stairs slowly, a quick trip to the bathroom, he dragged his feet to our dark bedroom. His eyes adjusted; he could just barely make out my form in the bed. The shape he saw didn't match what it should be. When he flipped the light on, he screamed. The top half of my body lay partially off the bed. When he ran over, he saw my lips were all wrong, blue. The lips of a dead woman. Then he saw the problem. The beers I'd snuck upstairs because I read when mixed with my medicine, of which I'd taken both bottles, could be deadly. I learned this much later, when he had nothing left to lose, my body convulsed, and he thought, *it's time to let her go. Goodbye Beverly.*

"It wasn't time.

"He dialed 9-1-1, stuck his fingers down my throat to try to make my body reject the poison, then performed CPR until the paramedics broke down our front door."

Forty Six

Before

I WOKE up in another hospital room. A failure.

"Here we are again," Henry said.

The chair hadn't been pulled up to the side of my bed this time.

"Your throat will hurt. They intubated you."

"Why didn't you let me go?" I croaked, looking for liquid. My throat did hurt, like it had been rubbed with sandpaper.

"Maybe I should have. I've been here for hours and haven't slept. I wanted to make sure you didn't wake up alone. But I need to go home now. I need to sleep. You're going to be staying here for a few days. They'll call me when you're allowed to come home. I've tried to help you and failed. I hope the doctors here can do a better job. I love you."

And with that, he got up and left.

For the first time in our relationship, I felt alone. The unbreakable chain holding us together had snapped. The emptiness in the room left by his absence was heavier than the weights that had been holding me down for so many months. I hadn't realized how much I relied on Henry's unwavering presence. Even Bill had gone. The girl who wanted nothing but to be left alone finally got what she wanted. And I didn't like it, not one bit.

Forty Seven

EVERYTHING about the hospital was cold. The air, the colors, the people. Doctors and nurses came in and out of my room, checking machines, writing notes, barely addressing me. I'd lost my status as a human, rendered nothing more than a pile of meat bound by their Hippocratic Oath to keep alive.

Once physically stable, they moved me to the section of the hospital fit for people like me, for the mentally unstable.

Clarissa the nurse oversaw my intake. She looked down her beak-like nose at me. A bird observing a worm. Her beady eyes so dark it was hard to discern her irises from her pupils, only added to her hawk-like appearance.

She flipped through the pages of my file. "I see you tried to take your life using prescribed medications and alcohol."

"Well, yes, but were you aware a side-effect of those medications is depression and suicidal thoughts? I believe my case was one of an inadequate doctor versus a problem with my mental health. Really, I'm fine. Can I go home now?"

Her piercing eyes fixed on me before returning to the pages filled with inaccurate opinions of my mental state. A label of insanity is an interesting predicament. You can tell people you aren't insane, but as an insane person, your word isn't credible, negating any declarations of sanity. It's enough to drive even the sanest person mad.

"Suicide attempts earn an automatic three-day stay here in our lovely accommodations. After that time, the doctor will re-evaluate and determine if you're fit to go home or need longer-term care. In that case you'd be transferred to a more appropriate facility. I have no choice in the matter, so don't bother begging."

She stood and walked behind my wheelchair and pushed me down the hallway. It could have been my imagination, but the lights seemed dimmer here, the walls grayer. No happy paintings dotted the walls of these halls like the rest of the hospital; instead, they had the wrinkled look of a face weathered by time. The peeling paint and stains told the stories of patient intakes that didn't go as smoothly as mine.

From somewhere deep in the belly of that forgotten section of the hospital came a muffled scream. As I squeezed the wheelchair's arms, images of shock therapy and lobotomies flashed through my mind.

Nurse Clarissa wheeled me into what would be my home for the next seventy-two hours, potentially longer. I shuddered. The front wheel caught on the door jamb, jerking me forward.

Without an apology, the nurse simply reversed the chair, corrected its course, and continued pushing me into the room. I would have appreciated an apology, but apologies were for respectable humans, not mentally unwell people like me.

I panicked. I was a prisoner, and this was my cell. A single frosted and barred window concealed me from the outside world, or the outside world from me, depending on which side of the window you were on. And right then, I was on the wrong side. A small bed with wheels made of plastic resembled an over-sized child's bed. Besides the bed and a tray, also on wheels, the room was barren. Very similar to the room I'd come from, only emptier.

"All right. Up now." Clarissa walked into my view and indicated with her hand that my ride was over. I pushed myself up and tested my legs before fully committing.

The bed looked clean enough, but thoughts of how many strangers had spent sweaty nights on top of it made me wince. I took two unsteady steps and lowered myself down onto it. The rough nylon fabric of the heavy blanket did not bode well for a good night's sleep.

"You're on suicide watch, so the door stays open at all times and checks every fifteen minutes. If you close it without permission you'll be restrained to the bed, so I highly recommend staying put. The psychiatrist will be here in the morning for your first appointment. Bathroom is behind that door." She pointed to a swinging door. "Another nurse will be here momentarily to give you something to help you sleep. I highly suggest you take it as requested."

"What am I supposed to—"

She was gone before I could finish.

A few minutes later, a kinder nurse entered. She carried in a tray arranged with a small white cup and two blue pills. Her features were rounder, less bird-like. I took the medication without argument. The less time awake in that cage, the better.

"Open up, let's see your mouth," she said.

I stuck out my tongue and let her inspect my mouth.

"Good job. That should take the edge off. You'll be asleep in no time. Is this your first time here?"

I nodded once, my face felt frozen in fear. Like a photo had been snapped of me right before my killer had attacked.

"Don't worry, you'll be fine. And if all goes well, you'll be home before you know it."

The thought of home sent tears running down my face. Not because I missed it and wanted to be there, but because I had no idea if it was still my home. She must have been used to tears because she smiled and left without a further word.

I laid down on the suspicious bed listening to the sounds of the hospital. Doors opening and closing. Random screams, sometimes discernable enough to make out the words. FBI, murder, and a lot of cussing. I stared at the open door wishing for more protection from the source of those sounds. They were the last things I heard before the pills made my eyelids heavy. I gave in and fell into a deep, dreamless sleep.

EARLY MORNING, a new nurse carrying a new tray walked in.

"Morning. I have your breakfast. Have you used the bathroom? You can brush your teeth and do your business, then eat."

I grabbed the toothbrush and toothpaste from my jailer and dragged out the tasks for as long as possible.

A knock at the door. "Hurry it up in there or I'll have to come in."

I opened the door and shuffled back to the bed. She had wheeled the food tray over to the bed where my feast awaited me.

I sat on the bed carefully. I wasn't given any utensils. A fork—even a plastic one—could be a very effective weapon. Probably for the best. I had been contemplating how effective cutlery would be against skin while brushing my teeth. I knew I had tried to commit suicide, but I wasn't suicidal. Not until they locked me in that room. I scooped up a yellow clump of eggs with my hands and forced myself to eat the whole plate. I'd need my strength to figure a way out of there.

With nothing better to do with my time, I rotated between lying and sitting on the bed and pacing the room. Every once in a while, I'd poke my head out into the hall, but I couldn't stand the way the staff stared at me when I did, so I avoided temptation. How could anyone believe this was an effective solution to treat mental illness?

I laughed, remembering all the times I'd complained in my head, bored at the bookshop or at home while Henry was at work. Stupid girl, so naïve. All the diversions available to me then. I wanted to go back and shake myself. I looked around to see if cameras were watching me. Surely, standing alone laughing at nothing would earn me a one-way ticket to the long-term care facility hawk-nurse mentioned.

I wanted to scratch my face, rip my eyeballs out, pull at my hair. Anything to feel. I was *not* better. I was feeling significantly less healed, in fact. Already angry my attempts at taking my life had failed, now that I had been locked away, it was infuriating.

Every time a nurse came in to do a check or bring a meal or medication, I wanted to fling my arms about their neck and never let go. Finally, after lunch—what time I couldn't say because there was no means to tell the time in my cramped chamber—the doctor came to see me.

With a manic smile glued to my face I answered his questions with what I hoped were words that would set me free.

They were not.

Forty Eight

Blythe Hospital. A private facility. Best in the area the doctor had said while Henry nodded enthusiastically. Despite my protests, I sat in his truck being driven to my new home. I glared at him from my peripheral vision. He practically hummed with glee, so happy to be rid of me. I was no longer his burden.

"You're upset now, but this is what's best for you," he said.

"Everyone knows what's best for me. When did my opinion on the matter stop being consequential?"

"Of course you matter. If we didn't care, then we wouldn't all be working so hard to get you better. One day you'll look back on this and realize that. Besides, you heard what the doctor said about this place. It's nice, like a vacation! It's not like the psychiatric ward at the hospital."

I harrumphed and turned my head from him. Staring out the passenger window, enjoying my last moments of freedom. There was one positive in this mess I'd gotten myself in. This was the first time I'd ever been excited to spend time amongst a crowd of people.

Finally, a group of people I didn't have to pretend for.

―――――――――

THE LONG-TERM HOSPITAL *was* more accommodating than the hospital's psych ward; at least they hadn't lied about that. Rooms were decorated to look more home-like and less hospital-like. My room had more furniture, a small desk, closet, and an end table, but the same uncomfortable plastic bed and same barred window. Meals were eaten in a room meant for eating.

"Don't. Say. A. Word." On day two, Carla, another inmate I was eating breakfast next to, wiggled her shifty eyes in her head.

"But if I don't say a word, what are we going to talk about?" It was the most fascinating conversation I could ever remember having. I might enjoy this place after all.

"Shh. They are listening. They are always listening."

"Who's they?" I asked.

She looked confused. "The people who always listen, you idiot!"

I laughed hysterically. Not at her mental illness. That wasn't funny at all. I was laughing at being called an idiot. I finally found a place where you could express your opinions on and to people with no repercussions. What a refreshing change!

"Shut up, Carla, no one is listening to any stupid thing you have to say," a girl sitting across from me broke in, not bothering to look up from her food. Food which we were allowed to eat with utensils.

She didn't look like she belonged. My gaze locked on her perfectly symmetrical face, beautifully styled chestnut hair, then traveled down from her blue eyes to her plump lips—and landed on her arms. Her arms told a different story than her face. Thick and jagged scars covered her skin. Some were an inflamed red, others pale and white. She noticed me tracing the scars with my eyes and went to pull down on sleeves that weren't there. An impulse ingrained from years of hiding her secret, no doubt. I understood that, having spent years hiding my own secrets as well.

"I'm Beverly," I said.

"I don't care," she replied.

"I've been locked in a cell for three days, you might not care, but if I don't talk to someone, I'm going to stand on this table and scream."

"Don't do that. You'll just get yourself locked up again. I'm Olivia. I'm not here to make friends."

I could certainly relate to that sentiment.

At the end of our table, a woman started smashing her face with her tray, initiating a stampede of nurses and orderlies. They gathered us up and marched us back to our rooms. Locked away again. I hoped the lady broke her nose. I spent the remainder of my morning weaving vivid images of trays crushing bones and the damage I could do to her face if I had been the one holding the tray.

They released us again at lunch time. I was pleased to find the seat next to Olivia open. Based on her sigh and rolled eyes, I don't think she shared in that pleasure.

"You're the only person I've found capable of carrying a conversation, so you're stuck with me until I go home. Which should be any day now. So, deal with it."

She barked a single loud laugh.

"What's so funny?"

"You think they're going to let you out of here? I'm going on a month. My parents are more than happy to let me rot here. I'm someone else's problem. They just keep signing the papers extending my stay."

"Well, that's terrible for you, but my husband wouldn't do that to me. The doctor will see I've learned from my mistake, and Henry will come take me home."

"Keep telling yourself that. What got you sent here, anyway?"

"I accidentally took too much of my medication."

"For starters, if you want to get out, you can't lie. They'll see right through that. Accidentally, my ass."

An excellent tip I was most grateful for.

"And second, you don't think your husband is sick of your shit? Happy to have you out of his hair just like my parents? How many times have you done this? How many times has your husband been forced to live through one of your mental breakdowns? People get sick of people like us. We're draining. Unless your husband is a saint, you can bet he's enjoying his peace and quiet without having to worry about you and your problems."

Henry *was* a saint. But notably an air of what she described surrounded him the last few months. And I certainly had depleted him. She had given me a lot to think about. I began to worry I would never get out of there. I pushed my tray away, my appetite gone. She laughed and finished her meal.

The sense of dread followed me to the recreation room where art supplies were set out for the women who wanted to pass their time drawing, and a television surrounded by mismatched couches was set up for people who didn't. The group shuffled in, taking their respective places. Some chose neither. Instead, they stood in corners, against walls, at windows, staring off with blank expressions and deadened eyes, ignoring the drool trailing down their chins.

I took a seat at the art table, figuring I needed to find something to keep my hands occupied. Olivia had the decency to look guilty when she took the seat beside me.

"Birthday crowns," I said, picking up the provided art project. "Who's the lucky birthday girl?"

"It's me," a woman called from the end of the table in a high-pitched, child-like voice.

"Happiest of birthdays," I said.

Her smile faltered at my flat tone. But she wasn't about to let me dampen her mood. She returned her attention to her project and hummed to herself.

Olivia shifted in her seat. "Look, I'm sorry. I didn't mean to scare you. And maybe your husband isn't sick of you like my parents are of me. He'll come pick you up, and you can put all this"—she gestured around the room with her scarred arms—"and all of us behind you."

"Perhaps. Or perhaps he'll leave me here to die." I grinned and picked up a red marker. My crown would be a homage to Carrie's, dripping with blood.

"Well, if he does, I promise to talk to you, so you don't

have to die in here alone." Her lopsided grin made me smile despite myself.

We finished our crowns and put them on our heads.

"Happy birthday," she sang, kissing the air.

"Settle down, Olivia," a bored orderly called from across the room, his boring bald head could use a crown.

We met each other's eyes and hid our giggles behind hands lifted to our mouths. This place could provide the healing I needed. No thanks to the doctors or nurses, though.

When the group was being herded back to our rooms —fun time over—a nurse placed a hand on my elbow and gently separated me from the pack.

"You have an appointment with the doctor."

Confused but happy for the change of scenery, I followed her down the long hallway toward the doctor's cramped office. She opened the door.

Henry twisted in his seat to watch me enter. I hadn't been there long, but I had acclimated. His presence, a paradox, made my skin crawl.

He looked well-rested. *Must be nice.* Color back in his cheeks, eyes alert and shining, no hint of red. I narrowed my eyes and pursed my lips. He was obviously taking full advantage of our time apart. Olivia's warnings whispered in my mind. While I rotted away in there, Henry had the look of a man who had been enjoying spa treatments. That traitor held the key to my freedom. I quickly replaced my scowl with the most pleasant smile I could muster.

"Hi," I said sheepishly. "I'm so happy to see you. I've missed you." I sat in the seat next to him.

"Hi Bev, how are you feeling?" he asked.

"Much better. I think the break was just what I needed," I said, trying my hardest to sound like a mentally stable woman who wasn't a burden.

"I've asked Henry here so the three of us could discuss your long-term treatment plan," the doctor explained.

The word *long-term* sent my stomach plummeting to the earth's core. It kept coming up, but for the first time I felt the gravity of its meaning. Was Olivia right? I looked at Henry, trying to gauge his thoughts on how long the long in long-term meant to him. His expression proved indiscernible.

"I think I would be better, happier—at home." I hoped I kept the shake out of my voice enough to convince the two of them.

"Henry, how do you feel about Beverly coming home?" the doctor asked. He looked at Henry, waiting for his answer, which took significantly longer than I would have preferred. I stared at the side of Henry's face, pleading with my eyes for him to agree and free me from that place. I watched his jaw muscle clench and unclench. Clench and unclench.

Finally, Henry broke his silence. "What do you think, doctor? When will she be ready to come home? Will she do this again?"

"I think Beverly is in a much better place than she was, but do I think she won't attempt suicide again? I can't be sure. I recommend we re-evaluate in a week and go from there."

"No!" I started to stand but realized a cool head was needed. Henry had to understand I wouldn't be a burden to him anymore, wouldn't be his burden. "Henry, please.

I'm begging you. I'll try harder, I swear." I grabbed his hand, hoping my touch would stir some former feelings he had for me.

Henry removed his hand from my grip and rubbed his face with his hands. The hands holding my fate. My old fears came roaring back to life from hibernation.

How did I get here? How had my life become so entirely out of my control? I prayed Henry wouldn't turn those hands over and smash my life on the ground.

"Beverly, I've heard this before. If you aren't better—"

"I am, or I will try to be. Please, Henry, I'm begging you. It's terrible here. I have no books. The women drool and smash their faces with trays. I don't belong here. I'm not one of them. I belong with you."

He finally looked over at me. I could see the decision swirling in his eyes. He looked back to the doctor and told him he needed a day to think about it.

My mouth dropped open. What was there to think about?

"I'm sorry," he said. "I'm trying my best here. I just want you happy. We've tried to do this on our own and look where it got us." He stood. "Doctor, I have your number. I'll call you tomorrow so we can discuss this further."

"I'll never forgive—" I growled.

"If it keeps you alive, I can live with that." He dropped his head and stepped around me. Before I could fully process all that had just happened, he was gone.

"You were right," I told Olivia later that night at dinner.

"Shit, what happened?"

I recited the conversation, annoyed I couldn't do it without crying. I used to be so much better at keeping my tears inside, one time, a long time ago. Before I met Henry.

She shook her head. "Damn, I was hoping I was wrong about you. But they're all the same, the families. Once they see what it's like without us, they have a hard time going back."

"It's not our fault." My raised voice received a few sideways glances from the jailers looking over us. I wanted to smash *their* faces with my tray.

"No, but what can we do?" She shrugged and continued eating.

"I'm just mad at the world. Mad at this life. Mad at this stupid brain. And mad the one person I thought would always be there for me has proven to be just like every other person in this stupid world," I said, pushing my food away. My stomach was too sour to accept food. "Everyone keeps telling me to be honest with myself and with them. Honesty has gotten me nowhere."

"Look on the bright side. You have me." She grinned.

"That is a bright side; two rejected loons, rotting together in the insane asylum." We both laughed. "What happened to the woman with the tray?"

"What woman?" She tilted her head in confusion.

"The one who smashed her face in. Surely that was dramatic enough to stand out from all the other events of the day."

"Oh yeah, that lady. She does it all the time. So not

very dramatic. I'm sure they have her all drugged up in a padded room until she can behave herself again. Which she can't, so the pattern will repeat itself again, over and over."

I shuddered. It could always be worse. Poor woman, and her poor broken mind. Was there hope for any of us? Or were we all destined to be damaged forever?

Forty Nine

I HATED HENRY. The doctor came to see me before breakfast. He told me he spoke with Henry, I would not be going home, I needed to accept my situation and open myself to the care I was receiving. Any talk of dates would only deter my healing. I looked around the room for something to throw. The emptiness of it snickered at me. My hands clawed at my throat, desperate to scream, but something had stolen my voice. I slid out of my skin and took two steps so I could observe my empty shell from afar. Beverly sat on the bed staring at nothing. The doctor kept talking to the empty woman.

"Looks like you've really done it this time, love."

I looked to my right. Bill had returned. My eyes narrowed, unsure if I could trust him.

"I don't think you're him."

"Are any of us really the versions of ourselves that others create of us?"

I grunted in frustration. "I don't have time for riddles. I need to figure a way out of here."

"The key to set you free lives up here."

He flicked my head and I jerked back into my skin. With my hands fisted I looked at the doctor and screamed.

Chaos ensued. Orderlies rushed in. A needle pricked. Hands all over me.

"I don't like to be touched," I protested.

Heavy limbs.

Tired.

Sleep.

Evil bracelets held my wrists captive. I attempted to sit up, to move, to do anything. Dejected, I gave up. I had to use the bathroom and was about to call for help when a nurse with kind eyes walked in. Her presence was enough to bring tears to my eyes.

Surely, she would unchain me.

"Help me." I craned my neck so she could see my face, so she could understand my desperation.

"Let's get those things off you. You fainted, and these were just a precaution. Nothing to fret over."

I sat up and rubbed the angry ring of red that encircled my wrists. This was all Henry's fault.

"Why would he do this to me?" I asked.

"It's procedure, don't worry, we rarely use restraints—"

"Not the doctor, my husband. How could he do this to me? I want to go home."

She looked at me with a sympathetic frown. "Sometimes we need help. It's nothing to be ashamed of, and I'm sure he just wants the best for you."

"I'll never forgive him for this."

"I think you'll find when you get your mind in a healthy, happy place, forgiveness will come much easier."

I wanted to rip her smiling lips off her face. I decided I was wrong about her. Her eyes weren't kind. She was a façade. A phony. Like everyone else in my life.

I walked to the bathroom and shut the door behind me. I sat on the toilet and ate through half the roll of toilet paper, hoping they didn't monitor those things.

LATER THAT AFTERNOON, a different nurse escorted me to the doctor's office. There were so many nurses and staff, I couldn't be bothered to learn their names. It was just him and me, no Henry.

"Have you called my parents? Henry may think it's appropriate to keep me locked away like a prisoner, but I'm positive they would disagree. I could go home with them instead?"

"I'm afraid not, Beverly." He shuffled through his papers. "Yes, here it is, I spoke with your mother. She agreed with Henry's decision."

I slumped back in my seat, refusing to look at him. My last hope was as helpless as a bug crawling across the floor, his words a shoe crushing it. I hated them all.

"The quicker you stop thinking of this as a punishment and think of this instead as the help you need, the quicker you'll get better and go home," he said, looking over his glasses at me. "I want to make your stay more pleasant, but I need some promises from you. There are rules you need to abide by."

"Can I have books?"

"Yes. Henry will bring some personal effects for you later this afternoon."

I cringed at his name but then slipped my affable mask back on my face, assuming the role of a complacent patient. Whatever it took to retain my freedom.

"Yes, I can comply with your rules."

"It's more than just complacency. You need to be open and honest in our sessions. Dig deep. That's the only way we will get your mind in a better place. I have faith in you. You need to have faith in yourself."

"I understand." My cheeks ached from my plastered-on smile. I tried not to fidget, but I needed to get out of there.

He droned on about my treatment plan, new rules, and other things I couldn't care less about. I half-listened. My mind exploded with thoughts—how I got here, how everyone I loved could betray me, and how I'd get myself out of this precarious situation.

Fifty

"Knock, knock." Olivia leaned against my doorframe. "Lunch time, let's go before the good seats are taken."

I followed her out into the hallway.

"Who's that?" I asked, nodding my head to a woman sitting in a chair by the window in another room. She was staring out the window, which you couldn't see through. I hadn't seen her at any meals, at group, or during rec time. She resembled a corpse, stiff and unmoving.

"That's Elise. She's been here forever. Her daughter died, drowning, I think, and she hasn't spoken a word since."

I inhaled sharply and clutched at my chest. Few people could understand Elise's pain—why it was easier to tuck back into yourself, why words were so trivial, not worth forming—but I could. I wished for a knife or sharp object, something to slice through Elise's neck and put an end to her misery. It's what she wanted; I was sure of it.

Olivia cocked an eyebrow. "You okay?"

I nodded. "Yes, sorry, I'm fine. That's so sad."

"Sure is. She's one of the only ones in here with an excuse. The rest of us were just unlucky enough to be born with broken minds."

"Unlucky indeed," I whispered to myself.

After an uneventful lunch I walked into my room, I was delighted to see a box sitting on my bed. A box full of clothing and books. I threw everything onto the bed, separating out the books. I cracked one open, covered my face with it, and breathed in the pulpy scent of the pages. Thirty of them, brand new, books I had never read.

I hated Henry just a little less.

I PUT my years of practice hiding my emotions to good use. I gathered my rage and placed it neatly back inside, out of the doctors' and nurses' prying hands. My brick wall back in place, easily constructed that second time. The minutes blurred into hours blurred into days blurred into weeks, and January was over.

Back in the doctor's office, Henry looked from the doctor to me. A 'family session,' the doctor called it.

"You're still holding back, Beverly," the doctor said. "You haven't fully confronted your trauma."

I squared my shoulders, glaring at Henry in my peripheral vision but not turning my face from the doctor. Jaw clenched and fingernails digging half-moons into my palms, I considered my next words carefully.

"Has there been any progress?" Henry asked.

"Yes, I would say there has been. But she needs to let me in if we're going to make a full recovery."

I couldn't stand the way they were talking about me like I wasn't sitting right there.

"I've been working hard. Attending every session, group therapy, and following the rules. I don't understand why you aren't recommending I go home." I hated how whiney I sounded.

The doctor cleared his throat. "I'm not diminishing the work you've put in. But you and I both know you haven't been completely honest in your sessions. You still claim the incident that landed you here was an accident."

"Fine, it wasn't an accident. I tried to kill myself. Happy?" I was now a petulant child.

"No, I'm not. But I'm pleased you are finally able to admit it. This will be the topic of our next session." He turned his attention to Henry. "I'm recommending another month's stay here. As you can see, Mr. Bonnefinche, we still have much to work on."

I sat on my hands so they wouldn't be tempted to smash his skull in with the paperweight sitting on his desk.

"Okay." Henry sighed. "I'm sorry, Birdie. But we have to think of the future. Our future. I'm not going to bring home a partially healed wife. I want you whole again."

I turned my head away and looked at the trees, the brick hospital, the grass, the path, the other people milling about beyond the window, anything but him. The whorled branches of the nearest spruce tree began to quiver, and a cardinal took flight. At least he had his freedom.

I was once again a bird with clipped wings.

Fifty One

I stood in Olivia's doorway, consumed by the suitcase opened on the bed.

"I'm going home."

My eyes grew as wide as the bottom of a coffee mug.

"What?" I asked.

"My parents do this every once in a while. Remember they have a daughter, feel guilty, come release Rapunzel from her tower, then turn right back around and dump me back in here when they get me home and remember why they originally got rid of me."

"Well, that's great. Good for you."

"Don't be angry with me. I'm sorry you're stuck here. Maybe you'll be next?"

"I'm never getting out of here. I guess you were right all along. Henry got his taste of life without me, and he finds it delicious."

I marched away from Olivia's frowning face, slamming my door shut behind me.

An orderly opened it. "Doors open during the day. You know the rules."

I collapsed on my bed and stifled my scream with a pillow.

WITH OLIVIA GONE, I fell into a deep depression. People were always leaving me right when I cared for them enough to be devastated by their departure. I had been right all along. Love wasn't worth it. Friendship wasn't worth it. I was perfectly fine back in the bookshop, alone and not lonely. And that attitude, and my insistence that I'd be better off dead, earned me six more months in that place. No release for good behavior.

The first three months were torture. I rejected culpability. Blamed Henry, my parents, humanity, anything and anyone that wasn't me. I sulked through sessions, refused to participate in group therapy, and envied Elise, who was allowed to sit in her room staring at nothing.

Henry and I were outside on a walk after one of our family sessions. Another privilege awarded to patients who had been there long enough. It was hot, even for June. I was sweating but didn't want to give up even a minute of fresh air.

"We all want you to come home, you believe that, don't you?" Henry said.

"It doesn't seem that way. I've been here for ages! Here, let's sit on that bench in the shade. It's too hot to walk."

We sat, and Henry continued, "You heard what he said in there. You aren't taking this seriously. You need to participate in your care for it to be effective."

I groaned. "You're starting to sound like them."

"You aren't helping yourself, and you know it. You antagonize the nurses and orderlies with your bizarre statements. Always talking about murder, threatening to kill yourself just to get a rise out of them. It's not helping your case. Is that really the only thing you can do to amuse yourself?"

"It's funny. I like to see their reactions. And frankly, you and your doctor friend should be pleased by this. In the past, I'd think these things in my head. You all are always telling me to *open up*."

Henry rubbed his face. "It's not *funny*, Beverly. It's disturbing."

Rude.

"What else am I supposed to do with my time? I'm surrounded by insane people—"

He cut me off. "That's part of your problem. You consider yourself better than everyone in here. You aren't. I'm not being ugly, but you're one of them. They are here for help, no different than you."

I refused to talk after that, and he left, cutting our visit and walk short. Later that night, I stared at my ceiling, thinking back on my conversation with Henry. Perhaps it was time to try something different. I had been kicking and fighting my entire time here, so sure I knew best.

Maybe, just maybe, I was wrong.

THE NEXT THREE months passed much faster.

I relented. Partially. Just enough.

I wasn't complacent, I tried, really tried. I told my doctor what I knew he wanted to hear. I was vulnerable. After each session, my discomfort sent me running to the bathroom, throwing up the day's meals, and replacing it with a feast of pulpy paper.

"I have to share something with you," I said during one of our sessions. "That one time Henry found me, the day I ate all the toilet paper. It wasn't a one-time thing. It's an everyday thing, actually. Something I've done my whole life." I grabbed hold of the chair's seat and braced myself for the horror, disgust, shock that never came.

"Thank you for being honest with me, let's talk about it. When did this first start?"

We unraveled my strange secret, much like the rolls of toilet paper I'd been unraveling and consuming my entire life.

By August, I could sit through group therapy, individual, and family sessions and share my feelings, hopes, and dreams without the need to purge my lunch. One day it dawned on me, it had been weeks since I ate toilet paper.

Henry continued to visit, but he didn't love me anymore. He didn't look at me the same. I was his burden. The only thing binding us were our vows, in sickness and in health. Did he realize how much that promise he made would be tested on the day he recited those words? Once again, my timing was off. My heart burst for him. I loved him freely and fully. I craved his affection and attention and wanted to give him mine in return. We'd chat and he'd smile, but it didn't reach his eyes. They no longer crinkled at the edges. I feared I'd lost Henry and had no one to blame but myself.

I could sense he didn't trust me or my mind, but he finally agreed to take me home.

Fifty Two

AFTER LUNCH, the day of my release, I sat on my bed on my hands. My skin crawled. I couldn't run far from this dreadful place fast enough. Henry had paused a bit too long for my liking at the doctor's release recommendation. If he didn't show up, what would happen to me then? Would I rot in this awful room? My skin flaking off in decaying chunks until there was nothing left. My gaze flicked to the door for the hundredth time since I'd sat down.

I didn't belong here. I relented. I healed. Now come get me, Henry. Save me!

My two old comrades sidled in. It had been so long since I'd seen them. The Beverly who wasn't Beverly leaned down and whispered in my ear, *"Liar. You've fooled them all haven't you, stupid girl. You've even fooled yourself. You think you're free?"* Her laugh pierced my ears. I slammed my hands to them, but the sound came from within. I couldn't get away from it. Bill stood back, looking at us. His head hung low, refusing to meet my eye. Then they were gone.

I jumped up from the bed when the friendly nurse walked in, not letting figments of my imagination ruin that perfect day. She was the perfect warden to release my shackles. I decided I liked her again.

"Ready to go?"

"Yes. Very much so."

The knot in my stomach loosened with each step.

We met Henry at the front desk, where he was signing paperwork. I was now Henry's responsibility. It was still hard to get over the unjustness of it all. Why my fate was not mine and instead a possession of all those people. People who had no clue what thoughts were in my head. Although if they knew them, they would not be letting me go. Sometimes stones remain best unturned.

If it meant I could get out of this forgotten forsaken place, I would play their games, let them all believe they could manipulate me, bend me, and mold me into their idea of normal. It wasn't fair, really. None of them had experienced so much loss, so much rejection. I'd survived a lot. I'd like to see them do the same and smile their way through it.

He didn't look up upon my arrival. I could sense the canyon between us widening. This may have bothered me a year ago, maybe even a day prior, but at that moment, all that concerned me was him signing the papers and getting me the hell out of there.

Shifting the weight between my feet, I wanted to sprint for the exit. So many papers, and Henry was taking too long. Finally, after the last document was signed, he put the pen down on top of them and handed them back to the receptionist. He looked at me for the first time since arriving, grabbed under my elbow, and told me to come with him.

I let him lead me as far as the nurses could see from their desk, but when the doors closed behind us, removing us from their line of sight, I wiggled my arm loose.

"I can manage from here."

"Are you sure about that?"

There was an edge to his words. That was new. Even on his visits, his words were much rounder, more cursive in their delivery. The canyon between us grew wider still.

The ride home wasn't much warmer. His chilly stare stayed on the road. I would have liked to thank him for his careful driving. But his attitude toward me was unnerving. I went to turn on the radio, and he spoke his first words since the hospital.

"No. I prefer the quiet."

I wasn't about to let his bad attitude dampen my mood, though. I rolled down the window and enjoyed the seventy-degree August air fanning my face, ignoring him when he asked me to roll it up. It was time to regain authority over my life, take back control, and I was starting with the air that I wanted blowing on my face.

We got home, and without a word, Henry went straight to bed. I stood at the bottom of the stairs staring up them. My hand tightening its grip on the railing. The nerve of him. I'd lost almost a year of my life, and this is how he treated me. I lifted a foot to the first step, then thought better of it. I'd have to choose my next move carefully.

Fifty Three

A CURIOUS THING happens in marriage. You enter into it as a person, and your moods, your energy, are influenced only by what happens to you. You're in complete control.

But once in the marriage, that changes. It's not immediate and evolves over time. After a horrible day, your spouse will come home, happiness radiating from them. They don't have to *do* anything. A process of symbiosis transfuses their happiness from their cells to yours. Suddenly you can't remember why you were upset to begin with.

There's another side to that, though. A perfectly pleasant mood can be ruined for no reason other than some internal turmoil your spouse is battling. They don't even have to say anything; you feel it. And it takes over. Perhaps this is what they really mean by soulmates. And they got the entire concept wrong. It's not that one person walking around amongst the billions of people was put on this earth for the sole purpose of mating with you. What it actually means is a nebulous concept too complex for the human brain to process. It's where you become so connected to someone that your two souls mate. Feeding off each other. This can happen with lovers, spouses, but it can also occur in friendships. Henry and I used to feed each other with positive energy and light. Then we became leeches, sucking the life from each other, feeding on the other's blood.

I woke up, neck aching, in the same spot I had sat down the night before to read. I rubbed my eyes and strained to hear Henry. Whispers floated from the kitchen, but I couldn't translate those whispers into words. The breaks in the conversation and lack of another voice suggested he was on the phone.

I stretched my neck to both sides in an effort to work out the kink before standing and walking toward the sound.

"Who are you talking to?"

His back stiffened. I had surprised him, which I found peculiar.

"Let me get off here, Beverly just walked in." He slipped his phone into his pocket, turned to me, and muttered. "Work stuff."

I ignored the guilt etched across his face, and asked, "Want scrambled eggs for breakfast?"

"It's past noon. I've already had breakfast. Besides, I have to go. I have some errands to run."

My toes curled in my socks. He gathered his keys from the holder and walked out the screen door.

Curiosity piqued. I walked to the front of the house and drew the curtain back slightly, watching him from the living room window. Strategically positioned so he couldn't see me.

Beverly materialized besides me. Her voice breathy, just above a whisper. *"It's done. It's over. Accept it and move on with your life. You've always known you were better off alone."*

My gaze followed Henry's car down the street, and I noticed Bonnie marching down the sidewalk toward my house.

"Oh look, one of the called friends who left you to die."

"Shut up, shut up, shut up," I said, grabbing the sides of my head. I closed my eyes and forced myself to smile. Deep breath in, deep breath out. Then walked to the front door and flung it open before she could ring the bell.

"Beverly! My gosh, you had us worried." She wrapped her arms around me, smothering me with large her chest. I surprised myself by not shrinking from her touch.

Once separated, I stepped to the side, giving her space to enter.

"Come in. Thank you for coming. Shall I put some coffee on?" I asked, a genuine smile brightened my face.

"Perfect, let's sit. Have a chat."

We cried together when I filled her in on my life. My downward spiral and time at the hospital. With every laugh and tear, the pressure on my chest lifted. All the doctors, Henry, everyone had told me with time it wouldn't hurt so bad, my chest wouldn't feel so tender. I hadn't believed them. But as the scream that had cemented in my throat since my baby died evaporated, I let myself believe I could make it through life without her.

"You're going to be alright Beverly, I'm sure of it." She

placed her hands on mine and squeezed. A warmth spread through my body, and I let myself believe her.

"I'm going to try." I smiled, hoping that saying the words out loud were enough to make them true.

"Now enough of this sappy nonsense. When can we expect to see you back at book club? Also, you need to call Jeanine before she loses her mind. She's been nothing but waterworks worried about you."

"I can come next week. What book are we reading?" I asked.

"Don't you roll your eyes. It's not one of those weird scary books you love, but this one is darn good. A classic, even."

She reached into her giant purse sitting on the floor next to her chair and started digging around. The book she pulled out was huge, making me wonder what else she had stored in there that made it so difficult to find. She placed the hefty hardcover on the table.

"*The Prince of Tides*." I read out loud. "Gosh, this is old. Not your usual pick."

"I stumbled across it on Netflix the other day, the movie. Figured a little nostalgia never hurt anyone."

I turned the book over to read the blurb. I had never read the book or seen the movie.

"I hope it's not too soon, but there *is* suicide." My head jerked up, and she quickly continued, "It's much more than that, though—love, affairs, healing. Savannah is Tom's sister, who tries to kill herself. You may relate to her; it could help you with your own path to recovery."

I enjoyed a sip of my coffee, pondering whether I was ready. I realized a core frustration I had been experiencing was not having anyone who *got* me. Plus, I'd always connected to characters in books more than characters in real life.

"I'll start reading tonight. Thank you for bringing it. And thank you for checking on me. It really means a lot."

We finished our chat, and I walked Bonnie to the door, promising to see her Wednesday. I couldn't bear the thought of Jeanine feeling even a fragment of what I had been feeling. Lifting spirits wasn't my specialty, but for Jeanine, I certainly wanted to try. I walked back to the kitchen and dug my phone from my purse.

"Jeanine, hello. It's Beverly, how are you?"

"Oh Bev, it's so wonderful to hear your voice. Are you doing better?"

"I'm much better now, really. I made an awful mistake. But I know it was a mistake. It's the wake-up call I needed. I have to find *some* way to get past this terrible thing."

"I can't imagine, none of us can really. Is there anything I can do for you? I've been checking in with Henry but trying not to be a bother. You both have had so much to deal with. Stuff no one should have to. We're here to help you. You're not alone. Remember that. Are you up to joining us at book club again?"

I chewed on the word *alone*. It had never been a state I disliked. Quite the opposite. I *preferred* to be alone. But hearing from my friends and listening to them tell me how much they cared, I understood why people needed other people and why they put so much credence in relation-ships. The filament in the proverbial light bulb above my head flickered to life. I needed these women—I needed people. With them, I would find the strength to recover from my unrecoverable injury.

I told Jeanine I would see everyone Wednesday, and I couldn't wait. I gave Kat a quick call as well. Like the other women, she was happy to hear from me and lavished me with concern and care. Not only was I pleased to have my spirits lifted, but I was also glad none of them seemed to hold my deplorable behavior against me. I guess a child lost and two suicide attempts earned you redemption.

My hand hovered over the phone for one final phone call: Quinn. But suddenly too tired to talk, I wrinkled my nose and decided I would call her tomorrow, choosing instead to start dinner for Henry—not that he deserved it the way he'd been acting.

Regardless, I smiled while I chopped the vegetables and peeled the potatoes. Hummed while I pounded the seasoning into the chicken. Determined to prepare a nice meal. I would prove to Henry and myself he had made the right decision. I wasn't a lost cause. I had simply lost my way for a bit.

"Oh! You're home just in time," I said when Henry walked in.

"Is that dinner? It smells delicious."

"It is! I can't imagine the amount of pizza and Chinese takeout you've been living off while I've been gone." I chuckled. "I thought you'd enjoy a nice home-cooked meal."

I put the dish down on top of the oven and walked

over to meet him, placing one hand on his back and one on his arm, I ushered him to the table.

"Sit, sit. I'm going to pop these rolls in the oven and heat them up a bit. Dinner will be ready in a minute."

After guiding him into his seat, I kissed his forehead. Eyes wide, jaw hanging loose, he watched me move around the kitchen.

"Looks like you had a busy day," he observed.

"Yes, Bonnie came over. We had a lovely chat. She gave me the book they're currently reading," I pointed at the book on the table. "I think I'm going to go back to book club next week. Try to get back into my routine. It should help, don't you think?"

The oven dinged.

"Rolls are ready!" I chirped.

I made each of us a plate and brought them to the table. I could feel Henry watching me eat.

"Eat, silly. Your dinner's going cold," I said.

He complied.

"Wow, you've really outdone yourself, Beverly."

My smile widened. "As good as your mom's?"

"Then some!"

"Where did you go? Didn't you have errands to run?"

He paused, the fork halfway to his mouth. "The store didn't have what I was looking for, then I ran into one of my buddies from work, and we got to talking. Next thing I knew, an hour had passed."

"What were you looking for? I could go tomorrow while you're at work and check a few other shops. It would be nice to have an excuse to go out."

"Well, turns out my friend had one he said I could

borrow. The tool, I mean, I was out looking for a tool. I'm going to grab it from him next weekend. Nice guy, may grab a beer or something with him after."

"That's kind of him," I said flatly. "I was thinking we could do something nice to celebrate my recovery. Rent a house on the Cape. The summer crowd should be cleared out by now, so it will be peaceful. And not hard to find a place to stay."

"Quinn has been saying how much she wants to bring Jacob to the beach. Should we invite them too?"

"Quinn will be fine without us for a week," I snapped. I wanted to see Quinn, but I didn't understand why Henry had to inject her into everything that had to do with us.

"Sure, sure. Of course, she will be. I didn't know if you wanted to spend some time with her too. She's your best friend, so I just thought—"

"I'll have plenty of time to spend with Quinn and Jacob. I want to go to the Cape with you. We've been apart for almost a year."

"Excellent point, love. I'll start calling around and find a cottage available to rent. I can check tomorrow with work if it's okay for me to take a week off. I'm sure they'll be fine with it."

"Lovely. I was actually thinking of calling Quinn tomorrow and checking in on her. How is she doing these days?"

"Fine, I suppose. I haven't chatted with her much. Been a bit busy myself." He smiled sheepishly. I'd known that face long enough to know when it was lying. My eyes narrowed. Was this because of that fight we'd had? It was so long ago. I thought we could move forward. A fresh start.

"It's a great idea to call her, though, and the vacation and going to book club. Dr. Clarke will agree, I'm sure."

"Ugh, do I still have to go to her?"

"What's wrong with Dr. Clarke? I figured you wouldn't want to start over with someone new. Since the two of you already have a history, it saves you the trouble of having to tell your story from the beginning. Starting over with a new doctor wouldn't be a good idea."

"Fine, you're right. I guess you took the liberty of making an appointment for me already?"

"I did. But if you want to handle the appointments yourself, I'll be happy to stand down and let you take over."

"I would. From now on, I'll be managing my own calendar again. Thank you for doing it for me, but I think I'm ready to do it for myself now. I'll even drive myself there."

"Sounds good. It will be easier for me to get time off work if I don't have to take you anymore. Good all around. You'll get out of the house, and I'll be able to take you on a nice vacation to the beach."

We finished dinner, and both did the dishes together, him rinsing, me placing them in the dishwasher. With the kitchen clean, we retired to the living room. I curled up on the couch with my book club book, and Henry leaned back in his chair watching TV.

I almost let myself believe things were back to normal and that we would be okay. My mind was so very good at lying.

Fifty Four

FOR ONCE IN HER LIFE, Bonnie was correct in her assessment. I thoroughly enjoyed *The Prince of Tides*. I stayed up most of the night reading. And much to my neck's chagrin, I fell asleep sitting up on the couch again.

Each page chased away worries over Savannah's state of mind and other various triggers. While Tom was the novel's protagonist, it was Savannah I furiously turned the pages for, waiting to hear more from the sensitive poet hiding among the New York crowds. The book was no doubt emotionally devastating. But being destroyed by someone else's trauma was a welcomed change. I immersed myself in the tragedies of another family.

Henry had already left for work. After showering and dressing, I much preferred to return to the couch and finish the book but couldn't put off calling Quinn any longer. I placed a filter in the coffee maker, and while I stood at the sink filling the pot with water, hazy images of last night's dream came back to me. Tom and Susan

Lowenstein—Savannah's doctor—ripping each other's clothes off with a hungry desire. Only Tom wasn't Tom he was Henry, and Susan wasn't Susan, she was Dr. Clarke.

I looked down at my red hand; the sink's steaming water overflowed from the pot onto it. I quickly turned off the water and poured the excess down the drain. Then I poured the remainder into the back of the coffee maker. After pressing the button, it gurgled to life. I stood over the machine watching the brown liquid fill the pot, wondering what to make of the dream. Henry's fidelity had never been a worry, but he was acting peculiar lately. Thoughts for another day. I would see how the trip to the Cape went and come back to them if needed.

The smell of coffee wafting from the pot brought my mind back to the kitchen and out of my head. I fixed myself a cup, then dialed Quinn's number.

"Well, I'll be. I've been waiting to hear your voice, Beverly. How are you?"

Sick of that question, I didn't answer.

"How are you? How's Jacob? He must be huge now."

"Still amazing. He's just started walking, keeping me on my toes for sure."

A shock of jealousy closed my throat. I swallowed it down.

"That's wonderful. I can't wait to see him."

"Me too. He loves his Uncle Henry, and I know he'll love his Auntie Bev too. We'll have to make plans to meet up when you get back from the Cape if we don't have the chance before you two leave."

The phone slipped from my hand and crashed to the

floor. I picked it up and checked the screen for cracks, then slowly placed it back to my ear.

"How did you know about our trip?" My words had frost on them despite my efforts to keep them warm and round. One hand clenched the phone, the other I placed on the counter to hold myself up.

"Oh, Henry called me this morning. He asked if I could recommend a nice cottage rental or bed-and-breakfast. Said he wanted to make it really special for you. So sweet of him, huh?"

"Yes," I replied. "So sweet."

Quinn was an excellent liar too. That piece of information was filed for future evaluation.

"Sorry to cut this short, but that's my mom calling me. Let's get together soon, 'kay?"

She hung up before I could reply. Which was fine, because suddenly words had escaped me.

I saw a man-shaped shadow from the corner of my eye and spun toward the mudroom door to confront Henry with my accusations. The closed door confused me. I was sure I'd heard it open, could swear I saw a person. The only sound in the house was the ticking of the grandfather clock from the other room. With images of Bill and not-Beverly Beverly already haunting me, I couldn't take any new demons lurking in the shadows.

I fell into a chair at the kitchen table, grabbing my head, hoping my hands could keep my mind in there. It couldn't desert me again. If I lost it, I wasn't sure I'd be able to find it this time. I focused my attention on the sound of my breathing and not the places my imagination wanted to run. Desperate to sprint to the bathroom and gobble an entire roll of toilet paper, I grabbed the sides of the chair, holding myself in place. I was *better*. And my best friend and husband were *not* having an affair.

After several minutes of shaky breaths, I calmed. The rolling thunder in my ears retreated. I slumped back into the chair. It was unfathomable for the two people who loved me the most to betray me, not in that way. I *knew* Henry and Quinn. They were good. Not like other people. Maybe it wasn't such a good idea for me to read a book whose character flaws were so real and so raw. I needed a comfort read. The new adaptation of Stephen King's *It* had me craving a re-read for a while now. An evil, child-killing clown was the sounder choice for my current state of mind.

I looked through my books trying to find my copy. It must have been lost in the move. I could order it online but getting out of the house for a few hours sounded nice. I called Jeanine and asked her to join me for a trip to the bookstore.

———

JEANINE's idle chatter in the car ride made me a much safer driver. My mind couldn't slip off and drag the vehicle with it. Her calming presence soothed me, I concluded I had spun the entire Henry and Quinn situation into something it wasn't. A combination of stress and devouring more than half of an emotionally charged book in one sitting. The happy ramblings from Charlotte, her daughter, in the back seat mixed with Jeanine's animated voice were helping.

At first, she was hesitant to come, worried I wasn't ready to spend time with a child. I surprised myself when I laid eyes on her. It didn't bring the rushing flood of despair for my own missing daughter with it. I scooped her up and twirled her around in a circle, making her laugh hysterically.

"What book are you after? Or are we just browsing?"

"*It*. I haven't done as much reading as I would have liked over the last few months, and I'm ready to get back to it."

"You and your scary books." She laughed. "I tried to watch the movie and didn't make it past the sewer scene. I *hate* clowns. They are scary, even the non-killing ones. I couldn't stand to read that book."

"What? Why clowns? They are goofy, and their entire job is to make people laugh. What could possibly be scary about that?"

"My grandma had this painting hanging in the bedroom I would sleep in on visits. Every night I would lie in bed, and this man, this clown, would smile at me from across the room. I think it was supposed to be a happy painting, but his mouth was all big and open, I was convinced he was hiding something evil behind all that makeup and funny outfit."

"You sound like me. I'm supposed to be the one who twists harmless paintings and people into evil killers. You're supposed to see balloon animals and flower lapels that shoot water."

"Ha! Next thing you know I'll be reading Stephen King books!"

"And I'll grow my hair out and start walking around barefoot."

"Ugh, shoes are the worst, so confining," she said, looking down at ballet flats. "You'll love it."

"And *you* would love Stephen King. Here we are now." I eased the sedan into a parking spot, and we made our way into the store.

My feet knew the way to the horror section, having traveled the path enough times before. Finger scanning the bindings, Jeanine chatted behind me.

"Even the books' covers make my skin crawl," she said. "Don't look, Charlotte, you may be scarred for life." She covered Charlotte's eyes with her hand.

"Mommy, no," Charlotte squealed, and we all laughed.

I found what I was looking for on the bottom shelf and crouched to grab a copy. When I rose, women's loud laughter broke out down the aisle. While sneaking a look at the source of all the noise, I made eye contact with them. They quickly turned away, one whispering something into the other's ear. They continued to glance at us, trying, but not achieving, to be inconspicuous.

"What are those ladies talking about?" I whispered. Placing my back to them, I gave a slight backward nod in their direction.

"What ladies?" Jeanine asked, scanning the store.

"The ladies *right behind me*," I said. "I think they're talking about us. And laughing."

Jeanine peered around me with her eyebrows knitted together. "What could anyone possibly have to say about us? Two boring women surrounded by every nightmare I've ever had."

I turned around, frustrated. They were gone.

"You missed them, they already walked away. How strange."

We walked to the cashier, the two laughing women now stood at the front of the store, browsing a display of coffee table books.

"There, right there." I elbowed Jeanine so she wouldn't miss them.

"Ouch! Oh, yeah. I see them. Are you sure they were talking about us? They don't seem to be too interested now."

Charlotte had pulled a few items off the front display, distracting Jeanine. Right when she bent down to pick one of the items up, the women's heads whipped toward us in unison, their expressionless faces and dead gazes locked on me, making goosebumps erupt on my skin.

"Oh my God, Jeanine, look at the way they're staring at me!"

She turned toward them, and they were intently staring. But not our way—one woman was pointing to something in a book she had opened, both were fixated on whatever she had found within the glossy pages.

"Something behind us must have caught their eye for a second. They seem more interested in whatever it is they found in that book than they do us," she said.

"Yes, yes, you must be right. I must be mistaken. Silly me." I laughed, but there was a tremor in it. I made it a point to avoid glancing in the direction of the two women when we walked past them out the front entrance.

Between the car ride home and an engrossing desire to start my new book, I forgot all about the women. Henry came home and, with a start, I realized I had been so entrenched in reading, I'd forgotten to prepare dinner.

Sliding my bookmark between the pages to mark my spot, I ran into the kitchen to meet him.

"I forgot to cook," I said, catching my breath.

He picked his keys back up. "Well, let's go out to eat. I'm starving."

He smiled, the hint of disgust that had been tinting his features since I came home no longer visible. At least for now.

"Yes, perfect. I haven't been out to eat in ages. Let me grab my purse, and I'm ready."

I WAS a bit nervous on the ride to the restaurant. But Henry wasn't snapping at me or ignoring my presence completely, which soothed my anxiety. By the time we were seated, and the waiter had taken our drink orders, it felt like I'd slipped back into my favorite sweater on the first cool day of fall.

Our conversation stalled at first, both of us feeling the other out, but things felt normal by the time dinner was over. We were the old Henry and Beverly. The stranger's face across from me had reorganized, and the familiar face-filling smile had returned.

Fifty Five

First Beach was my favorite spot in Newport. It was made up of a small strip of sand perfect for watching the waves crash. They fold in on themselves with their white-foamed fingers tickling the shore before retreating out to sea. Or you could crane your neck up to the right and admire the sheer, sunbaked cliff face, the steep rocky home to the famous Newport mansions, their inhabitants looking down—literally and figuratively—on the rest of us. Some people would gaze up at those mansions and wish they could live the life of their owners, but not me. I preferred the cliff to the homes on top of it.

Although, I wouldn't have minded being part of a society that would afford the opportunity to meet Newport's most infamous resident—Doris Duke. The wealthy tobacco heiress whose summer home—Rough Point—was one of those Newport mansions. It was in the driveway of that very mansion where her longtime employee, Eduardo Tirella, met his demise. Crushed beneath the tires of her station wagon. A tragic accident. If I had been afforded the opportunity to meet her, I'd sidle up to her and whisper in her ear, *you did it on purpose, didn't you?* We'd laugh and discuss all the other people who we've wanted to mutilate with our vehicle's wheels. I'd congratulate her for having the gusto to follow through —and the good fortune to get away with it.

Despite all Newport offered, both Henry and I—like most of New England—had been vacationing in Cape Cod our entire lives. It was a peaceful escape to enjoy the sleepy town and picturesque beaches, and just under a two-hour drive from home.

Henry rented us a quaint single-story cottage in West Dennis. In Cape Cod's center, West Dennis was on the bottom of the U forming the Cape. A convenient location, yet off the beaten path enough to feel like we were getting away from it all. I fell in love with the place the second the truck's tires crunched over the sandy street and rolled into the tree-lined driveway. Fallen pine blanketed the front yard, and the weathered brown siding gave it a cozy, charming feel. Inside, the rooms were small but inviting. Notes of sunscreen and the sea hung in the air.

Henry lugged our suitcases inside while I took a short walk around the exterior to explore. I opened the old wooden door to the outdoor shower, a nice convenience to spray off the sand from a day at the beach. I rocked on the shaded lounge chair using my toes to swing lazily, wishing I had a book. Henry came out and sat next to me, and I curled under his arm as he draped it across my shoulders. We enjoyed the cool air tickling our faces as we sat in an intimate silence.

After kissing the top of my head, he hoisted himself up. "I'm going to the grocery store to get some supplies, want to join me?"

"I'm enjoying myself. You don't mind if I stay here, do you?"

"Not at all, I'm going to grab a jacket and my keys. It's getting chilly out here. Need anything from inside?"

"My book and a blanket would be wonderful if you don't mind."

He returned shortly with the requested items and waved his goodbyes. I took a deep breath, inhaling the salt and sea and pine. I turned my face to the sky, letting the sun warm my face.

It was hard to process how far I'd come. When I stopped and remembered my life, a life scarred by tragedy, I couldn't imagine how I'd survived. It was even harder to imagine the transformation I'd gone through. From a girl who scoffed at the notion of love—even friendship—to a wife and almost a mother.

I'd suffered three major losses in my life; myself, my Bill, and my daughter. Two of those losses would leave permanent scars. Pangs of sadness still jarred my heart when something reminded me of Bill. A whiff of vodka, a man with a raspy loud laugh. And I still had my breath stolen when something reminded me of my daughter. It wasn't constant, and it was unpredictable. I imagine it will always be that way.

I smoothed the book's cover in my lap, before opening it to the page I'd left off. A loud smack made my head snap up. I inspected the back of the house, unable to discern the source of the noise. Curious, I placed the book on the swing, pushed myself up, and walked over to investigate.

When I got to the house, I found the source of the noise. A broken bird lay dying beneath the window. Was the universe sending me more signs? I had always been Henry's Birdie. He was always so confident, so sure I could fly. Maybe the bird realized how merciless this world can be and chose instead to leave it early rather than suffer through its games. Maybe I was never meant to fly in the first place. Or maybe he saw the reflection of the sky in the window and got confused.

I wanted to cradle him and nurse him back to health, but instead, I picked up a rock and smashed it onto his head, relieving him from any unnecessary misery.

THE TRUCK's slamming door stole my attention from the book. Henry, weighed down by grocery bags, ambled toward the door.

I jumped up and jogged over. "Here, let me help you." I stepped in front of him to let him in the cottage.

"There are a few more in the truck. Do you mind putting these away while I grab the rest?" he asked.

I entered the cottage's small kitchen and began putting the food away without a word. It's always best to check food purchased by someone else. You never know who could try to poison you. While I didn't fully believe Henry would poison me, I also wasn't one to take that sort of chance, so I scanned the items for broken seals and punctures as I put them away.

"I got some burgers to grill tonight if that's okay with you?" Henry asked, returning with the remaining bags.

"Yes, sounds delicious," I replied. I waited for him to put the bags on the table then leaned in to kiss him hello.

After I put the groceries away, I jotted down a list of all the items he forgot. I should have known he couldn't be trusted with the task. I managed the groceries at home. Henry's shopping trip filled the freezer with meat and the fridge with beer, and that was about it. It would have to do until we made another—more productive—trip to the grocery store.

Henry stood at the counter seasoning the meat and pounding them into burger-shaped lumps.

"I'm starving," he said.

"Me too. What do you want to do tomorrow?"

"Doesn't matter to me. We could walk down to the beach, go see the lighthouse, visit the shops. Whatever you feel up to."

"I guess we can play it by ear when we wake up."

"Yeah, sounds like a plan." He put the raw hunks of meat on a plate, washed his hands, and grabbed the bag of charcoal and can of lighter fluid from the table, then walked outside to the grill.

I set the table while Henry stood over the grill flipping the burgers. Opening the drawers one by one, I finally located a can opener. With some struggle, I pried the top off the can of baked beans and dumped them into a pot on the stove. Henry came back in a bit later with a plate full of steaming burgers.

"How many people are you planning on serving

tonight?" I laughed at the abundance of food piled on the plate.

"These, my Birdie, are going to be the best burgers you've ever tasted, so good in fact you're going to want thirds." I tried to hide my wince, the name bringing back images of the bird I'd murdered earlier.

After stuffing myself, I pushed my plate away and declared I couldn't stand to eat another bite. Henry grabbed a beer and went to relax in the living room. I told him I was going to take a shower.

I grabbed my toiletries and pajamas from my suitcase then proceeded to the bathroom. While waiting for the water to heat, a muffled voice traveled through the wall. I assumed Henry had turned on the TV until his distinctive laugh carried through the thin wall. I stood there in a towel, the shower's steam filling the bathroom with slow-moving waves, straining to hear.

An ear pressed to the wall I strained to make sense of the muffled sounds. Henry was absolutely talking to some-one, but what he was saying, I couldn't make out. My eyes narrowed and lips pursed. There was a fresh roll of toilet paper hanging on the wall, so tempting. I sat down, unraveled a handful, and stuffed my mouth, with not one single regret. Once I had my fill, I stepped into the warm, humid shower and cried tears of rage.

Whatever it was, *whoever* it was, they were *not* going to wreck this vacation. I earned this vacation. It was *my* turn to be happy. It was my turn to get what I wanted without it crumbling like dried dirt in my hands.

I hurried through my shower and joined Henry in the living room. Seated in the same spot, in almost the same position I had left him in. Tricky. Smart. I'd have to keep a closer eye on him. But not this week, not tonight—I cuddled up next to him on the couch.

We watched a few shows before both deciding to go to bed early, saving our energy for the next day's activities. As we were falling asleep, my self-control loosened its hold on my words.

"I wonder what Quinn's up to?" I prodded.

"Dunno, I guess we'll find out when we get home." He laid down and, within seconds, began snoring. I pushed him on his side to shut him up and rolled over with my back to him. The moon created a small sliver of light in the room's corner. That horrid version of myself stood in the corner barely lit. She stepped forward, and evil smirk splitting her lower face. Helium filled, I floated from my body and suddenly slipped into my evil twin's skin. Now I stood in the corner of the room, observing the couple sleeping in bed. Nothing felt real. It was all a movie or a dream or a something I had no words for. Meaningless time passed without meaning, or it didn't. Fear and confusion reigned, but my feet firmly planted to the floor, I could do nothing but stand there and watch. An unwilling audience member forced to sit through the performance of my life.

Fifty Six

I woke up cranky, which only made me crankier because this was my vacation. I should be enjoying myself. Henry suggested a walk down to the beach. I figured it may lift my mood, so I agreed without argument and went to get ready.

It was still early and off-season, so we shared the beach with a few seagulls diving for their breakfast and only passed two other couples on our walk along the shore.

My hair whipped around my face and I lifted my chin to the blue cloudless sky.

"It's so healing, isn't it?" I asked.

"The beach? Yeah, for sure."

"Not *just* the beach." I side-eyed him. "The salt coating your skin, the wind in your hair, the sun kissing your skin, the grains of sand molding to your feet with each step, like they have spent their entire lives patiently awaiting your footsteps. And that sound. If I had to pick only one sound to hear for the rest of my life, all other sounds being muted, I would pick the sound of the waves crashing. A close second would be rain pattering on a tin roof."

Henry stopped and closed his eyes. I felt so close to him in that moment. I faced him and we stood there with our eyes closed letting the sounds and smells wash over us.

"The seagulls, too. I've always loved the sound they make. Mixed with the roaring of the ocean, it's like an amazing song," Henry added.

My eyes popped open, and our gazes locked.

"They are vile, annoying creatures. They steal your food and poop all over your car," I said.

And the moment was over. Henry laughed. "I stand corrected."

After our walk on the beach, we took advantage of the outdoor shower to rinse the sand off our bare feet.

"Thinking further about it, the beach is, in theory, this amazing place. When you're there, it can overwhelm the senses. But once you leave, the sand itches and you're sunburnt on at least some area you didn't apply sunscreen to diligently enough. If it's the summer, you're hot and the sun has depleted your energy. And the ocean itself. Riptides that can come from nowhere, drowning the most experienced swimmer. Storms that sink ships. Waves form that are large enough to wipe out entire towns. And the creatures lurking beneath the surface, ready to inject you with their poison or eat you bit by bit. It's amazing how something so healing can be so deadly and destructive and downright annoying, isn't it? There are many people who are like the sea, charming you with their good looks and personality, then bam! They're robbing the life from you, dragging you under, filling you with their poison until there's nothing left." I locked eyes with Henry, waiting for him to agree.

"Well, let's get that sand fully washed off, fresh coffee in your cup, and some aloe set out just in case."

He left me in the shower rinsing my feet, wondering which of us would drown the other fastest.

I walked into the kitchen to Henry at the table, an array of colorful brochures spread before him.

"I know we've both been here a million times," he said. "But I passed the rack of these at the grocery store and thought it would be fun to experience the Cape from fresh eyes. Pick out some places to go and play tourist."

I joined him at the table and grabbed one of the colorful booklets.

"This one looks interesting," I said, holding one up for the Whaling Museum, which according to the brochure, had opened in 1930, and offered interesting exhibits on— as the name suggested—whales.

"I remember going there as a kid. You take a ferry ride to get there. It takes a few hours to get there and back so we can make a day of it. Find a nice place to eat and walk around and check out the other nearby Nantucket sights when we're done."

After getting ready, we piled in the truck and were off to explore the Cape. On the ferry ride over I stood at the railing practically the entire trip feeling the cool breeze on my face.

We both enjoyed the Whaling Museum, where we took turns reading the informative plaques at each of the exhibits, then quizzing each other on the new fun facts we'd learned over lunch.

After lunch, we walked around checking out the various historic landmarks and homes dotting the streets, taking goofy photos, enjoying the day and each other. I spotted an ice cream shop and dragged Henry by the hand into it.

A banana split sitting between us, I peeked over the colorful scoops of ice cream drizzled in chocolate sauce.

"Do you think we're all right, Henry?"

He didn't answer right away, I stuffed my mouth with a spoonful of ice cream wishing I could stuff the question back in with it.

"No, I don't think we're all right." My eyes dropped to the table, but he continued. "But that doesn't mean we can't be. We've been through a heck of a lot, haven't we? I know you've been struggling. But you're not the only one. It's been hard on me, real hard. And I'm alone here. I know you *feel* alone. But when you're in your head, when you're not getting out of bed, or snapping at me, or a bag of bones wearing a skin suit, eyes glazed over, staring off into space, I'm there with you. I'm real, solid. But you aren't, and that's why I'm alone. I really feel like I've done my best for you and by you. But there have been a lot more days and months where I'm doing most of the heavy lifting in this relationship. You've depleted me, Beverly. My resources are gone. I'm not sure how much more I can give without getting something—anything from you in return," I finished.

"But what if I'm not capable of that? Of giving you what you need."

"Well, we won't be all right. And eventually, we'll grow apart, and one day, we won't be us anymore."

"You mean you'll divorce me?"

"I can't live like this forever. I need more stability in my life. I need to know the person I'm with loves me, and I can count on them as much as they can count on me. I used to feel like that with you, every minute of every day, without question. But I'm not sure if I do anymore. I get what you went through was traumatizing, I really do. And the depression, all of it. It's not that. I meant it when I said in sickness and in health, mental health included. It's just, you don't appreciate my sacrifices and everything I do for you. It's like you don't care about me. You only care about yourself. Like you've reverted to who you used to be. And to be honest, it makes me think maybe people don't change. Not fully."

"It's hard to care about people when you don't care about yourself," I said. "And that's where I've been since I lost her."

The scoops of ice cream melted between us. A fine metaphor for our relationship. Once it melted, you could put it back in the freezer and try to turn it back into the delicious dessert it started its life as, but it never would taste the same again. The texture would never be exactly right, the taste off. Melted ice cream refrozen is a subpar version of the tasty creation it began as. Was that our destination? A shoddy imitation of a beautiful marriage.

Henry sighed. "Since *we* lost her, Beverly. *We.*"

I studied Henry over the melting balls of ice cream.

"I understand. It's not fair what I've put you through. I'll do better. And I know we both lost her. That you mourn her loss as much as I do. It's not fair that I didn't leave room for your grief. I'm sorry."

It wasn't the first time I had to beg him not to give up on me. I hoped it wasn't too late. I resolved to do better, to focus on Henry and his needs. I loved Henry, and I loved what we had before. Once again, my own issues were coiling around my insides, making it impossible to give my attention to those around me. I needed to be better.

He dug into the sundae with his spoon, letting a large scoop of ice cream melt into his throat before answering.

"I appreciate your understanding. Let's work on it. We've had a nice time here, that's a start."

We could only finish half the dessert. Both exhausted from a day on our feet—and the emotionally draining conversation—we headed back to the cottage to relax until dinner. I dozed a bit on the ferry, and before I knew it, we were back at the truck and on our way back to the cottage, collapsing into bed, and passed out within what felt like seconds.

The next morning, while looking for something to make for breakfast, I declared a needed trip to the grocery store.

"I already went. We need to go again?"

Laughing I replied, "We do if we want to survive on something other than meat and beer for a week."

"That sounds like a diet I can get behind."

A few more pieces of the strain between us scattered out the window. I eased back into my seat, smiling. *I can do this. We can do this.*

As Henry eased the truck into a parking spot, I was proud of myself for not complaining about how far he'd parked from the entrance or pointing out how many spots we passed on the way to it. He got out and opened the door for me, taking my hand in his. We walked into the store.

I pushed the cart lazily through the aisles, with Henry following behind. We were in no rush. Without the tourists, we had the store to ourselves. Our idle chitchat and good-natured arguments over flavors and selections broke the silence. I even let Henry win most of them. We piled all his favorite snacks into the cart. I commended myself for being able to follow through on my promises so quickly and easily.

With the shopping almost completed, we turned into the frozen food section. The temperature plummeted from the rows of freezers keeping the frozen food solid. I shivered, wishing I had brought my jacket.

Without warning, sweat began dripping from my pores, which made no sense, seeing as I was shivering with cold. I halted and gripped the cart's handle. The two freezers on either side of me morphed into waves and crashed over us, blinding my vision. Then almost immediately, they regained their form and snapped back into place on either side of the aisle.

"Something wrong?" Henry asked.

I blinked my eyes rapidly, looked down to ensure the ground was stable, then nodded my head slowly.

"Yes, everything is totally fine. I think I'm still worn from yesterday. Maybe I should lay down for a bit before we go do anything today."

"A lazy day. Sounds right up my alley."

I breathed a sigh of relief. He was no longer looking at

me like he knew at any minute I would do something unhinged. It was the stress getting to me. The thought of Henry leaving. I had come a long way, but I was still me.

An overabundance of interactions and the strain of putting Henry's feelings in consideration before my own were more than I could handle without a break. I needed a lie down. A refresh. We finished our shopping without incident, paid, and drove back to the cottage.

Fifty Seven

THE REST of our vacation was lovely—I hoped Henry felt the same. Sadness coated my heart as we crossed the bridge departing the cape. It's funny how a thing can contradict itself without changing. When arriving, that bridge is the signal that everyday life is paused, it brings joy, anticipation—then when you cross that bridge the second time, your vacation is over. All that remains is sun-kissed skin and memories.

We didn't discuss our relationship any further in our remaining days. I took everything Henry said to heart, though. I worked extra hard to show him I could think of other people's needs. I'm sure I went overboard to the point of annoying him. If I were Henry, I'd have been annoyed. But I kept reminding myself, I'm not Henry, and Henry is not me. His wants and needs are different.

It's hard. Everyone is *so* different in every way. I'm convinced it's the most challenging aspect of maturing, finding the ability to slip on someone else's shoes and walk without stumbling. There are plenty of people who die without figuring out this complex skill. People who don't have a Henry to help teach them how to do this. I was lucky to have him, he lit my blind spots, forced me into being a better version of myself.

The problem is—and has always been—anger and anxiety are much stronger beasts than logic. While logically, I knew how I *should* react. But a trigger, any trigger —large, small, or anything in between—would awaken those sleeping giants who would throw logic away with the ease of a thrown dish. A dish sitting in your hand one minute, smashed into a thousand pieces the next, slicing your hands and feet while you try to clean up the shards.

Exhausted from the drive, we shuffled into the house dragging our suitcases. Henry told me he'd take everything upstairs, and I was more than happy to let him.

WE SETTLED back into our routine. I would wake up with Henry every morning and make the two of us coffee. We'd sit and share a few sparse words before he'd leave for work. I reclaimed my daily schedule, cleaning, reading, and eventually preparing dinner when it was time for Henry to come home. His late nights and work dinners lessened, and I was glad that I had successfully proven myself worthy again.

I looked forward to Wednesdays, and the chance to break free from the monotony of my chores. I wasn't foolish enough to take my dull days for granted ever again, though. After an extended stay in the mental hospital, even the dullest of days—the ones that were gray from rain, where I had nothing to do but sit and stare at the wall —were adventurous compared to what I had been through.

I thought of Olivia occasionally and hoped she was well. Had she found a way to process her pain without raking a razor blade down her arms? I hoped her parents found it within themselves to work with her, believe in her, like the gift Henry had bestowed on me. We weren't too different, Olivia and me. It's hard to trust untrustworthy people like us. But we were worthy. All humans are flawed, all humans deserve grace. I believed in her. I hope she knew that.

That Wednesday, we were meeting at Jeanine's house. This meant comfortable seating, and no arguments over things as trivial as coaster usage. She was a terrible cook, so it also meant store-bought snacks, which I much preferred. While they may not have the same charm as homemade, I could at least be sure of attention to cleanliness during preparation. Not that I didn't trust Kat or Bonnie. I'd consumed plenty of food prepared in their kitchens. I'd seen their kitchens with my own eyes and both more than met my standards. But my mind couldn't help itself. Conjuring up images of fingernails in dips and hairs in casseroles. I had to remind myself not to think about it too hard for fear that I'd gag and offend someone.

"Hello!" Jeanine welcomed me by pulling me into a tight hug. I was able to accept hugs without tensing. So much growth. "Come in, come in. Kat is already here."

I had been hoping to steal a few minutes alone with Jeanine and tried to hide my annoyance behind a smile when I entered the living room and greeted Kat, who sparkled with perfection as always. Perched on the end of her chair, she took a sip of wine and greeted me.

The other ladies had gotten past my minor incident—well *incidents*–but it seemed Kat still held a grudge. She didn't outwardly treat me any differently than before, or different from any of the other ladies, really. But I always got the feeling she was more cautious around me now. She was looking a bit further down her nose at me than before.

"Hello, Kat; how are you?" I said, sitting on the couch across the room from her. I could be cordial, but the distance gave me a false sense of security.

"I'm well. Busy, of course, but when am I not?" She laughed, taking another sip. "You're looking much better. Your time away must have been good for you."

"Yes, most definitely. We had a lovely time, in fact."

"Mmm," she replied, looking more interested in her wine than she was in hearing any further details of our trip.

I focused my attention on Jeanine's décor and clutter as if they were as interesting as paintings in a museum. I longed for Jeanine to return, or even Bonnie to come bounding in and fill the silence. Tapping my fingers on my lap, I could feel my old friend anxiety curdling in my stomach. The doorbell made me jump, and Kat took another long sip of wine.

"And here she is," Kat said, her words as flat as the table in front of us covered in children's toys. I laughed a high and staccato laugh.

"Ladies! Hello! Beverly, welcome home, can't wait to

hear all about your great escape to the Cape," Bonnie hollered, strolling into the room.

"We live at the beach, Bonnie, and it was the Cape, not Tahiti," Kat said, rolling her eyes. She then glanced at her glass, dismayed by its lack of wine. My stomach tightened more.

"Someone's in a mood," Bonnie snorted.

Kat burst into tears. The bustle of the room froze. We all turned our heads to Kat with mouths and eyes circled. I was hoping someone else would react because I had no clue how to proceed. While I was no stranger to sudden outbursts of emotion those days, they remained an area of mystery to me when coming from someone other than myself. Even Jeanine was at a loss for words. Bonnie walked over to Kat and scooped her out of her seat and into one of her smothering hugs. Jeanine looked on— frozen in the room's threshold with a cheese and cracker tray balanced in her arms, and I sat wringing my hands in my lap.

Emotional outbursts didn't fit my character—however, over the last year that seemed to no longer be true—but they were even more foreign to Kat's. The woman who had her entire life planned out to the second. Her meticulous attention to detail and careful control of every situation rivaled even my own—well, my own before I lost all control, of course.

After putting Kat down, Bonnie lowered into the spot on the couch nearest Kat, shuffling into her seat and patting Kat on the leg. Jeanine placed the charcuterie board onto the coffee table and took her own seat. I didn't move.

"All right, spill it, Katherine," Bonnie said, grabbing one of Kat's hands. It took me a few beats to understand who Bonnie was speaking to. The use of her full name didn't register at first.

After several attempts, Kat composed herself enough to continue. Jeanine passed her a tissue. She made a failed attempt at cleaning the black streaks of mascara from under her eyes and blew her nose. That alone was shocking. A disheveled Kat was an image I'd never thought possible, having never seen so much as a hair misplaced on her head.

"He's cheating on me."

Déjà vu smacked me in the forehead. The women coming into the bookshop who would rattle on and on. The ones who were so annoying, bothering me with their relentless chatter, who I had convinced myself only needed to talk to because their cheating husbands didn't have time for them. A very uncomfortable feeling of shame crawled over me.

Watching Kat now, I realized how terrible I was back then. Henry's lessons penetrated deeper. Kat was those women. Those women were Kat. And maybe they needed support from someone, anyone, even a social derelict like me.

"That asshole. Why do you think that?" Bonnie asked.

Kat's chin fell to her chest. "I got a call from a woman the other day. She told me everything. Said they had been seeing each other for months, and she just thought I should know. So very kind of her, don't you think?"

"Did you confront him?" Jeanine walked over to Kat's other side and lovingly rubbed her back.

"I did." Kat's face contorted with anger. "I took the kids to my sister's and sat at our dining room table waiting for him to come home. That bastard walked in and had the nerve to ask *me* why dinner wasn't ready. Ha!" Taking a fresh tissue, she blew her nose and continued. "I told him to sit down, and the second he did, I unloaded. I screamed at him that I knew, and that his little secret called and told me all about what he'd been up to."

"What did he say?"

Everyone turned to me in surprise. I'm not sure if the source of their confusion was from the fact that I was joining a conversation about something other than books, or that I had paid enough attention to someone other than myself to be able to ask a question. The moment passed quickly, and Kat continued.

"Well. He confessed it all. Told me he made a terrible mistake with a woman from work. It was a short fling, only a few months, and he had broken things off with her recently and she had been furious. Which is why she called me."

I wanted to ask what the woman—the other woman—looked like to put a face to the image my mind was conjuring up. But I knew the ladies wouldn't like that at all. I pictured her husband, whose good looks had always garnered extra attention from the other moms at the school functions and the ladies in the neighborhood. The charming smile, broad shoulders, head of thick hair. He would laugh along with the harmless flirting, but always put his arm around Kat, or shower her with some show of affection, proving where his loyalties lay—or so we all thought.

Then I imagined him meeting some young—because they're always young—blonde bombshell in a seedy motel. The charm gone, replaced by animal instinct. Clothes ripped off and devouring each other on the disgusting bed used by thousands of other cheating husbands. Kat, bursting into the room to find her sweaty husband pumping on top of his prize. Then I see it, a gun in Kat's hand, she raises it and pulls the trigger, over and over and over again. Their surprised faces collapsed into mush. Brain matter, blood, and bones splattered around the room, painting the walls red.

I quickly replaced the smile from the thought with a look of concern. I hoped no one noticed—I didn't want the ladies to accuse me of reveling in someone else's misery. I had my suspicions of Henry, ones I had tucked away for a later date, and the feelings those suspicions gave me were terrible; I wouldn't wish them on anyone.

"What are you going to do about it?" Bonnie asked. "We don't have much room, but you can always come stay with me. We'll make it work. You and the kids."

Kat sighed, her tears dried up. "We're going to try to work it out. I know that makes me a fool. But I love him, and our life, I'm not ready to give up yet."

"Once a cheater, always a cheater," I said.

All three glared at me. I mumbled an apology.

There was a lull in the conversation, soon interrupted by Kat laughing.

"You're exactly right, Beverly. That is what I'm most upset about! How can I ever trust him again? Now, all because of his idiotic actions, I'm the one who suffers forever. I'm the one stuck always wondering where he is, who he's with."

"It's not fair," I replied.

"You're gosh damn right it isn't fair," Bonnie jumped in. "Ugh, men are pigs. All of them!"

"Not all of them," Jeanine chimed in. We all looked at each other and burst out laughing, including Kat. Discussions of books put to the side for the evening, we laughed, we cried, we drank too much wine. For once, the off-topic diversion didn't annoy me. It hit me while walking home how wrong my earlier assumptions had been. How selfish of me to assume I was the center of Kat's entire mood. So many life lessons to learn.

Fifty Eight

I woke up with a ball of pain pulsing behind my right eyeball. Hot waves of nausea swept through me. With eyes squeezed shut, I blindly reached for Henry's side of the bed but found it unoccupied. After opening one eye, I saw the wrinkled bedding pulled back, and the indent his sleeping body left from the night before.

Inwardly groaning, I realized I had overdone it with the wine. I closed my eyes and gave the ball of pain form, imagining my hand grabbing it and tossing it away from the space between my eye and brain.

Once in a sitting position, I swallowed down the bile that simple gesture brought closer to my throat. I stood, stumbled, then grabbed my head with one hand and the nightstand with the other. When the room stopped spinning, I dragged my feet to the bathroom, vowing to never drink again.

Yet another example of the thousands of empty promises we make to ourselves, to trick our brains into recovering faster from whatever self-inflicted misery our bad decisions have caused.

I tried not to gag while I brushed my teeth. I knew I had to eat and drink to recover but putting anything into my mouth was a chore. Desperate to feel better, I turned on the shower, pleading internally for my body to respond to my futile attempts. Watching the water with barely functioning eyes, I prayed for it to heat quickly and aid my recovery.

Once inside, I leaned my head against the cool tiles and let the hot water wash over me. The only benefit of a hangover—which thankfully I didn't experience very often —is that it is all-encompassing. When hungover, it is nearly impossible to think of anything else other than your hangover. I'm thankful this realization hadn't previously crossed my thoughts. Who knows what a mind like mine may do with that type of information—the most likely of outcomes being that I would have drunk myself stupid every day chasing a blinding hangover to hide my pain. A raging drunk and a woman on the precipice of sanity was a horrible combination. Maybe this is why Bill chose to reach for the vodka each day?

I accomplished very little with the rest of my day, but did manage to bake a delicious sausage casserole for dinner.

Henry walked in as I was pulling the casserole from the oven. It wasn't his favorite dish, but it was mine. And I needed to feed my hangover.

He chuckled. "You and the ladies have fun last night?"

"I'll get our plates made up and tell you about it."

I set the table and wanted to devour my serving in two bites, but I had much to tell him.

"Kat's husband cheated on her." I examined his face.

"Yikes!"

"Yes, she had quite the come-apart last night. We did little book clubbing as you can imagine."

"What's she gonna do?" he asked through a mouthful. I ignored my irritation at him not waiting for his mouth to be empty before opening it to speak.

"Apparently nothing. Well, not *nothing*, but she's not leaving him if that's what you mean."

"I meant nothing. Not my business really, what Kat and her husband do with their marriage, or their spare time."

"Obviously not. I assumed it would be of interest to you though."

"I guess. I'm glad they're trying to work it out, though. Especially with the kids and all."

"Yes. Well, Kat is devastated, obviously. I can't help but wonder if it also has to do with the fear of her image being tarnished. She does bask in the attention from her admirers."

"I doubt her image is the thing keeping her up at night."

"You don't know her as well as I do."

"That's true. Anyhow, how was your day?"

"It was fine. I don't know if I could get over it so easily, though. An affair, that is. It was with a woman at work. He says it's over, but how can she believe him? He's proven himself to be a capable liar. How can she believe anything he says, really?"

"I imagine it takes time, like with most things."

"*Time.* Why does everyone always say that? As if time is some universal remedy for all that ails. Husband cheats? Take some time. Broke a bone? Ah, here's some time for you. Dead baby? I have just the thing, here's some time!"

Henry paused, his eyebrows wrinkled together. "Are we talking about Kat here or you?

"Kat, of course." I flicked my wrist to dismiss any other possibilities.

"Okay, just seemed like you were veering off in a different direction there for a minute and wanted to make sure I was keeping up."

"No, no. Simply trying to make my point. It's awful, really, the whole thing. They are going to try counseling. I've never seen her like that, though. So—" I searched for the right words. "So unwound. It was quite unlike her. She's normally so composed."

"Well, Bev, the image people portray on the outside is not always the full picture. It's usually what they want people to see, not who they actually are."

I squinted my eyes and squeezed my fork a tad tighter.

"I suppose you're right," I said. "Have you talked to Quinn? I really need to call her and make plans."

"Funny you should suggest that because I talked to her today and she said exactly the same thing. Must be some sort of best friend mind reading thing." He chuckled.

"Yes. Must be," I replied slowly.

We finished our meal and spent the rest of the evening in the living room. Henry sipping a beer, recliner extended, the lights from the television that held his attention flickering on his face.

I sat next to him on the couch, reading, but finding it hard to concentrate on the words. Feeling my gaze on him, Henry's eyes met mine. I smiled, letting him believe the smile was for him and not for myself, knowing I would learn his secrets soon enough. I couldn't lose Henry, or our marriage, but I also didn't like to be lied to. How I would react to and handle the truth, whatever it may be, I hadn't quite worked out yet.

Fifty Nine

In an unusual show of promptness, Quinn beat me to the coffee shop, where we agreed to meet 'for old time's sake.'

"Bev, over here," she said. Her loud voice carried through the small room, attracting a few stares from the other customers. I gave her a curt nod and got in line to order a black coffee.

"Do you have to cause such a scene? I hate people staring at me like that," I said, sliding into the chair across from her.

"Stop it. Nobody cares about you or anyone else. They're too wrapped up in their own stuff. You look great, Beverly. The color is back in your cheeks, your eyes, everything. I'm so glad to see you in such a better place."

I fiddled with a napkin and thanked her.

"How's Jacob?"

"He's growing like a weed. You wouldn't believe how big he is now. You need to come by the house and see him. I'm finally done with school. Put my resume out, so hopefully I'll get some interviews soon. It will be so hard to leave him every day, different from school which is only a few hours at a time. I need my own space, and I want to give him the life he deserves. That requires money."

"Congrats, that's great news. I'm proud of you. What companies have you applied to?"

"One of Henry's clients owns an advertising agency. He has a meeting with him sometime this week, so that's the most promising one. Fingers crossed." She held up both hands with crossed fingers.

I took a sip of my coffee before my lips had a chance to purse.

"That's very kind of him, I'll thank him tonight."

We stared out the window and sipped on our coffees. That was one thing I did love about our friendship. We could sit together in silence, and it never felt weird or awkward. We moved onto much less frustrating topics and were thankfully able to end the coffee date on an agreeable note.

"I'm sorry to run out on you, but I am hosting book club tonight and have a few last-minute things to collect for it," I said.

"You don't have to apologize to me, darling. Sounds like fun."

"Yes." I perked up. "I made the ladies read Stephen King. I'm excited to see what they all thought of it."

"Brilliant. It's great to hear that you're really getting back into the swing of things."

We stood, and she pulled me into a hug, squeezing too

tightly, then kissed me on the cheek. My arms remained stiffly at my sides.

"Don't be a stranger, Bev. I miss your million calls a day." She winked and waved over her shoulder, running out before I'd even had a chance to gather my purse.

I WANTED to make this book club meeting special. Show my appreciation for everything the ladies had done for me and perhaps cheer Kat up in the process. The ladies had finally let me pick the book. I didn't go easy on them either, we were reading *Misery*. Me, for the fifth time. This was our first night discussing the book, and I was eager to hear their thoughts.

After meeting Quinn, I rushed back to the house to get to work on preparations. Baking all my favorite desserts, preparing appetizers. For drinks, I made hot buttered rums, a stray from our usual wine, but one that I hoped they would enjoy.

Kat was the first to arrive. Her appearance startled me when she knocked on the kitchen door and walked in. Her hair was pulled back from her makeup-free face into a ponytail, and she wore jeans and a simple green sweat-shirt. I wasn't aware she owned a pair of jeans. She was comfortable and beautiful. I'd never seen her so relaxed. She sat down and placed her copy of *Misery* on the table.

"It's very good," she said.

"What's good?" I asked, looking up from the pot of water I was waiting to boil.

"The book. I thought I would absolutely hate it. My

real life has enough misery in it right now as it is." She laughed sardonically. "But that isn't the case. Is it wrong to enjoy someone else's misery as a way to forget yours?"

She was staring at the wall.

"Not at all. Why do you think I love books like that? Let someone else suffer for a few hours. Besides, they aren't real people. We can hope for their world to collapse around them guilt free."

She dissolved into laughter, genuine laughter. When she finally composed herself, she said, "You're right, Beverly. We should have been listening to you all along. Here we were, worried the crazy books you read were making you insane, but that's not the case at all, is it? They're the escape, the cure. I'll never doubt you again."

"It would be best if you ladies also agreed not to talk about my sanity behind my back again as well." I looked into her startled eyes and started laughing. Soon we were both in hysterics, with tears streaming down our faces. I was compelled to do something entirely out of character, so I walked over to the table, picked Kat up by her arms, and pulled her into a big Bonnie-style hug.

Bonnie walked in and cried, "I want in on this!"

She lumbered over and pulled us both into an even bigger hug, making Kat and I laugh harder. After a few minutes, Bonnie peered over our heads and announced that my water was boiling over.

"Oh, shoot." I peeled myself away and ran over to the stove, moving the pot onto a cold burner.

"It looks like you've outdone yourself here, Bev," Bonnie proclaimed, glancing around the kitchen at all the dishes laid out on the counter. "What do you have going there?"

"Well, I figured we could use a bit of cheer in our lives right now, all of us, and there is no better way than to eat our feelings. Also, if you notice, I've prepared some dishes to go with our book discussion tonight." I pointed to the special portion of tonight's spread. In the center of the tray was a crystal dish filled with black balls of caviar and surrounded by sliced toast, next to it there was a plate with wedged lemons, and a third crystal bowl held grated egg. I waited to see if Bonnie would understand, and she howled with laughter. I smiled, she read the book.

"Amazing! A themed meal, how creative. You aren't going to cut off our legs before we get to enjoy it, will you? Poor Paul."

"What's so funny?" Jeanine came into the kitchen and looked between each of us.

"Look at what Beverly made us," Bonnie said and pointed to the tray.

Jeanine started laughing, "Oh! I get it! It's what Annie made for Paul—from the book." She clapped her hands. I drank in each of their smiling, beautiful faces, grateful for every single one of them.

"I also made hot buttered rums for us. If everyone could grab a tray and help me bring the food into the living room, I'll get these drinks finished."

The ladies each picked up a tray and settled around the living room. I grabbed the bowl of batter from the fridge before distributing it into four cups then adding the rum and boiling water into each cup. Garnishing each with a stick of cinnamon, I joined the ladies in the living room and passed out the drinks.

Kat gripped her steaming mug with both hands and inhaled deeply, "Oh my God, this smells amazing." After taking a sip, she declared, "It tastes amazing too! You must give me this recipe—I'm going to add this to my holiday menu."

"What are you doing for the holidays? Spending them with *him*?" Bonnie spat out the word him with her face puckered like she had eaten one of the sliced lemons.

Kat sighed and put down her drink. "We're still trying to work it out. I don't trust him. Maybe I never will. But I love him, and some days I hate myself for that. It would be so much easier, you know? If I could just *stop* loving him. Just walk away, start over with my life."

"You're a better woman than I. I'm not sure I could do it. I want to punch him in his stupid face as it is," Bonnie retorted.

"I mean, I'm not saying that thought doesn't cross my mind at least fifteen times a day." We all laughed with Kat, then her face got serious.

"Do you all think I'm a fool?" Her pleading eyes met each of ours.

"I don't," I said. "People make mistakes, and sometimes they do things because they are selfish and don't think about the repercussions or what affect their actions have on their loved ones. I know my situation is different, but I have personal experience in that area."

"You're no fool, Kat," Bonnie said. "You're one of the strongest women I've ever met. It takes a lot of guts to do what you're doing. Forgiveness is way harder than holding a grudge."

"We're here for you, whatever you decide to do," Jeanine said with a reassuring smile.

Kat wiped a tear that had fallen from the corner of her eye. "I always thought I could never put up with something like this. An *affair*. I never in a million years imagined having to deal with one. And I was always the first one to say I'd leave him immediately for any indiscretion. But then it happens, and you realize that the decision isn't so cut and dry. Not with kids. Not when love tangles it all up." She sighed, took another sip of her drink and continued. "I'm not saying we're out of the woods, I could still change my mind and leave him. My sister is ready to come scoop us up and move the kids and I into her house. She's pretty annoyed at me right now for not taking her up on it. But we'll see. He's going to have a lot of regrets, and I can't live the rest of my life like that. Regretting. I'm going to give myself the chance to forgive him, and try to move forward, and if I can't, then I'll move on without him. But at least I'll move on knowing I did everything I could."

We all nodded sympathetically, wondering whether we could do the same. At least that's what I was wondering. Could I be so forgiving? The suspicions I'd been holding in, tingled within my mind. I wondered if I could handle Kat's situation with the same level head.

Probably not, based on my history.

"Now, let's talk about this book," Kat said, letting us know she was ready to move on.

"I must admit, Beverly, I expected to hate it. I only read it because you've suffered through enough of my choices." Bonnie jumped in. "But I couldn't put it down! Stayed up all night reading."

"Me too!" Jeanine added. "And thank you for not picking the one with the clown." She shuddered.

"I was telling Bev that before you ladies came in. I think we were all pleasantly surprised. Thanks for forcing us out of our comfort zone," Kat said.

I was so pleased with their reaction to the book. The women loved it so much we actually spent book club discussing the book, which in itself was a miracle.

Henry came home to us, still deep into our discussion.

"Hello ladies, I didn't expect to find you still here." He greeted them all in his friendly manner.

"Your wife picked such an engaging read, we have completely lost track of time," Bonnie replied. "But it's late, so we should get out of your hair."

"Do you need help cleaning up?" Jeanine asked.

"'Course not," Henry replied. "I can help get this sorted, Beverly."

We all said our goodbyes, and the ladies left for home.

"I'm so glad that you enjoyed yourself tonight, love." Henry smiled at me. "You deserve it."

He leaned in and kissed me on my forehead.

Sixty

"I'll go get the coffee started while you finish getting ready," I said, sitting up in bed. Henry's stirring woke me up. "Do you want me to make breakfast too?"

"No breakfast, coffee would be great, though."

I put on my robe and walked downstairs to start the coffee. I rejoiced at how different I felt. Light, free. It's like when your nose is stuffed, you forget how it feels to breathe normally until it finally clears, and you take that first full freezing intake of air. You knew you weren't breathing properly, but it didn't occur to you until that very moment how different it was. I sat there watching the coffee—breathing fully and freely.

Henry, with his perfect timing, entered the kitchen right as I was placing the mugs down on the table. He sat and took a large gulp.

"I hate to do this to you, but I have an early meeting. Wish I could sit and chat, but I need to run."

"Oh," I said, frowning. "Don't even worry about it. I'll see you tonight and we can catch up over dinner."

"Er, well, I actually have a work dinner tonight." He at least had the decency to look upset and quickly followed with, "but I'll cancel and come home for dinner."

"No, no. Don't be silly. I can manage fine on my own. We have plenty of breakfasts and dinners to look forward to on other days."

"Exactly. Many more days." He stood, leaned down, and kissed me. After placing his cup in the sink, he walked out the door.

I squeezed the sides of my mug. "Would it be so hard to have rinsed your cup and put it in the dishwasher?" I said to an empty room. Three deep breaths. I reminded myself that I was happy, and this petty annoyance wasn't worth getting upset over.

I wanted to leverage this renewed energy and do a deep cleaning of the house. A fresh house to go with my fresh outlook on life. But first, I needed to call Quinn. I wanted to repair our relationship—find a way back to the way we were. I knew she wouldn't be able to give me the attention she had before with Jacob in her life. But that was okay, I didn't need her so desperately. I had Kat, Bonnie, Jeanine, and Henry.

"Hey, good to hear from you, Bev. What's up?"

"Nothing special, I wanted to call and check on you. I woke up today feeling happy, really happy. It's nice."

"That's so good to hear. Time heals all, they say, and I guess that saying proves true again."

I closed my eyes and counted to three. There was that

word again. Time. It wasn't time that had cured me. It was self-reflection and hard work.

Not in the mood to debate, I continued, "Yes, when you're in it, though, whatever thing that needs healing, it never seems that way, does it?"

"No, it never does. You need to stay diligent, though. Not to be a downer, but you need to tell us if you start to feel worse again, promise?"

"What's this? It's my job to be the pessimistic friend in our relationship," I said.

She laughed. "All I'm saying is that if you feel a bit sad or anything, you need to tell Henry or me. Don't let it get that far again. I love you, Bev. I don't want anything to happen to you."

"I won't need to tell you anything, I promise. I'm past all that, I'm sure."

"I hope so, I really do. I'm not trying to be mean—I hope you know that. But if you need more help, there are some really nice places out there. More like retreats, not like the hospital you were in."

"That won't be necessary."

"Oh, that's the baby crying. I need to go see what he's on about. Call me later, 'kay?"

I stared at my phone. Retreat? What was she even talking about? Why suggest such a thing after I'd just explained how perfectly fine I was? I paced the kitchen, feeling myself overthink. Before I could unlock my phone and fall down an unnecessary internet rabbit hole, I decided to get to work.

Upstairs, I started dusting, scrubbing the floor, then wiping down the baseboards. The weather hadn't turned cold yet, so I opened all the windows and let the October air in. The faint scent of campfire filled the house. I took a deep breath in and smiled; I didn't like the cold air it brought, but the smell was always one of my favorites.

After finishing upstairs, I carted my supplies down to conquer the first floor, starting with the kitchen. Counters scrubbed, fridge and pantry cleaned out, I walked over to the oven to place it on cleaning mode, remembering what a different place I had been in not too far in the past. When I had willed the burning air to melt the skin from my face and end it all. I smiled once again, elated to be past all that.

The formal dining room went quicker. Barely used, the bulk of the work came from dusting the various décor in the built-in display cabinets. I treated the table with a fresh layer of Pine-Sol and wiped it down, making it shine like new. The crisp scent of pine trees mixed with the smokey air reminded me of Christmas. It would be nice to enjoy the holidays this year with Henry and our parents.

The last room, the living room, I knew would take me the longest, being the most used. I started by walking around and picking up various trash and papers that my lackluster cleaning the night before had missed. After circling the room, about to move on to the deep scrubbing, my eye caught something white poking out from between the seat cushion and arm of Henry's chair. I realized it was a napkin. It must have fallen out of Henry's pockets and crept down into the spot it was now lying in. I reached down and grabbed it. About to crumple it up and toss it into the trash bag, black markings on the napkin stopped me.

I smoothed it out and recognized Quinn's loopy handwriting immediately. More fitting for a teenager than a grown woman, especially a mother.

IT'S time to tell her. I can't wait any longer.
It's not fair to her, and it's not fair to me.
I love you,
Quinn

I HAD to read the note three times before I could process what I was seeing. No longer able to hold the napkin in my shaking hands, it floated to the floor. I stumbled to the couch in shock. My mind flooded with flashes of every interaction.

Henry meeting her alone.

Quinn knowing things that only Henry could have told her.

Henry's sneaky conversations at the Cape.

All the extra time Henry spent 'at work' or with 'colleagues.'

And the worst of them all, that last conversation with Quinn, the one where she tried to encourage me to consider retreats. The perfect way to be rid of me. It made sense now, why she responded that way when I told her I was better than ever. Much easier to sleep with my husband when I'm locked away—again.

The second Beverly returned, her breath tickled my neck. *"If you'd have only listened to me. How can you be surprised? You didn't deserve him. You don't deserve anyone. Not those book friends, not Henry, not Quinn...not Bill. Worthless girl."*

Bill materialized on my other side. I looked at him, waiting for him to tell her she was wrong. That I was worthy of happiness. His mouth opened and closed, and I was alone again.

I looked at the napkin and considered eating it. It wouldn't be as soothing as toilet paper, but it would make it disappear, go away, dissolve this problem, never to be thought of again.

The betrayal stole every bit of oxygen I had. I could hear myself breathing, but my lungs were too full to benefit from those breaths. The shaking in my hands spread to my entire body. I couldn't function. The shock was too much. I became part of the couch, melded into it, I couldn't move—trembling and staring at the spot on the floor where the napkin had landed.

When the shaking wore off, I pinched my left arm with my right hand. The pinch proved I was still alive and not dreaming—I hadn't inadvertently fallen asleep on the couch during cleaning and entered a horrible nightmare. I glared at the napkin again and the loopy black writing.

Still there. Still real. Still happening.

I stood and walked stiffly upstairs to the bathroom. I knew I needed to think, figure out what to do next. But I needed help. I needed my old friend, the friend that hadn't slept with my husband. I sat on the toilet and began eating. Enjoying the familiar feeling of the paper melting on my tongue. Eyes closed, head tilted back, tears silently fell down the sides of my face. I ate and ate and ate and ate while a plan formed.

Sixty One

WITH HENRY, my face was a window into my soul. He knew me too well for me to try to hide anything from him. If he saw me, he would immediately guess something was wrong and begin prying. I figured the best way around this was to take a sleeping pill and fall asleep on the couch with a book in my lap. He would see the clean house and assume I was so worn out from my work I passed out. I had fallen asleep enough times on that couch reading, it wouldn't be an unusual sight for him to come home to.

Book in hand, I sat on the couch in my staged position. Picking up the glass of water with a shaking hand, I took a large gulp and swallowed two pills. My hands tapped the top of the book. I closed my eyes to see if it would help—it didn't. A sigh passed through my lips, I got back up and retrieved another sleeping pill from the kitchen cabinet. I turned the kitchen sink on, filled my mouth with water straight from the faucet, and swallowed back a third pill.

Back on the couch and still wide awake, I picked the

book up, planning to read myself to sleep. After reading the same sentence five times with no comprehension, I closed my eyes. When I woke, it was still dark, but it was at least the following day.

I thought I'd feel something after a good night's sleep. That the anger would erupt like a thunderstorm, but I was numb and oddly calm.

I sat up and let my subconscious take over. It brought me upstairs to the bathroom, where I got showered and dressed. It then brought me back downstairs with a bottle of pills in hand. My movements mechanical and calculated.

The other Beverly stood beside me whispering encouragements in my ear.

I put a cutting board on the kitchen counter and retrieved my rolling pin. And one by one, I crushed the pills into a fine powder. With the task completed, I stood in front of the pile of powder, waiting and listening. Water rushing through pipes. I started the coffee. While it was brewing, I rinsed the rolling pin and hid the empty pill bottle in the bottom of the trash can, then stood very still and listened some more.

When the pipes silenced, I prepared two cups of coffee, then poured the powder evenly into each cup. I almost changed my mind but pulled the napkin out of my pocket and read the note. Beverly looked on, arms crossed, smiling and nodding. I rinsed the cutting board and put it away.

The spoon tinged the sides of the cup as I stirred the coffee, ensuring every grain dissolved fully.

With the coffee mugs placed behind our chairs, I sat behind mine and continued to wait.

"You're up early."

I gripped the napkin in my pocket and plastered a smile on my face to hide the truth swirling behind it.

"I fell asleep on the couch early reading again." I shrugged a shoulder. "Sit, have a cup with me before you go."

He shuffled to the table and sat across from me, taking a sip. His face screwed up, and he sucked in his cheeks.

"My gosh, Beverly, this is sweet!"

"Apologies, my mind was wandering, and I must have gotten heavy-handed on the sugar. Drink that one, and I'll make you a fresh cup."

He finished the coffee and I swallowed back the last drop of mine.

I whipped the napkin out of my pocket and slammed it on the table between us, writing side up. After smoothing the edges, I stared at him intently, waiting for his confession.

"I'm confused. Are you upset about something?"

He tilted his head, a puzzled look on his face. An actor giving his best performance.

"Am I upset about something? Of course, I'm upset about something." I smacked my hand on the table next to the napkin, making us and the coffee mugs jump.

"What are you talking about? It's a napkin. A wrinkled used napkin."

I blinked and tried to understand how he could deliver such an egregious lie without looking the least bit guilty.

"A used napkin? That's what you have to say about this?" My finger jammed down on the writing.

He shook his head with his eyes wide, but it wasn't fear in them, it was confusion. My gaze moved from his eyes to my finger, and I watched in horror as Quinn's looped handwriting disintegrated—like the letters had been lit on fire. They curled in on themselves and dissolved into nothing.

I rubbed my eyes with clenched fists and looked down again. Still blank. I blinked rapidly and shook my head.

"I don't understand. It was there." I flipped the napkin over then pushed it closer to him before grabbing my head in my hands.

"What was there?" he asked, still looking confused.

"The note, the love note. From Quinn. It was there, right there on the napkin!"

I picked it back up and continued flipping it over to examine both sides more closely. The napkin remained blank. The writing, gone.

I began searching under the table, lifting items up and placing them down. What had he done with the real napkin? The one with the writing.

Bill appeared in one of the empty seats. "She's a liar," he hissed.

"No, she's not a liar. I saw it," I argued.

"THAT'S RIGHT, Quinn's not a liar, and neither am I. I don't know what is going on with you, but this is crazy! A love note from Quinn?"

"Yes, yes. That's exactly what it was. A love note.

Quinn and you are having an affair. You're in love. She's said you must leave me for her.

"Quinn and I are *not* having an affair. This is—I don't even know what this is. You've gone too far, Beverly—" He stood and paced the kitchen. "I need a minute."

Henry trudged into the living room shaking his head.

I sat at the kitchen table staring at my hands gripping the napkin, trying to make sense of it all, not knowing what to do.

My eyes met Bill's. "It was there, right on the napkin." My voice had lost all conviction.

He looked sad, devastated, even more than I felt. "Open your eyes. You've been tricked. Not just today. So many lies. I wish I could have saved you."

"I wish I could have saved you," I told the empty chair.

Finally, I gathered the courage to find Henry and confess my sins.

I sat on the couch and looked at him, not sure where to start. I didn't have to think for very long.

He finally looked at me. "Has this all been an act?"

"No, I found the napkin, it—"

"Not the fucking napkin," he screamed. "This." He swooped his arms. I didn't understand. I had no idea what he was asking me.

"The promises to do better. The 'I'm so happy nows.' The everything. What have you been hiding?"

"Nothing, I swear nothing at all." My voice lowered. "Apparently you have—"

"Shut up, shut up, shut up. I can't take this. It was a napkin, Beverly. A blank nothing of a napkin. I can't even tell if you're messing with me or if you truly believe it.

This is insanity." His eyes widened. "I feel like I'm the one losing my mind. I can't even tell what's real anymore."

"Now you know how I feel. Yet you don't feel sympathy. Why? That's how I feel every single day. It's terrifying."

"Then why wouldn't you say anything?"

I slapped my hands to my ears. The yelling. The chaos in my mind. Too much. But softening.

He dropped his face into his hands.

We sat there for seconds, or hours.

My thoughts settled. The senseless became full of sense.

He looked up with heavy eyelids. "I don't feel well." He rubbed his face and shook his head, as if trying to wake himself.

Oh no. No no no no.

The image of me crushing the pills and pouring the powder into his coffee, mixing it with sugar and cream to hide the taste.

The realization of what my mind had done formed a boulder in my stomach. My mind was the liar, not Henry, not Quinn. I could picture it laughing at how easily I had fallen for its tricks. Not taking my eyes from Henry, I sat on the floor with my back against the couch. My eyes wandered lazily around the room, the drugs took effect, and the blackness took over.

Sixty Two

Now

THE STORM HAS PASSED, but thankfully the lights have stayed on. Electric is so unreliable in this new home of mine in the Vermont mountains.

"And now you know the bad things I've done. The very bad thing. The reason I'm here alone. No longer married. Well, alone except you. Though you may leave me now, too. I wouldn't blame you, now that you see what kind of person I am."

"Yet here you sit before me, looking exactly like the same person you've always been. My friend."

My breath hitches. It's been an emotional evening. One I was sure would end with him walking out, never to return.

"What happened to Henry? He's not..."

I swallow. I've come so far. It's time to finish. "The sleeping pills did what sleeping pills are supposed to do.

Despite the large amounts over the recommended dosage, Henry awoke hours later to a darkened room. His limbs heavy, his mind slow, his heart still beating."

I can see the relief in my friend's eyes. Would he still be here if things had ended differently?

I continue, "Henry survived, but the pills still held him in their grip. All this he of course had to explain to me later. He felt pinned to his chair, some invisible mass holding him in place. Even the simplest task like rubbing his eyes felt impossible. He widened his eyes, willing the softness of his vision to sharpen. He didn't even realize where he was. The room, he knew it, he'd been there before, but he couldn't figure out why he knew it, when he'd been there, or how he got there.

That's when he saw me, lying on the floor. *What's a wife? Does she have a name?* he thought, then realized those shouldn't be questions, these were things he should know. Everything was moving too slow. He convinced himself he was dying or dead. But thankfully my Henry was very much alive."

HENRY STARED AT THAT WOMAN. *His wife.*

I think I hate her, he thought.

The source of the hate was an enigma. A tingling skittered across his skin as the feeling in his body returned, moving became less impossible. He slipped back into his skin and forced himself into a sitting position. Still weak, he leaned to one side, using the chair to hold himself up, his stomach convulsed, and he threw up over the side. Finally, able to reach his hand to his face, he jammed the heels of his hands into his eyes.

The source of his hate crashed into him. Beverly, my wife, tried to kill me—to kill us. *She was sprawled on her back on the floor, not moving. He wished her dead. The fragments of knowledge began clicking into place.* Beverly accusing me of having an affair, her throwing a plain old blank napkin at me as proof.

There had been so many hints of her unraveling mind; he shouldn't have been surprised. The grocery store, the barbeque, the strange story she told him about the women in the bookstore, the odd flashes of fear that would take over her face, each time brushing the incidents off, pretending they hadn't happened, making excuses. They'd missed the signs, everyone, even her.

Anger gave him the energy he needed to regain the function of his body and mind.

He heaved himself from the chair and ambled to her. A groan escaped her lips when he tapped her with his foot.

Not dead.

She could be arrested for this, thrown in jail for years. But is that really what he wanted? She needed help, medication. She'd get neither of those in jail. He needed to think, but not in the same room as her. He didn't trust himself with her defenseless body so close. Didn't trust his hands not to grab a pillow and put an end to this madness once and for all.

Sixty Three

THE COFFEE MUGS clatter on the small saucers they are balanced on. I open the screen door with my back and step out onto my wrap-around front porch. Roger sits rocking in a chair, gazing out at the Vermont mountains.

"Beautiful evening now that the storm's cleared isn't it, love," he says, gently rocking, not taking his eyes off the endless view of the rolling pine trees.

"It is," I reply, sitting down in the chair next to him. Ending our evening where we started it. I let my eyes drink in his face for a few extra beats. For a moment, I see Bill rocking in the white wooden rocking chair beside me. Not a Bill figment. Bill only visits me in my dreams these days.

I would never wish to replace Roger, but I would do anything to have Bill here with us.

I live in a cabin nestled in the mountains of Vermont now, courtesy of Henry and my parents. Roger is my closest neighbor; he reminds me of Bill in so many ways.

He drinks too much and has too many opinions. But he is his own man too, and I cherish our time together.

"Thank you for listening," I say.

He smiles and nods. "Thank you for sharing those pieces of you."

Beverly Bonnefinche is dead. At least the Beverly I had always been and the Beverly Bonnefinche I became after marrying Henry.

I believed I'd been cured, truly I did. But like the ocean, my bottom was too far deep to fathom. I assumed wrong that the suicide attempt that sent me to hospital was my lowest point, there was still so much farther to sink.

My demons hadn't left. They had just burrowed themselves in the darkest caves of my mind, playing their tricks on me when opportunities arose.

My belongings packed, I left Henry's house that night and stayed at Jeanine's. Henry was kind enough to fund a long-term mental health facility, which Jeanine drove me to the next day. I'm sure having me locked up, not able to kill him, was a good thing in his opinion, so he was happy to help.

It didn't happen overnight, but I got better, *actually* better this time. The doctors at the facility were very competent and helpful, the nurses too. My new doctors gave me a proper diagnosis. I did have postpartum depression, but that only hid the true illness that slowly overtook me. Made it easier for it to hide. Bipolar schizoaffective disorder. It explained so much. The diagnosis came as a relief. I had a reason for all the things happening to me and words to describe those experiences that had been scary and confusing: disassociating, manic episodes, depression, hallucinations, delusions. Most importantly, I had a treatment plan. Methods to recognize these things which had names, medication to stabilize my mood and keep me happy and functioning. It took a few weeks but once I adjusted and my mind settled, the change was indescribable. The static in my head cleared. I could think, I could laugh, I could feel without feeling too big or too wrong. I've even stopped eating toilet paper—mostly. There has been the occasional slipup on particularly bad days.

Minds are so fragile; it turns out mine is more fragile than most. With lots of therapy, I gained a firmer grasp on how mine works and learned how to function properly in this world. My mind will never work like most minds, but that's okay. It's my mind, and it's beautiful in its own chaotic way.

With lifelong therapy and proper care, I will never hurt myself or anyone else again.

I used to think love wasn't worth it. That the heartbreak and pain love caused were too much to bear. My opinion on love has changed. I don't regret my life with Henry. I needed him. Without Henry, Bill, my parents, Quinn, my book club ladies—all of them—my journey wouldn't have started. Without them, I wouldn't have found myself here, and here is a very good place to be.

Do I regret how things ended with Henry? My actions eventually leading to our intended demise? I regret my attempt to kill him, yes, but I learned and grew so much from the situation. I'm a different woman now. I'm not sure I would have grown into this woman, not fully, if everything had worked out perfectly. I would have kept people at arm's length, never letting them in. And more importantly, I would have never realized that some of the things I was seeing and hearing weren't actually there. Who knows how far my mind would have taken things? And who knows if I would have perfected my murder and suicide skills?

I'll do things differently in my next relationship if there ever is to be a next one.

I still talk to Jeanine, Kat, and Bonnie. Even Quinn, who graciously forgave me. We aren't as close as we once were, but I do enjoy catching up with her and hearing about Jacob. Through them, I learned Henry met someone new, sold the house, and moved—to where exactly, they don't know. I hope he's happy. I hope she's good to him. He deserves it. I've also re-connected with Olivia. Like me, she has found a way to ward off her demons, or at least keep them at bay through a successful and ongoing treatment plan. She's at home with her parents, attending university.

Perhaps one day I'll move closer to civilization. Try my hand at love again. But for now, I've found my joy. For now, I am alive.

"Have I ever told you about the time Bill stood in the square and danced until he fell over?" I ask.

"You have, love, but why don't you tell me again. It's one of my favorite stories," Roger says.

And so, I do.

The End.

Acknowledgments

After my dad read my last book, he called me and raved for an hour, then told me how unprofessional it was to curse in my acknowledgements. So, this swear-free, super professional, very authory acknowledgements section is dedicated to my dad.

First and foremost, big thank you to Phyliss who told me to stop talking about it and just write the book already.

As always, Alexandria, my editor and friend, I look forward to finding new and improved ways to annoy you. And yes, I'm working on my book and not scrolling the internet.

Tina, the other, better (Alex will stop reading after her name, so I can say that here) half of Rising Action.

Thank you to Ashley Santoro for the beautiful cover that fits Bev perfectly.

Mar Fenech, an amazing editor and person. Your feedback always brings a better story out of me.

Kathleen Fox, because it truly does take a village, big thanks for being the final check to make Bev's story shine.

A special thank you to my sister-in-law, Shelly Davis, one of the smartest, hard-working women I know, thank you for allowing me to tap into your endless knowledge of mental health.

And finally, to everyone whose mind has lied to them, tricked them, and made them feel different, you are seen, heard, and perfect the way you are.

About the Author

Kristen Seeley is the pen name for Marie Still, which she uses when she wants to write stories with less murder and more heart. She grew up obsessed with words and the dark and complex characters authors bring to life with them. Now she creates her own while living in Tampa with her husband, four kids, two dogs, and a very grumpy hedgehog.

Book Club Questions

1. In one of the first scenes Beverly is reading *Carrie*. Are there any parallel themes with Beverly and Carrie's stories?

2. Beverly can be very judgmental; do you believe this is a coping mechanism or is she just not a very nice person?

3. Trust is hard for Beverly. Why do you think that is and who/what in her journey has taught her to trust?

4. Oftentimes when people are experiencing mental health issues, they don't reach out for help. Why do you believe it took Beverly so long to realize she needed help?

5. Beverly didn't receive a proper diagnosis, not allowing her to get the treatment she needed. Who is to blame for this?

6. Had Beverly received the proper diagnosis, how would her life have been changed?

7. Mental health disorders not only impact the person with the disorder, but those closest to them. How did Beverly's mental health affect her loved ones?

8. Beverly's mind conjured up two images: her reflection, this not-Beverly Beverly, and Bill. Why do you think it chose these forms?

9. How did Beverly's story impact your feelings toward mental health?